Cameron
IN
THE GUARDIAN

1974—1984

Cameron
IN
THE GUARDIAN

1974–1984

JAMES CAMERON

Hutchinson
London Melbourne Sydney Auckland Johannesburg

Hutchinson & Co. (Publishers) Ltd
An imprint of the Hutchinson Publishing Group

17–21 Conway Street, London W1P 6JD

Hutchinson Publishing Group (Australia) Pty Ltd
16–22 Church Street, Hawthorn, Melbourne, Victoria 3122

Hutchinson Group (NZ) Ltd
32–34 View Road, PO Box 40-086, Glenfield, Auckland, 10

Hutchinson Group (SA) Pty Ltd
PO Box 337, Bergvlei 2012, South Africa

First published in this collection 1985

Phototypeset by Wyvern Typesetting Limited, Bristol
Printed and bound in Great Britain by
Anchor Brendon Ltd, Tiptree, Essex

ISBN 0 09 162710 9

Contents

These pieces are a selection from the four hundred or so columns and other articles which James Cameron wrote for the *Guardian* between 1974 and 1984. They are arranged according to subject matter. Within each section the order is chronological, except in a few cases where continuity of argument, or the need for contrast, suggested otherwise. The titles of the sections are all taken from the columns themselves or from other articles or books by James.

Martin Woollacott

My Life and Yours

Beating about the Bush

If you turn this page of your *Guardian* to the other side (not *now*, silly; in a minute) you will discover the regular feature of the left-hand columns which increasingly gives the paper real meaning. The main editorial? Yes and no. The second leader? Maybe, but. Get lower. When you have reached the ground floor and can descend no further you will find the cream of the newspaper, since only here does the cream stay at the bottom. I mean, of course, A Country Diary. There comes a time in every journalist's life when he covets that job more than gold. Not, I imagine, that there is much equation. I am a fairly new addict to this anodyne slot, which I now realize is not only more valuable but clearly more enduring than the rest. Elsewhere in the paper, from the masthead to the imprint, bones rattle, storm-clouds gather, the end of the world grows daily higher, costly pages of newsprint are filled with the chilling chunterings of the Experts on Everything. They are written on the wind, as none should know better than I.

Ever since I can remember, blundering up Fleet Street as the original barefoot boy from Beaverbrook, democracy has been disintegrating, diplomacy doomed, Parliament pooped, capitalism collapsing and socialism sunk. Alliteration's artful aid is a great substitute for sense. But A Country Diary, the least meretricious and obtrusive few sticks of type in the whole street, continues with an equanimity that I am only now beginning to appreciate.

Possibly the reason is that I have only recently come to terms with being a landowner and, at least by proxy, a cultivator of the English soil. I doubt if our estate would be held considerable by the standards of, say, the Duke of Sutherland; it occupies some 60 feet by 28 feet of the London Borough of Hammersmith. Such a holding does not encompass much grouse shooting, nor do we maintain many tenants' cottages on our lands; we offer few problems to the European Agricultural Commission. To tell the truth, even the radishes have to queue up for *lebensraum*. Nevertheless our seigneurdom of even that much of the planet entitles me now to read these rustic jottings with critical care and affection. I am a countryman, if you can call London W12 the country, as I can and do, and never stop repeating that I am still the local President and indeed sole member of the Shepherd's Bush Agrarian and Peasant Party. For some time I have urged that our locals should be obliged to wear smocks and carry crooks; I even promoted the idea that we should employ an Oldest Inhabitant to sit outside the Bush tavern and drool out anecdotes for tourists, until it occurred to me that the one best qualified for the job was myself. We have made little headway recently. No shepherd has been seen around our Bush for some ninety years, but I have not abandoned hope; after all it is only a generation ago that President Woodrow Wilson had sheep grazing on the White House lawn to dramatize his fantasies of country pleasures. I see no reason why the peculiarly hideous architecture that has grown up around our last remaining meadow should impede my ambition one day to return the Bush to the Shepherds.

In the meantime we have had a good growing season out in Hammersmith this year; maybe a little on the dry side, but the combine harvester depot along the Goldhawk Road is standing by for a fair crop. We are reckoned to be dandelion and dead-grass country, by and large. This of course makes for a good natural balance: if you compost the dead grass carefully in a proper compost-thing, as we do, it provides excellent nourishment for the dandelions, and indeed vice versa; thereby nature's great cycle is maintained and her mighty ecological purpose revealed. It is true that difficulties arise in finding profitable markets for either crop, but this is not disabling; the dandelion and dead-grass market has been quiet for some time, and come the day we can doubtless live on it ourselves.

Right now it is our herds and our flocks that are giving concern, and this is where A Country Diary tends to let one down. In our grounds we maintain an establishment of two tortoises, some thirteen fish (goldfish, shubunkin, scavenging tench and a predatory catfish) and a floating population of sparrows, starlings, thrushes, and two professional blackbirds, employed to sing in the early hours. Some time ago we were given a present by David Attenborough of a breeding pair of horned toads, but they went to ground on arrival and are rarely seen. There is also a pair of truly obese and arrogant pigeons, the size of ducks, very vulgar and offensive, so corpulent they can barely fly, and assume that the garden path is only there for a take-off runway. One day, when they cease to be nimble, I shall have them for a pie.

I do not hate them, however, as much as I hate my cats. They are not my cats, but they exploit us. They claim to have angling rights in our pond. Our fish are now so foolishly amiable that they eat from our fingers; their error is they cannot distinguish my fingers from those of the bloody cats, which have spikes on them. I have lost three fish in the past fortnight, namely Fred, Gladys and Les. I cannot stand sentry on the pond all day. I begin to understand the attraction of blood sports, like cat-hunting. A Country Diary gives me no help in this matter. Come to think of it, A Country Diary is on the whole pretty cavalier towards gardens in general, which I suspect it regards with some contempt, and even more so us urban yokels trying to make the desert bloom under the shadow of Television Centre. It is to be sure a long way from the late Evelyn Waugh's famous Mr Boot, of *Scoop*, whose gentle vole slipped plashy-footed through his fenny ways, or words to that effect. Yet it does go on about leafy shades of Cotswold woodland and a clump of greater butterfly orchids with blackcaps fluting above, and crawling through masses of sweet-scented white-flowered amaryllid (pancratum) when what I want to know is how to deal with criminal cats. Or for that matter tortoises: they are presented with expensive and succulent shop lettuces, which they spurn and amble off to eat our own miserable little lettuce sprouts almost before their infancy. Considering how long tortoises are obliged to live they are very improvident.

I read last week that the *New York Times* carried the headline: 'Ford Vegetable Garden Off Till Next Year.' It seems that some time ago President Ford exhorted Americans to grow vegetables at home to save cash and energy, and proposed to set an example in the White House. It didn't come off. The Presidential spokesman's explanation rings an echo in every gardener's heart. 'We talked about it a lot and were going to, but the final decision was never made. Now they say it's too late. Maybe next year.' The editorialist of the *New Yorker* magazine wiped away a sympathetic tear. 'We're with the President in this. A garden is a lovesome thing, but it is most lovesome in November, when it's asleep. About two minutes after the winter solstice the seed catalogues arrive, fat and snappy, with pictures of improved varieties for next growing season; by the time you've sorted them out it's March, but the ground is too hard. Then it rains for a month. Then it's just too late. . . . '

What a decent and emollient article this has been. Begone dull care. *Ave atque vale* to the political jeremiahs and the dismal record of our imperfections, as one removes oneself, either gracefully or clumsily, from the tedious tangle of type to the wonderful wilderness of weeds. (Really, the man should be Swinburne.) Like

Voltaire's Candide one should cultivate one's garden. And here I go.

14 July 1975

A Sudden Month of Fundays

I got a bit of news last week that took weeks off my life. Four, to be exact. It came to pass that for some damnfool official purpose I had to have my birth date verified from the Registrar General's records, and the certificate shows that I was born on 17 July of a year that I need not specify except to say it was the year in which King George V was crowned and some joker pinched the Mona Lisa from the Louvre.

That is all very well. Except for the fact that for my entire life up until this moment I have supposed that I was shown the light of day on 17 *June*. This trifling statistic, admittedly of no great importance to the chronology of man, is nevertheless recorded on every official paper, minute, chronicle and file that bureaucracy has accumulated about me over three score years, it is endorsed on every one of my sixteen passports, it is enshrined in mouldering stacks of *dokumenti* in dozens of countries, it is a date hallowed by the years and accepted without question by one and all – except, it now seems, the Registrar General. As a revelation it hardly ranks with Watergate, or Joanna Southcott's Box, and at my time of life I cannot see one month making much odds to my prospects of making the *Guinness Book of Records* as the oldest boy wonder in the world. It is none the less an odd feeling to be officially that much younger than one had for so long believed. There is a curious, meaningless mystery about it.

How, for example, could my parents have believed to the end of their days that they had had their firstborn in June, and not July? It is not the sort of mistake that one would expect a mother to make. It is true that I sprang a bit untimely from the womb, a trace premature, perhaps a little foolishly impatient to join the human race, but my parents would presumably have been aware of this. Unless of course my arrival was so inconspicuous that nobody even noticed for a month. This theory does not square with the family legend that I howled horribly and virtually without a break for the first year of my life, and that in fact we were required to move house at the instance of our exhausted neighbour. I still find it difficult to believe that my father and mother would have waited four solid weeks before trotting along to the East Battersea sub-district of the Wandsworth region of South London to get me on the index, and then to have falsified the entry. There could hardly have been the conventional reason for this, since they had already been married for three or four years, or so I have been reliably told. Could the above-mentioned coronation have had something to do with it? This happy event is recorded as having taken place just five days after my supposed debut, that is to say on 22 June. Could it be that my parents were thrown into such transports of royalist fervour that I wholly slipped from their minds for a full month? It does not sound in the least like my old man. But if so, some infantile anti-monarchical resentment on my part could explain a lot.

Anyhow, that is the technical situation. The question is what to do about it now. To put the record straight I should have to correct about a million dossiers all over the world, arousing suspicion wherever I went, and doubtless getting myself blacklisted by all the barmy little bureaucracies that take these things seriously. It hardly seems worth it for a simple month. I think the answer is to keep the whole thing quiet, a harmless secret between me and the Registrar General. Certain personal adjustments will have to be made. I shall have to come to terms with being not a Gemini but a Cancer, which I could have done without. I shall have to wait another month for my old age pension, but that will make little difference since I am told I'm not getting it anyway: to pay one's compulsory £2.41 a week for absolutely nothing is the cherished privilege of the self-employed.

Some questions about this June-July business still haunt me. Why didn't my astrologer in India spot the discrepancy? Why have I been kidded for so long? Could it be that I was some changeling, possibly of noble blood, the truth of whose birth had to be obfuscated in this way? Can my parents have both had a simultaneous attack of amnesia? Was I, in fact, *ever born at all*?

Meanwhile, what shall I do with my borrowed time? It is like the beginning of one of those Edwardian novels in which some stricken fellow steps out into Harley Street having been told that he has but a month to live. I have been told I have an *extra* month to live. So, anyone for tennis?

Unless, of course, the Registrar General has boobed. It was, after all, quite a time ago.

10 May 1976

Cross Purpose

Will anyone swap me two Peter Hains for a Paul Johnson? Or the other way round if you like. What about a couple of Nicholas Scotts for a Conor Cruise O'Brien? What am I bid for a batch of hardly used Reg Prentices?

The Lord giveth and the Lord taketh away. Cross-defections are in the air, and the lefties and the righties play politics like musical chairs. If anyone is thinking of changing allegiances with the maximum of petulant publicity this is the chic time to do it. I cannot do it myself. I'm afraid, since I have no party to defect from, and certainly none to defect to. The Shepherd's Bush Peasant and Agrarian Party came to nothing; the Chalk Farmers Union is moribund. I am too radical for the Communists; the Anarchists consider me too inconsistent. The Tories have got that peculiar lady. I do not know any Liberals. Like Groucho Marx, I could hardly bring myself to join any club that would admit the likes of me.

Nevertheless I know where my duty lies. Memo to the Minister of Defence; I have momentarily forgotten his name, but it will come back. I am sorry that I owe your gallant and steadfast Army £11.73, but I do not know here and now, at this moment in time, in what you might call an ambiguity-situation, what to do about it. I have just received from the Officers' Mess, HQ3 Infantry Brigade, to wit: Wines £10.47, VAT Wines 84p, Telephones 42p. It was directed to my proper name at my proper address, and there is much in it that puzzles me, but the one thing of which I am absolutely sure is that you are not going to get paid. You can therefore tell Dr Luns, or whoever it is of NATO, that our mean and niggardly Government is going to skrimshank a bit more on its Army obligations, up to and including this £11.73. I do not know what £11.73 buys in the way of military gear, maybe a handful of ball bearings or a very small bomb, but whatever it is HQ3 Infantry Brigade is out of luck. Many things elude my flagging memory, but one is engraved forever, and that is that I have never in my life set foot in the Officers' Mess of 3 Infantry Brigade. I have never bought so much as a dram there, let alone ten quid's worth of wine, plus VAT. I do not know the Mess Secretary. I do not even know where he, or it, is to be found. One of the oddities of this bill is that even if I proposed to pay it I could not, since it bears no hint nor suggestion of an address. Is the location of 3 Infantry Brigade a military secret? Or is everyone supposed to know it, as a matter of course? Just as, apparently, they knew mine?

The fact is, I am obliged to own, that I have not been a member of a British Army Officers' Mess for nearly thirty years, indeed as far as I recall since the days of the Berlin Blockade. Was that 3 Infantry Brigade? Perhaps. But one did not drink wine. Instead they initiated me in my innocence to a gross and gruesome competitive game called Cardinal Puff, which involved the forcible consumption of huge quantities of beer, the effect of which was to put me off beer forever. In any case, such was the temper of the times, *nothing* cost £11.73. This was just as well since that was what most of us made in a week.

The Navy, now, that was a different matter. Some years ago I did a sort of professional holiday cruise in the great aircraft carrier *Eagle* ('the last of the gunboats') from Singapore to Hong Kong, a trip normally done in a couple of days but which we spun out for a fortnight, circling round and round the China Sea at the taxpayers' expense. I was most warmly welcomed to the wardroom, where I found to my satisfaction that while mineral waters were extremely dear, gin cost about tuppence a tot. At journey's end, to repay all the comradeship and hospitality, I gave a wardroom party for about two hundred officers at which most of them, or if you wish it us, got stoned out of their, or our, minds, and the following day I was asked to pay a bill for about £8. I certainly never submitted that bill on my expenses; it would have created a most unwholesome precedent.

So you see, Mr Mulley (I finally got it), I owe you, and 3 Infantry Brigade, and HM Government, the sum of £11.73, and shall continue to owe it until your chaps tell me what it is for, where I incurred it, and to whom I should send it. How you are going to square it in your Defence Estimates of £2,000 millions, or whatever it is, I do not know; I imagine your accountants are even now racking their brains. Let them rack. All I wonder is: who got that wine?

26 September 1977

Theatre of Fear

A funny thing happened on the way to the movies, and a nasty thing inside. Since our going to the cinema is an event that comes up maybe once a year it is worth recording. We went to see *Annie Hall*, and while we were waiting in the queue to get in a small nuisance developed behind us, some talkative young bore with a penetrating voice being troublesome. It was of no matter. We got into the theatre, and about the first comedy sequence of the show – if you have seen *Annie Hall* you will know it – was a couple in a cinema queue getting aggro from a man behind them, some talkative young bore with a penetrating voice. Talk about art imitating nature. I said: we just had this act, for free. Or was it precognition? Anyhow it made me very uneasy; I really hate coincidences.

At that moment someone moved into the row in front and said to his neighbour: 'Is this your case?'

'No,' everyone said, 'never seen it.'

'Oh well, better leave it then,' said this man, and settled down, having successfully wrecked the show for me, conditioned as I am to worry about unattended cases. This was day four of the Lufthansa hijacking.

Did I then ostentatiously seek out the management to remove this potentially perilous bag? I did not. I sat there quietly waiting for the bloody thing to go off. I showed no sense of public responsibility whatever. I would sooner have martyred myself than cause a scene in a crowded hall in order to unmask, doubtless, a bag of Marks and Spencer's fish fingers. This is the British disease: thou shalt not embarrass thy neighbour; better connive at his disintegration.

As it turned out, nothing happened, but for the next hour or so Woody Allen laboured for me in vain. So even did the wonderful Diane Keaton, albeit she is clearly the freshest female talent to hit the screen since Carole Lombard. I salute her evermore. But on this occasion she had to compete with that goddam bag.

My plucky demonstration of moral cowardice in that movie house sent me home in a proper frame of mind to reflect on the goings on at Mogadishu. I had always had a vague feeling (easy enough for one who has never been hijacked) that the passengers in these beleaguered aircraft never do quite as much for themselves as perhaps they might, that a resolute and concerted action by seventy or so people could surely overwhelm four captors, even at some cost. It was a very priggish speculation. The assembled passengers were strangers to each other, with no experience of concerted action, even if the physical circumstances in an aeroplane made concerted action possible, which they do not. They were unnerved and terrified and leaderless, and as incapable of initiative as was I in the middle of *Annie Hall*.

The abduction of planeloads of uncommitted civilians seems to me a particularly cowardly and beastly way of making a political point, however valid that point may be, and the one thing about this Lufthansa drama was that the precise political objective was never clearly defined anyhow. It will take a lot of persuading to make me believe that Baader took his own life in a high-security cell by shooting himself in the back of the neck with an unsuspected gun. It does not seem to matter particularly. But if the Germans wanted to execute their hostage, why did they not do it sooner, and abort all this hijack melodrama and deprive the terrorists of their one post-mortem success? The only sure conclusion is that evil begets evil, and that both sides will accept the inevitability of cruelty, until the world is populated by hostages.

What on earth is then to be done? Lord Duncan Sandys in *The Times* suggests an international boycott of the nations that have chickened out to the terrorists, and paid them off – that in fact a Japanese or Algerian passport should be a bar to any international air travel. I am inclined, probably for the first time in my life, to agree with Duncan Sandys. A vast number of blameless people would be inconvenienced, and the airline industry would be catastrophically affected, but it would be a start. The *New States-man* proposes a terrific tightening-up of passenger-control security, which has indeed got very sloppy of late, especially in tourist resorts. Why, it asks, when Israel is a major terrorist target, are El Al planes never hijacked? Because the Israelis make joining an El Al flight like getting into Fort Knox, with a two-hour check-in and a really scrupulous search, not to speak of armed quasi-passengers on every plane. For all innocent travellers it is a tremendous nuisance, but I have never heard an El Al passenger complain.

The lunatic paradox is that the easier and cheaper international air travel becomes the more troublesome it is bound to be, and the reduction of flight schedules will mean a drop in airline profits and in consequence a rise in fares, so easier and cheaper will become dearer and more difficult, and so we go round and round. One almost wishes the Wright brothers had never been born. Doubtless they were saying this in the stage-coach days – the highwayman menace, the ever-present threat of Dick Turpin on the roads. Then it was a simple matter of your money or your life. Now, unfortunately, it is both.

24 October 1977

Watch This Space

Most of us are uneasily aware that empty outer space is nothing of the kind: the empyrean would now seem to be as crowded with manmade ironmongery as the M4 on a Friday evening, and the crash of a Russian satellite on northern Canada was of course inevitable sooner or later. That it did not fall on Piccadilly Circus or the Pentagon merely shows that the devil looks after his own. Some of us would rather have preferred that it had done, since neither place would have been greatly missed. I say people are uneasily aware of this situation, whenever they give it a thought; I am not, I am both scared and resentful. The idea of several thousand machines, satellites and rockets and their debris, circling overhead gives me no comfort whatever, my theorizing extending only to the principle that what goes up must come down.

I am not your Science Correspondent (as you may well have noticed) and I am no authority on space adventures – though oddly enough I spent some time with N A S A in Houston, Texas, trying to make sense of the Apollo programmes, which were absorbing but in no way like *Dr Who*. I am no expert on atomic weapons – though again I am obliged to say that I am one of the very few people around who has actually seen three of the damnable things go off, a thing that after many years still gives me unexpected nightmares. I know just superficially enough about this preposterous and arrogant human exercise to know that I know so little of its implications, that you know so little, and that, I am increasingly sure, *they* know so little.

The notion of outer space is infinitely (in its exact sense) consoling; out there where you measure milestones in light years and there is no ceiling, no boundaries. There must be room out there, one would assume for all the uncountable billions of fanciful vehicles man could devise; there could be no traffic jams in eternity. And yes . . . when the first man was sent into orbit I chanced to be in New York and passed by the facade of the *Daily News* office where was displayed a big global model illustrating the space-man's progress. He was about an inch and a quarter above the globe's surface, which is to say that he was orbiting around 120 miles overhead. I was shocked. The vehicle I had assumed to be careering in limitless space, at least halfway to Heaven, was in fact no further away from me than Philadelphia, to which I was going that day by simple railway train.

It was then that I lost my illusions; I stopped being awestruck and started being scared. If it were held to be miraculous to shoot a man no further than the distance from London to Birmingham, there was clearly no chance whatever of man ever reaching the moon. I may have been proved wrong in that. I say may have been because I am still far from persuaded that this event actually did take place, and even if it did, I cannot see how man has benefited tuppenceworth thereby. I cannot look at the moon on a clear night now without slightly shuddering at the thought of its litter of abandoned hardware and plastic bags of astronauts' excreta. I cannot think of any way in which space travel has advantaged anyone. As I get on a bit I begin to wonder if in fact any sort of travel does any good to anyone, except travel agents. Indeed in my moments of real dissaffection the idea grows on me that man's declension began with the invention of the wheel. Then I reflect that even that is not enough, since the wheel seems to be the one device that space machines do not use, so perhaps it all began to go wrong with the invention of man.

These sorrowful considerations have been revived by the crash of the Soviet Cosmos thing on Canada (probably the first noteworthy event that has happened in Canada for two generations) but they have been lurking around for a long time – I think ever since I discovered that NASA in Houston has actually got a public Museum of Antique Spacecraft, dating back to the old Gemini. Is it imaginable that we are already in a generation of *antique* fantasies? Is it possible that already there should be veteran spacecraft, exhibited as interesting curiosities to the heedless young? Can we now look towards an Old Crocks race from Cape Kennedy to Mars, with drivers clad in the quaint old costumes of the 1960s? How seemly and proper it was that the Director of Space Flight Operations who took me round was called Christopher Columbus Kraft.

Now I am told (but in this field anyone can tell me anything) that there are upwards of 4300 vehicles of one sort or another at this moment encircling the earth. Many of them are nuclear- or isotope-powered, therefore a source of radioactivity whether they burn up in the high atmosphere or whether, as with the Russian Cosmos, they don't. This does not in any way appeal to me. There can be no purpose for a satellite, whether it be Russian, American, British or

Albanian, other than espionage. Satellites are supervising other people's troop movements or nuclear installations or submarine activities; that is to say they are spying. If they are weather satellites, they are spying on the weather. If they are astronomical satellites they are spying on someone else's planet. If they are communications satellites they are spying on our conversation. They are the great regiment of metallic nosey parkers in the sky, and every now and again some of them are going to tumble out of the sky and onto our heads. It is too much to hope that this will always happen in the wastes of north Canada.

30 January 1978

Hold Me for Questioning, Officer

After reading Jill Tweedie's page the other day I felt like giving myself up. Come to surrender, officer. For what? For the crime of being a man. I can't help it, scout's honour, but I accept that is no excuse. Nor could my parents blame the television, because there wasn't any; if there had been I might not have been here at all. So I plead guilty to rape, violence, making war, debasing women, lewdness, muggings, incest and murder. Hold me for questioning, officer, in connection with every male wrongdoing since the Great Apple Robbery in Eden. Only just keep me safe from the avenging Eve.

Jill Tweedie has reached the parts most Libbers miss. Her

15

argument is irrefutable. Most violence, most crime and most vice *is* committed by men. When a woman chances to perform an unsocial act – as, for example, luring her husband to a beach to be throttled by a couple of lovers – it is always at the instance of the vile impulses of some non-woman or other. This is statistically provable. Jill Tweedie's challenge cannot be gainsaid. Men are the root of all evil. No wonder they look so sheepish.

The fact that men have also been responsible for all the world's major art, all the great painting, literature, architecture, sculpture, science, music and philosophy is a gigantic cover for their original sin. For every William Shakespeare or Michelangelo there are ten thousand murderers, bank robbers (leave out Patti Hearst for the moment), wife beaters, pornographers and pimps. For every benign male statesman there are a dozen male dictators. (Leave aside Mrs Gandhi; she was son-fixated.) For every Desdemona there are scores of Othellos. The odd Jezebel and Lady Macbeth are exceptions that prove the rule.

Jill Tweedie must in no circumstances think that I am satirizing the issue; I am wholly sincere (in so far as fallible man can be) in my agreement with her conclusions. 'If we really wish to attack the rotten roots of our society it will do us no good to obscure the issue. Human nature is not the cause, male nature is.' Well, as Humpty Dumpty would say, there's a right knock-down argument for you. It cannot, of course, be denied. Every major social calamity originated in mankind rather than womankind. Men invented the sovereign state; men invented international conflict; men created wars (we can safely ignore Boadicea and the Rani of Jansi); men created the nuclear bomb. The first human assassin, Cain, was by all accounts a man; Attila the Hun was a man; Hitler was a man, sort of; I am told that God is generally held to be in male form. (The Hindu mythology takes a rather broader view, in that the Supreme Goddess of Destruction, Kali, is represented as a particularly unpleasant woman, but that is doubtless another symbol of male chauvinism in its natural home, which is Asia.)

Since Jill Tweedie has an unanswerable case, why is it then that I am not overcome by guilt? Alternatively, why don't I have her up before the Race Relations Board or whatever it is, for exacerbating hostility between the tribe that has balls and the tribe that hasn't? Because, I fear, I am a bit of a quisling in this sex-war matter. I tend to take the easy course, since for domestic harmony I better had. But the conflict wearies me. I have heard Jill Tweedie's argument so often (though to be sure not so succinctly put) and when it is reasonable I agree and when it becomes strident I shut up. Male and female created He them, whoever He might be, and for the life of me I do not know what I can do about it.

An old-time friend and colleague of mine did in fact do something about it: he went and had some discreet surgery and had himself turned into a woman, into which state he has ably accommodated himself. You would think that such a person would have been vigorously articulate about the sexual cause, but not so: he/she is a private and thoughtful person, and what is more has tried both sides, which is more than Jill Tweedie or I have done; he is interested now only in the Person Lib campaign, which I must say in my advancing years attracts me more and more. My friend solved his own conundrum in his own way and for his own reasons; he defected from the team but he did not denounce it.

Why do the males of the world virtually monopolize politics, commerce, diplomacy and crime? Why is the wolf pack led by the dog and not the bitch? Why do men commit so many violences and women so few? Why in fact is it necessary to make this abrupt query of the obvious? Simple – because nature ordained it, as it ordained so many preposterous things. Men on the whole are bigger, stronger, less vulnerable, marginally brainier, they inherit their dominance without necessarily seeking it. There might well be an element of what some mad psychologist could call Venus envy. With a tiny minority of exceptions men are not considered as sex symbols: Perhaps they wish they were.

Miss Tweedie says: 'The motivation behind prostitution is male and the law that punishes prostitution is male-conceived.' (I don't think there is any law that punishes prostitution, as a matter of fact.) 'Women do not take indecent photographs of nude children.' (How on earth do we know that this is so?) It is, I would have thought, manifestly true that the exploitation of the pornography trade is almost exclusively male, but it is hard to see how this could be accomplished without the willing cooperation of women.

I began by acknowledging the total correctness of Jill Tweedie's theorem: most of the world's violent crime is committed by men, or at least most of it that becomes publicly known. When was it ever otherwise? Man is almost always the sexual aggressor (with the exception of the odd Mormon allegedly screwed while chained to a bed, a bizarre concept of which I am told we shall soon hear more in *Penthouse* magazine; order your copy now, it is owned by a man). Those of us who can honestly claim never to have been a sexual aggressor will modestly say that we never had to be.

I concede the game, set and match to Jill Tweedie. The world would be better off without men at all. But it wouldn't last long.

2 May 1978

Empire Gains

Days of dilemma. Days of brine and posies. The other day the Prime Minister was good enough, or rash enough, or absent-minded enough, to give me a CBE, and I was impulsive enough, or vain enough, to take it. It caused much honourable dispute among my family, and mirth among my friends. I was told that by taking an Establishment gong, however mysterious its meaning, I had joined the Establishment and supinely surrendered all values of importance. This may well seem so, but it was not intended to be so. In any case they say, what say they, let them say.

I must admit that at the outset the situation seemed to have a most attractive irony. To be made a CBE, of all things – that is to say a Commander, no less, of an institution I had spent years of my time trying to diminish, or even abolish – seemed to me to argue an official whimsicality that I had never associated with our mirthless administration. I took it in that sense, assuming rather hastily that this inference, of a somewhat far-out joke, would be generally understood. Sometimes it was, sometimes it wasn't.

I was of course flattered. In all the years of my life I have received no official recognition for anything I have done (reasonably enough, since I did little enough for them), nor expected it, nor required it, nor asked for it, nor even wanted it. When it came, in my sixty-eighth year, it came in a form – a CBE – so comically preposterous that I thought nobody could possibly take it seriously. Many did – with generosity, with reproach, with hilarity. I was urged by my nearest and dearest to turn the thing down. It seemed to me that to do so would be a gesture of extraordinarily petty arrogance, inflating the obviously routine affair ('Well – anyone else would you say, PM?') to a piece of ludicrous pomposity. Downing Street had offered it in goodwill, for reasons I know not; I am not big enough nor important enough to be convincingly churlish about something done with good intent. I am not even a Beatle.

It has always seemed to me that the honours list is one of the dottier and more harmless eccentricities of our undefined constitution. Former paid-up members of the Communist Party accept peerages without batting an eye. Happily married old gents become Knights Bachelor. Lifelong anti-colonialists become Members of the British Empire. Charming and gifted girls become Dames (that which we know there is nothing like). Middle-aged servants of the Royal households join the Victorian Order, whatever that means.

I cannot imagine that my flinching from his nice CBE would have brought a tear to the eye of Mr Callaghan or sent him sulking to his tent. The list of people in this order of the civil list took nearly 48 column inches of microscopic type, squeezed into the page as tightly as the stonehand could ram it. I can't be bothered to count us but there must be hundreds and hundreds. Let me rationalize it once again; I am clearly part of a mass movement. CBEs of the world unite; you have nothing to lose but your – what?

Clearly it won't get you tickets for Wimbledon, nor bows from head waiters, nor free homes in tax havens. It carries no title, thank God, and, unthank God, no dough. What, no silk knee breeches? No funny hat? Not even a little rosette for the buttonhole?.

The State, which denies me the pension I have paid up for years because I obstinately insist on continuing to work for my living, now permits me to Command the British Empire. It is interesting, and nicely pointed, that it waited until I was entitled to command something that vanished years ago. *Qui s'excuse, s'accuse.* Woe unto them that draw iniquity with cords of vanity. (Solomon, that old prig.) However, you may henceforth Call Me Madam.

8 January 1979

Living on Peanuts, Bread and Scrape

The Post Office takes 165 square inches of *Guardian* newsprint space, not to speak of appropriate acreage in lesser newspapers, to ask us *not* to post letters. This is an interesting development in the field of advertising: the negative sell. The Post Office proclaims: we are providing an absolutely lousy service, so don't be fool enough to use it. This is rather troublesome since, at least for the time being, it is the only Post Office we have. A postage stamp will soon cost you a couple of bob; why write? Why not send a telegram, which will cost you a couple of quid. On posters everywhere the repulsive Buzby enjoins us to ring up anybody, anywhere, any time. What for? To make them happy. This is preposterous psychology. Few phone calls from me make anyone happy. I ring up only at times of stress or need, and whenever I can I call collect.

What is our dearly beloved Post Office up to? Losing money, so spending money in order to lose even more. My father used to tell me that when I was born, which I assure you was not yesterday, a letter mailed in London on Monday would reach Edinburgh on Tuesday morning, and it cost tuppence. Boy, bring me my cleft stick.

Now that I can no longer afford to drink, smoke, drive a car, or even post a letter, thanks to seven weeks of Tory benevolence, I have decided to round the thing off by giving up eating. This is a fact a lot easier than most people imagine. I have been practising for some time. To abandon breakfast is no hardship, since at that time the stomach is not in training for solids. Luncheon is a troublesome interruption of the day's work. By dinner time the question of food is academic; one has got out of the habit. I know a man who claims to have lived for years on the olives from his dry martinis and nothing else. All physicians, among whom I number my best friends, insist professionally that food is as necessary for the human body as petrol is for a car, but since I have no car the analogy as far as I am concerned is academic. I have not been hungry for many years. Not long ago I was in a hospital and I was fed through a tube that went from my nose to my inside. The bliss of it. No tiresome mealtimes, no irritating choosing from a menu, no wasteful effort of mastication; every now and then someone poured something in and that was that. In fact I did begin to feel like a car, which accepts its nourishment without question, and I cost a lot less per gallon.

All this arises from a day spent at Hintlesham in Suffolk with Robert Carrier, that celebrated restaurateur, gastronome and guru of the gut, king of the kitchen and prophet of the pot, who has written *far* more best-selling cookbooks than I have had hot dinners, or want to have. He is excellent company, but it could not have been a meeting of true minds, since as far as haute cuisine is concerned I do not approach an O-level. I described to him my own creation in the food field, the staple I have come to subsist on for a long time. This delicacy, which for some reason has to be taken at about five in the morning, has the following recipe: you take a slice of bread, preferably home-made, and on this you spread a thin veneer of Marmite. Over this you place a layer of peanut butter. (Sir James Goldsmith and President Carter will receive their accounts for this commercial in due course.) Finally you top the whole thing with an onion chopped as finely as you can. Then you eat half of it. Experts have told me that this *pièce de résistance* contains virtually all the dietary elements required for the fruitful sustenance of the human frame – protein, calories, vitamins, the lot. But when I defined its detail to Mr Carrier his face fell into a rigor of disbelief, or even pity.

'You *like* that thing?' quoth he. 'You eat it all the time?'

'Three or four days a week, at five in the morning.'

'I'll be damned.'

Then the great man fell into what resembled a momentary reverie, as of a towering artist unexpectedly stimulated by the stumblings of a babe and suckling. 'I'll try it,' he said, 'but I won't sell it.'

Can it be that by accident I have provided a footnote for some future Carrier *chef d'oeuvre?* Why not: one might as well be remembered for something. Dame Nellie had her peach melba. Arnold Bennett had his omelette. I want my *tartine aux peanuts*. Even if nobody else does.

2 July 1979

Life Begins at Forty-two

This young woman opposite me on the Northern Line of the Underground suddenly leaned over and said: 'I love you so dearly, can I come and live with you?' She was wonderfully attractive.

I was beginning to say: 'But of course; when do you suggest; I shall have to clear it with my wife.'

Then she gave another incandescent smile and got off the train; it was Euston, an absurd place to begin and finish an eternal relationship.

This sort of thing is starting to happen to me often these days; I presume I am becoming either vulnerable or safe. Perhaps it is the change of life, although I confess I notice little change. I have often wondered why the liberated ladies haven't long ago protested about this. They call it the menopause; surely it should be the womenopause? Must men be associated with the one thing they can't have? Personapause is preposterous. Poor old Moon, what he is blamed for. Or possibly she. However, if maturity – and I refuse to admit to more than that – causes pretty women strangers to make advances in trains, or indeed anywhere, then I have no complaint. Some day one of them is in for a big surprise.

As a *Guardian* reader I have noticed that recently my good and *cher collègue* Philip Hope-Wallace has started to muse a bit about getting on in years, or anyhow feeling as though he is, or indeed more properly feeling that other people feel he is. I know exactly what he means. Well, let me tell you that Philip Hope-Wallace and I are almost to a day of the same age. I happen to know this. Ours was a pretty vintage year. I would not have it changed. It was some time ago, to be sure, but it had one great distinction. It was the one year of the century when *absolutely nothing happened*. If I may quote myself from a book I once had the impertinence to write: 'Neither glory nor drama, no especial rejoicing and no memorable regret; no lights went out nor were illumined; no journalist ever evoked the year as a punctuation mark of any consideration. How fortunate and decorous, then, to have been born into an age of such tranquil anonymity. . . .' Thank goodness I did not have the gift of prophecy; by and by things turned out much otherwise. That anodyne year of my debut, which I leave you to work out, provided what I suppose were one or two moments of casual interest – the coronation of a king, the theft of the Mona Lisa from the Louvre. For some long-forgotten reason Italy declared war on Turkey, but apparently little came of it. My father was to tell me later of his outrage and dismay when the income tax soared to 1s. 10d. in the pound.

Many years ago I made a resolution, which I warmly commend to my cordial contemporary Philip, to stay at the age of forty-two for the rest of my life. That is a proper moment at which to petrify. If Marlene Dietrich can do it, why cannot I? There are many advantages in sticking at forty-two. One is young enough to be sprightly, yet old enough to be solid. I have many years' experience of being forty-two, and I see no reason to improve on it. Life begins at forty-two, and there it stays. There are, of course, minor drawbacks. It is hard to get a pension. It is hard to get a travel card on the buses or a senior citizen's railway concession. People will not ask you, 'What did you do in the Great War, daddy?' The BBC will not interview you about the brave days of the music hall, nor consider you for *Yesterday's Witness*. The appalling lapses of memory that beset one are less easily explained away. These are small disadvantages.

The late George Bernard Shaw, on the other hand, was a great one for bragging about his age. He treated it as one more of his talents, another aspect of his brilliance, of which he talked with increasing admiration until in his eighties, he talked of little else. Nevertheless in a radio talk to sixth-formers in 1937 he admitted that 'If a person is a born fool, folly will get worse, not better by a long life's practice.' (He hastened to add that this had not happened to him.) On his ninetieth birthday, in 1946, he went on the television and insisted that he was not only brilliant, and famous, and rich, but also popular. 'I am told,' he said, 'that I haven't an enemy in the world, and that none of my friends likes me.' He was proud of being brilliant and famous and rich, and of having lived so long, but clearly he didn't altogether enjoy it. That was probably because young women no longer accosted him in trains. If indeed they ever did.

I have just celebrated my twenty-fifth forty-second birthday, and it feels great. Long live Peter Pan. Not to mention, alas, Walter Mitty.

7 July 1979

Heaven Raiser

Until a few days ago I had an uncommonly good friend, just about a quarter my age. He was called Nicky, and we got on remarkably well, considering he was only sixteen when he died last week, and I am a bit older. Whenever we met, we argued on wholly equal terms about the affairs of the world, about which he cared at his age perhaps more than I do at mine. The world for Nicky was something that needed to be put right, as soon as he got the hang of how. I mention this just because these days it is the done thing to shoot down teenagers for their selfish and careless frivolity. Maybe I have done that myself in my time; I shall no longer.

Several years ago they diagnosed a cerebral condition that was terminal, or so they said. Nicky would have none of that stuff. He not only survived but also vanquished it. You would have thought he almost scorned it, because from then on he engaged himself most cheerfully in learning and reading and studying the antics of the society he was to inhabit for such a short time. Proper young junior wrangler was Nicky. All the things our lot, the journalists, wrote about as though everything were to be measured in column inches – as everything is – he took seriously, or at least carefully. Even as a small vivacious boy, he took politics to heart. That is unfair: not politics; he just in his merry way felt part of the human condition, which contains much to enjoy, but also a hell of a lot to question. When there was time from his schoolwork, or indeed his games, he got down to considerations like confrontation, refugees, nationalism, deprivation, injustices – all the things we think teenagers reject. Probably most do. He sometimes exasperated his thoughtless grown-ups by talking far too much about things of which children are not supposed to care – like apartheid and racism and disarmament. He argued even then that if he, young Nicky, did not care, nobody else would. Nobody listened enough, except sometimes I did. As far as I was able, I egged him on. That was how I got to know him then, and why I sorrow for him now.

As a schoolboy he was sufficiently curious about something – I have forgotten what – to write to the President of the United States requesting some sort of explanation of whatever it was. The President was discourteous enough not to reply, but it was hard to discourage Nicky. He wrote, at intervals, to Margaret Thatcher, to Secretaries of State. He wrote to Field Marshal Auchinleck, who was and is a family friend, albeit just eight decades older. Some came off and some didn't; the determined young inquisitor realized that you can't win them all. So he would sit down and write some more.

'What do you think,' said Nicky to me quite recently, 'can anyone ever change anything?'

I said: 'I've been trying for a damn long time, and I never brought anything off, but you may.'

'Why?' said he. 'Because I'm younger?'

'Yes. And I dare say brighter. Anyone's brighter than me.'

'Not anyone,' said Nicky. 'Probably quite a few.'

In retrospect I think his parents know that he felt he had so much to say because he had so little time in which to say it. We may be thinking in hindsight, but I do not believe Nicky thought that way. Strange that a sixteen-year-old should leave concerned not about his future but about ours. He brought more verve and care into his sixteen years than most of us do in thrice that time. I shall never again sell teenagers short, anyhow.

This little boy – as I first knew him, and young man as he came to be – was full of zest and love of life, and he enjoyed the things kids enjoy, and he wrote to Washington because he had something to say to the President of the United States. Sometimes he telephoned me to ask what on earth I meant by something I had written, and really wanted to know. Unless you are in this crazy business, you cannot imagine what sort of reward that is.

That is why I am writing this total irrelevancy today, forgetful of a hundred things of greater importance, because one vigorous and questioning life has been untimely quenched, and no one will ever know why.

Now you are in Heaven, Nicky, give 'em Hell.

Save a place for me.

29 July 1980

Ethereal Spheres

Spring has come a little early this year, and the academic air stirs to the sound of a hundred cuckoos. They are mostly dons, and not a few are Quixotes too.

An assumption of false innocence is a well-known way of appearing to be smarter than one is. I have made use of the ploy as often as most, but here my hand is on my heart. It could be immaturity or it could be advancing years, but I have begun to hate new words, especially daft ones. What is this 'structuralism' that seems to be on everyone's lips, especially in Cambridge? Who is this post-structuralist Foucault, who argues that the discontinuities between our own and other ages vitiate the attempts of reconstruction of the 'contextualists'? Why do we need the specialized techniques of the structuralist anthropologist or linguistic philosopher? Just tell me, I need to know, if I am ever again going to hold up my head in the Mucky Duck.

I have always been uneasy in the presence of ostentatious intellectualism. Also, of course, ostentatious anti-intellectualism, such as perhaps I am showing now, though not aggressively. The noble *Guardian*, ready as ever with the hospitality of its columns to men and women of goodwill, however nutty, has been having a ball, defined as a spherical mode of evaluation resulting, as with billiards, in balls. 'Semiotics' are not, as one had always supposed, the study of the half-mad ('You must excuse him, poor soul, he was born semiotic.') It is the study of signifying systems of which language, a structure of phonemic and conceptual differences, is but one. God forfend I find out about the others, or I shall never write again.

It has to be admitted that there is a vaguely hypnotic quality about all this serious folderol. Only this past weekend, for instance, I read that 'according to the idealist principles of structuralism, the secrets of human nature may be unlocked through the contemplation of language'. As though that were not enough – that human nature communicates through words – 'the ultimate aim of such scrupulous intellectual hygiene is not truth but transcendence, not knowledge but nirvana'.

Actually I am rather fond of jargon. I do not derive the obfuscations of, for example, advanced mathematicians, or specialized disciplines which obviously need a technical lingua franca. Just as a newspaperman needed – or at least in my days as a sub-editor, briefly after Caxton – to use trade shorthand and go on about 30-point Cheltenham Bold across three-into-two and long-forgotten typefaces like sans serif and nonpareil and pica and bourgeois, pronounced burjoice. Printing was a literary trade in those days, even if journalism was not.

But that were just to tell us fellas what to do. Didn't tell us what to *think*. Didn't insist on no scrupulous intellectual hygiene. Or did it? There are terminologies wildly difficult, but they are specific and taut and precise and used, as a rule, only among specialists for specific purposes. Good doctors never blind you with science. I cannot imagine my own telling me that I am suffering from pharyngeal dysphagia. Since it means difficulty in swallowing it is in any case unlikely to affect me. I could, I suppose, fall victim to pityriasis dysphagia which, as we all know, is characterized by continuous desquamation. Desquamation! Now there is a word I could cherish, if I knew what it meant. 'Pity Riasis, old comrade of days. I hereby desquame that he did not live in vain. . . .' But my Black's *Med. Dic.* is even older than I: maybe desquamation has gone the way of ladies' vapours or the gout.

All these things were not nonsense; they defined something that could not be defined otherwise, they did not draw vaporous rings around something that can never be otherwise than an abstraction – the process of language – and by doing so turn communication upside down. 'In representing himself in this eirenic light, Dr MacCabe has sought to obscure the substantive issues at stake.' You bet he has; he was glowing through an eirenic light darkly. But this is the currency of semantic argument. In the beginning was the word. In the end was the eirenic light.

I ask pardon of my learned gentles, the academics. By admitting freely and frankly to the dons and donesses – I too can invent words – that this preceding stuff can be shrugged off as the easy satire employed by the Philistines to deride what they do not properly comprehend. I clearly reveal my insecurity. 'It is a structure of phonemic and conceptual differences that divides our world.'

There could, perhaps, be other things, forgotten by the colleges of Cambridge. What's in a name? That which we call a rose by any other name would smell as sweet. Would it? Even if that rose were called *esquobarbulos feetida,* as it has been in my family since the supernatural concept was an immature male human, or, alternatively, since God was a boy.

It is easily seen that I never went to Cambridge.

10 February 1981

Sacred Blues

Another bunch of slickers is monkeying about with Holy Writ, and I deplore it. The Bible is too Good a Book to need trendifying. Thou hadst not thought to read such words from me, but there thou ist.

I do not go to the kirk, and I am one of little faith. I am what my late Wee Free grandad, of whom I brag continually (and who himself wrote a Doric translation of the Psalms) would have called a flawed Christian. Yet I read, or dip into, the Bible more than I bet most of thee, my brethren; it is one of my bedroom books, along with the papist E. Waugh and the impious Orwell. I do this not for spiritual comfort or moral reassurance, since I am reckoned to be now beyond the reach of either. I read it to help me in my job, the only one I know: I read it to learn how to write.

Now another group of saboteurs ('more than 130 scholars from eight countries working for seven years') has just published another rejig of the Authorized Version. That seems to me to be a lot of time and manpower to corrupt and devalue an antiquated manuscript that, even from a sensitive pagan point of view, needs no improvement. It reminds me of a well-to-do acquaintance of mine who, to conform with his ghastly decor, painted a Sheraton sideboard white.

According to my revered colleague Martyn Halsall, the *Guardian's* Churches Correspondent (now there is a daunting job), the scholars decided that more non-stop and reverent activity was required, and commissioned the new version. Literature in their view must not be left to the literate; it is time that the Philistines got in on the act. This indeed may be right in the case of railway timetables or daily newspapers; I question if the judgment holds in works of, however minor, art.

For me, in this case, the medium *is* the message. Why else should heretics read the Testaments unasked, but that they value the words more than lessons? The religious do not have to be cajoled or convinced by poetry, though poetry must make it more persuasive. The unbeliever will not be seduced by words, however graceful, but he will read them with pleasure, to which even agnostics are entitled from time to time.

Of course crude parsons can corrupt the words into liturgical parody, and that is their fault, not their script's. My namesake, the late Scottish turncoat King James VI (I) in the seventeenth century commissioned a better pride of poetry than did the editor of this anodyne version, Dr Raymond Brown of Spurgeon Theological College, whoever he may be. He is far from the first to know better than his betters. Only last year the Gideons International, purveyors of Holy Writ to the world's hotels, put out their own Bible Mark XV, which is less abrasive than the new one, but still a mockery of the old dignities. Why do they do this?

Can it be the churchmen are running scared? Today we also have a revamped *Hymns for Today's Church* from Hodder's, a work of crushing banality that even attracted the derision of the well-known iconoclasts' journal *Private Eye*. Even that does not make it acceptable.

Always one to get in on an act, I am in process of preparing an updated *Works of Shakespeare,* or the *Moron's Bard.* I have not yet got very far, but I submit these examples of how all that Elizabethan waffle can be fined down to a reasonable economy:

Hath not old custom made this life more sweet
Than that of painted pomp?
Revised Version: Weren't you better off the way you were?

W.S.: Weariness can snore upon the flint.
When rested sloth finds the down pillow hard.
R.V.: A certain physical tiredness can doze off in a third-class railway carriage, while the unemployed man has difficulty dozing in the Ritz.

W.S.; Give thy thoughts no tongue,

Nor any unproportioned thought his act;
Be thou familiar, but no means vulgar.

R.V.: Keep your mouth shut. Give them a chance, but play it straight.

W.S.: To be or not to be, that is the question.
Whether 'tis nobler in the mind to suffer
The slings and arrows of outrageous fortune
Or to take arms against a sea of troubles
And by opposing end them.

R.V.: It's a matter of priorities. Either put up with your bad luck, or you do something about it.

I am in good company. In last week's *Guardian* a Yorkshire vicar, Peter Mullen, was sounding off in angry criticism of this new hymnal, too. To be sure, much of the old one was doggerel, but it was fairly decent doggerel, even accepting that it had a few superfluous thees and thous. Poor old Cranmer and Newman and Wesley would writhe at all the 'can'ts' and 'won'ts' and pidgin poetry, as though they had been adapted for the *Sun* newspaper.

This is not of much importance, since it is unlikely that anyone will take this 1982 hymnbook seriously. Many youngsters, however, may well come upon this Dr Brown's new Patent Bible and take it to be the thing their elders have been for years telling them to read for style and will take us to be crazy. As I see it, 'testament' means 'covenant'. That means you do not break faith. Whatever that may be.

23 November 1982

Silly Season Fans Start Here

Let us get the year off to a suitable start: 1982 is less than a week old and already five funerals have engaged our household. Could one ask for more? Whether it be the cold weather or the well-known Cameron Curse I know not, but one after another the old-established residents of our fishpond are giving up the ghost as never before and being buried with full piscine honours, whatever they may be. Five in a week. There is some mystery here. Our fishpond has sustained a population of about two dozen for at least ten years without loss; indeed it went from strength to strength, in so far as one is able to assess the enigmatic society of fish. My own fortunes fluctuated. But the fish waxed fat and prospered. Until now: why?

I cannot believe it was anything personal. Indeed it was very cold, and I would not have chosen personally to spend the last weeks in a pond, but in the past the fish have spent many a winter under the ice and taken no ill; why should they cave in now? I can only believe that in the last year they have learned to read the papers. This, as we all now, is the step before the last.

The fish are called, variously, Victoria, Michael, Yvonne, Groucho and Adar, named after friends whom they resembled, either in appearance or character. The leader was a dominant Prussian carp whom we had reared from infancy to a robust pound and a half. His name was Bismark, and I had hoped one day to see him stuffed and framed over the mantelpiece, not disintegrating in a nameless grave under the apple tree. He was the last to keel over, only yesterday, and we shall not see his like again. I am seriously concerned about this sudden mortality among this hitherto able-bodied colony. Where, after all these years, did we go wrong? I would seriously value an authoritative opinion, and you will agree that is something I rarely ask.

I am not an especially zealous pet-person. Dogs are troublesome and demanding; cats are contemptuous; rabbits are simply foolish; horses are expensive and resentful; goats eat everything except that which is offered to them. Only fish and reptiles fulfil a proper domestic function, which is to be there when you want them and to disappear when you don't. Tortoises are the best of all at that. When fish are happy they do not yell or bark or mew; they merely assemble in their chosen corner of the pond and hang about trustingly; if they are fed they are doubtless grateful; if they are not they do not repine or make a fuss, or not as far as anyone can detect. When I contemplate my fish in their little watery ghetto I feel like a sort of rather kind Hitler. This is good for my ego and bad for my soul.

Similarly, with snakes, man's ideal companion, since they neither give affection nor demand it. Many a time and oft have I told the tale of Christopher, the faithful old grass snake, who travelled thousands of miles over the world in my overcoat pocket, emerging at nights for a routine romp, partly for physical company and partly for intellectual stimulation, until one day he lost himself forever down a radiator in the Pierre Hotel, New York, and for all I know is there still, among that legendary colony of lost pet alligators who are said to multiply annually in the labyrinth of the Manhattan sewers, which must now resemble the Amazon. If one is to believe the recurrent stories in the New York press, which I for one do not.

Truly the Silly Season begins earlier every year. T. S. Eliot was wrong: April is not the cruellest month; it is January, breeding no lilacs out of the dead land, mixing memory and desire, stirring bull roots with spring rain, pretending to start a new year but only ending an old one, showing fear in a handful of dust, and where I meant to write about fate I find myself on about fish. All those 360 days over the hill.

So cheer up my lads, 'tis to glory we steer; only fifty more weeks till the end of the year.

15 January 1982

Yuanupmanship

You will agree in your charity that I rarely weary the customers with the analysis of economics or the stockmarket, for the same reason that I do not go on about Test matches or Wimbledon or the binomial theorem – which is that I know little about them. That I become a financial expert now must mean that I am growing up, or we are growing down.

The sterling crisis is of great and growing concern. The value of the pound is not a matter to be taken lightly as the flippant journalists tend to do. I have for many years been preoccupied with the pound sterling, not so much for its relation with the dollar (which is no longer of much moment to me because I no longer nip off to the US as in days of yore); my concern with the pound has largely been about how to get hold of one or two more, nor can I recall any time when this was not the case.

The sterling crisis is nothing new to me. True, I do not go on and on about it on the radio half a dozen times a day like Sir Geoffrey Howe; likewise I do not requisition enormously expensive public-owned aircraft to ferry me on PR jaunts to the Falklands for a few days' Rejoice-session – and then, if you please, come home and argue about 'sound money' as though the stuff started to dissolve the moment she turns her back.

Which, of course, it does, and has been doing for years. The first pay I ever earned, as a provincial newspaper office boy, was thirty bob a week. It was not affluence, but I cannot remember going hungry. Not with beans on toast for fourpence. I survived. I prospered. By the time I was making £9 a week I was rich enough to get married. My affluence astounded me. I thought nothing of taking someone out to dinner and paying 25s. for two, plus a carafe for half-a-crown.

By and by I came to London and climbed instantly into the lower middle class at a salary not unadjacent to 900 solid pounds a year. Even dizzier heights awaited me, when I was recruited into the late *News Chronicle,* owned then by Laurence Cadbury, who also made chocolate and was known in the trade as 'Mr Hard Centre'. There my meteoric climb to fortune came to a pause, because Mr Cadbury believed strongly in reporters' spiritual wellbeing, and saw no reason to tempt his staff with filthy lucre. His foreign editors, however, had fewer inhibitions, and after some years working abroad it occurred to me that I was getting about eleven times more in expenses than I ever saw in a pay packet. Then, of course, the poor old *News Chronicle* got the chop, its owners tearfully explaining that they couldn't afford to keep it going. Mr Cadbury himself died not long ago and, as I read at the weekend, left £981,560; so I am glad to say that my selfless sacrifice was not in vain.

Being translated so often to foreign parts had the inevitable result of causing me to think only erratically in sterling terms, because from then on it was funny money all the way. There were anomalies. When I first went to China in the fifties, the fluctuating exchange rate of the local money was, as I recall it, something preposterous like 68,000 yuan to the pound. This made a handbag almost imperative to carry around the great wads of disintegrating paper needed to buy a box of matches. I suggested to a senior finance ministry man that there could surely be no harm in changing the rate to something more reasonable. Patiently he sat me down and explained how this would cause untold financial complications and, in short, could not be contemplated. Within a matter of weeks, long before I left, it was announced that with a daring inspiration China was about to change the yuan rate to something like 60 to the pound. So do not keep saying that I am no economist: I changed the money value for 600 million people, or so I like to believe. Just ask my friend Mr 'Cadger' Dow Jones, who never indexes anything without consulting me.

There is a telling little scene in the Attenborough film when Gandhi, freed from gaol by South Africa's leader Jan Smuts, asks if he can borrow a shilling to pay his fare home. Smuts searches his pockets and finds he hasn't got one. They have to borrow it from the footman. Or witness the tale of Nubar Gulbenkian, the enormously wealthy Armenian who lived in the Ritz and who rode round London in a custom-built replica of a London taxi – 'because,' said he, 'I'm told it will turn on a sixpence. Whatever that may be.'

I like currencies that have odd names, or odd shapes. It pleased me when Israel went back to the 'shekel', though I understand you need a great many of them. I lived in Ireland some years ago during an interminable bank strike, when paper money literally ran out through being worn ragged, and at a County Cork petrol station I was given my change in three herrings. How J. M. Keynes would have approved. I first arrived at Bangkok for the first time in the middle of the night. I could not remember what currency they used. I asked the hotel clerk as I checked in. 'In Siam.' he said, 'you get forty tickals to the pound.' He was in fact underrating it.

Nevertheless it is a nice thought, to remember the pound. Whatever that may be.

18 January 1983

Dressing Down

Today, as all true unbelievers know, is the Feast of Saint Jacobus the Saintly Sceptic, who long, long ago was appointed by the Almighty (as has been said about all good mullahs) to find a difficulty for every solution. I cannot honestly say that the situation obsesses me. I have spent much of my life in the society of Muslems, Hindus, Jews and Christians, not to speak of their multifarious by-products and sub-divisions, that ages ago I accepted the usefulness of their schisms, for them, while insisting on the infallibility of my own curiously exclusive Cult of Aporetic and Humble Sceptics, whose symbol is the Revolving Signpost.

All this sounds preposterous, of course, to those who believe vigorously in God or vigorously otherwise. I am in neither camp from indifference; quite the contrary: I have tried too hard for too long to accept any sort of dogmatism. I am not devout enough to believe nor confident enough to deny, and formal agnosticism seems to me as arrogant as either. I have tried to explain this so often that I can even bore myself, but I know what I mean even if no one else does. I once got the late Archbishop of Canterbury in such a dialectical mess over this that he suggested we change jobs. That would have been a turn-up for the Good Book.

35

It must be something to do with the time of year, or the crazy climate, or the change of life (which whatever the doctors say is every bit as important to men as to women), but even the crudest materialists, like me, get occasionally drawn into metaphysics. Why otherwise, I ask myself, should I suddenly start thinking about Elizabeth Taylor?

Miss Taylor is a film actress and, it is fair to say, makes no great secret of it. I think I can claim to be one of the few male human beings who has never married Elizabeth Taylor. I feel therefore an impulse to salute her on her eighth (or is it eighteenth?) go at the blessed state. Not having married Elizabeth Taylor is a distinction granted to few able-bodied men, and I respect and indeed brag about it. However, there was one narrowish escape, which I can now reveal exclusively for the first time, and naturally for a fee so huge that it would keep even Miss Taylor for a couple of hours.

You will perhaps be aware that I rarely intrude my personal life into this public column. This is because my personal life is of a dullness so excruciating that if I were to go on about it all *Guardian* readers would instantly hurry off for light entertainment to the *Times Educational Supplement*. Miss Taylor was at the time passing through London, and I was despatched to 'interview' her, as the phrase went in those days, in her suite in one of the posh London hotels that even in those days only the employees of film companies could afford. It was not the sort of job that often came my way, and I repaired with diligence to the umpteenth floor of wherever it was. This was, I repeat, some twenty-five years ago, when I was in my prime, and Miss Taylor not too far beyond hers.

She received me with considerable grace, even, I felt, enthusiasm. She was costumed in what Hollywood would probably define as Informal, but which I took to be a Negligee to the point of negligence. In my innocence I felt already that we were starting Scene 10 Take 12 of *Antony and Cleopatra,* and I was deeply conscious of my M & S shirt, which I would have unbuttoned had I been more confident of my undervest. Miss Taylor offered me a glass of champagne (what else?) which, then as now, I find difficult to enjoy, having cruder Caledonian tastes. I gobbled it up with simulated delight, and got busy with the 'interview'.

I was at the time much more accustomed to middle-aged Asian politicians, who wanted to talk about emergent economics of the third world. This was only too clearly not to Miss Taylor's taste – nor, as the moments passed, to mine. Cross purposes is hardly the phrase to define our little chat. I became growingly interested in decolletage; Miss Taylor less and less in me. How were the economics of the Hollywood industry affecting her?

'Well, eff that,' said the lovely lady, 'we are talking about your proposition for the new contract.'

From that moment on it became clear that the lovely Miss Taylor had totally mistaken me for someone else. Her dates had got mixed; the man Miss Taylor had been expecting, and for whom she had beguilingly undressed, was a movie agent of some importance whose name had a vague resemblance to mine. Once this important fact had been firmly established, I was out on the landing in no time.

I don't know how I got on this silly subject; the Archbishop would certainly have ticked me off. Won't happen again.

16 August 1983

Nightcap on the News

In this Westminster institution – the hospital, not the political Palace of Varieties up the road – the only place where we patients are tacitly allowed to smoke is the TV room. Newcomers learn this by the sign 'No smoking' just discernible through the tobacco reek from the elderly addicts, momentarily escaping from the disciplines of the day. In the corner is the Box, forever locked on ITV, offering at least a few images other than our own boring, old, grousing, querulous faces across the ward. The telly is life, the world as it should be. *Coronation Street* is a vision of wonderland. Bruce Forsyth is the Voltaire of our time. Anna Ford is our oracle. Or at least they would be if anyone paid the slightest attention to any of them.

With our lot, the medium is not the message. The telly room is the sanctuary of the forbidden fag, the tiny clubhouse where old boys and girls in our dressing gowns can cosy up and chat about the things the doctors do not want to know; where no one is going to ram things into you, or pump stuff out of you. God bless the cathode ray tube – that gives us the evening off. On the little screen the comedians joke in desperation, the police cars scream skidding round Californian corners, the commercials tell us how to care for cats and how to fly to Singapore. They jest and skid and urge in vain. They are there, wherever that may be, to give us an excuse to discuss our bowel movements, our operations, our homesickness, our in-laws. Now and again, by chance, attention turns briefly to the television, because that is supposedly why we are here. Sometimes the image is powerful enough to quench conversation for a minute or two. There is a programme about the ghastly famine in Uganda; a couple of heroic English nurses trying to cope with the spectacular miseries of Karamoja. They hold the skeletal, almost lifeless frames of tiny children; horrifying. For a while we looked.

'My, aren't they skinny? They ought to feed the poor little buggers up a bit. Blacks, I should say. African or Chinese or something. Someone ought to tell their mums to make them eat a bit more. Listen, did I tell you our Janet's lost 8lb? About time if you ask me. And by the way. . . .'

The telly fades away; something subliminal remains.

'I tell you, Maureen, you can't deny the council is giving all the flats to the blacks. Why I'll never know. You'd think they'd some sort of rights, just being here. You've only got to look. . . .'

We look, and a demure little black nurse comes in with a tray of cocoa. 'Or would you like a cup of tea?'

'Why, thanks dear; very nice I'm sure.'

There is no way of reconciling this sort of thing, and I am far too tired to try.

How busy one is kept doing nothing. Gently and forcibly detached and insulated from the real considerations of the world, one feels everything outside blending together in one remote irrelevance. The other day Jewish New Year got itself somehow mixed up with arguments about the Pope's threatened visit to England. Neither circumstance had much moment for any of us; it made a change from talking about our insides. By and by it began to pall. Is there a world outside the ward?

There is of course the radio ear-set. For a few seconds the pop music is punctuated by a breathless bulletin of news. It seems there has been some sort of a coup d'état in Turkey. I don't know; is that news? I freely admit that to me the politics of Turkey defy analysis. I never liked the place; I never understood its convoluted wranglings, and long ago I gave up trying. Here, however, I might possibly catch up a bit. No go. By the time the newspaper trolley arrives here, it is left with a few copies of the *Tit Times* and the *Mammary Mail*. If they care about Mr Bulent Ecevit or Mr Necmettin Erbakan or General Kenan Evren, they do not make much of it. If they are concerned about Mrs Thatcher's fiscal policies they do not force them on their customers. This is a pity, because I need help there too, and how.

My next-bed neighbour is a well-meaning, considerate gentleman. He detects withdrawal symptoms in me, and tries to help.

'So what do you do for a living, Mr C.?'

I find this hard to explain even to myself, let alone to a kind stranger.

'I write bits and pieces for a paper.'

'Well, I never.' Interest leaks away. I strive desperately to retrieve it. 'I sometimes do bits for the telly.'

'You don't say! Like Anna Ford?'

'Yes. I like Anna Ford awfully much. Except that in that bloody TV room you can't hear a word she says.'

'Well, that don't matter much, does it? It's the way she says it.'

'The way she says *what*?'

'Any bloody thing.'

He must be right. No good asking him to explain the Turkish situation. Certainly no good asking me. Back to square one. Back to the page three ladies. Could they help? Doubtful. It is curious how indistinguishable are the torsos of naked women. But so are fingerprints, except to experts. So are Turkish coups d'état.

Welcome visit by good friends Martin Woollacott and John Cunningham. They are off to the office to find someone to explain the Turkish situation. It is not high on their priorities. By now it has totally vanished from mine. Roll on Horlicks time. I suspect that Martin and John are already pausing at the pub. I do not, repeat not, hope it chokes them.

'Thank you, staff nurse, I am absolutely fine and I'm going home tomorrow. Tell me, where are you from?'

'Long ago my family originally came from Istanbul.'

And so to bed.

16 September 1980

These
Semi-Sceptred Isles

It's a Long Way from Vladivostok

Among the many little truisms we learned at our mother's knee, or across our father's, and which we must now forget, is the one that says that crime doesn't pay. Crime does pay. It has paid off all over the Middle East, in Europe, in the UN, and now in England, for whatever happens to the senseless barbarians of Birmingham the fact remains that they have succeeded in putting the liberal way of life back by decades – and *for* decades – and since that is what they wanted to do, their crime has paid. If we start hanging these murderous creeps it will have paid even more. At least it will have made the rather ignoble point that it took four years and the Birmingham bombs to arouse us to the desolation and fear the Northern Irish have suffered so long, and to make Roy (The Modern Draco) Jenkins aware that Ulster is a different place with different rules to which undesirables can be transported, as if it were another Botany Bay.

Before I leave this luckless land forever, as I shall have done by the time you read this (well, perhaps forever is a big word for the ten days I shall be gone, but the mood is the same) there is yet time to reflect on the oddity that at the very moment when local murder is becoming increasingly unpopular, global war is now an occupation for gentlemen. Which is much the same thing as saying that Birmingham's a long way from Vladivostok.

Mr Jenkins responds to the activities of the anonymous and cowardly IRA bombers by imposing a new social dimension on the country, the half-hearted likeness of a police state, for which in some ways we may be obliged to him. At least we can recognize the context in which, in a word, we are all suspects now, since any brave boyo can now carry our destiny in a shopping bag, and if ordinary life becomes extremely irksome now I do not see how we can reasonably complain. I have worked in so many countries where the carrying of identity cards and *dokumenti* is an accepted obligation that it won't worry me. It is really small stuff.

The interesting paradox to me is that the same week that we started worrying about shopping bags and mail boxes, President Ford and Mr Brezhnev in Vladivostok were coming to an agreement on how most economically to blow up the world. Or not, as the case may be, since whatever these two great leaders did actually decide, or even discuss, so far remains very misty even by the standards of these opaque men. So far as any of us are concerned – those of us, that is, who read the bits on page two – it appears to amount to 'an agreement on guidelines for negotiations', on, when the time comes, the precise methodology for one half of the planet destroying the other.

It appears to be a very gentlemanly arrangement. The last World War will be run almost on Queensberry rules, or better still the conventions of a formal eighteenth-century duel to the death. There will be an agreed limitation on the deployment of multi-entry doomsday machines, but the US will be allowed to keep a long-range bomber capacity, while cutting down a trifle on nuclear submarines, at the same time conceding that the USSR may keep a marginally superior stock of the dreaded SS18 which, I am given to understand by my Dracula-type friends, can do anybody in within 200 miles. It sounds like the ultimate in nuclear clubmanship. *Que messieurs les assassins tirent d'abord.* Dr Kissinger, in one of his engaging turns of phrase, said: 'We are in the same ball park.' It is one of the troubles with Dr Kissinger that he will use unwise sporting analogies; they make me uneasy, particularly when you consider the balls he is both talking and talking about.

However, to extend the Vladivostok metaphor to our local situation would suggest that the IRA would be permitted to operate up to and including 55lb of gelignite, recognizably packed, provided that the police agreed to carry handguns up to 22mm, and to hang only those terrorists actually caught on the premises of Buckingham Palace. Translated into these terms the proposition is of course bizarre, and might probably be difficult to enact through Parliament. Nevertheless it is more or less what President Ford is trying to steer through Congress (which is actually being consulted, for a change). Mr Schlesinger, the US Defence Secretary, says that America has the option of selectively destroying Russian missile sites or obliterating cities, and he sounds as though he is doing us all a favour. We debate whether we should hold bomb suspects for 48 hours or five days. It is a most interesting set of double standards, and wholly comprehensible, since we know nothing about MIRVs in the stratosphere and we know about little bombs in pubs. Or some of us do; perhaps too few. I have in my life seen three atom bombs go off. I have never seen anyone blinded in a four-ale bar. Perhaps I would be a better witness if I had.

For the past year or so the news has brought us visible evidence of continuing violence – from Israel, where schoolgirls are shot in their beds, from Lebanon, where equally innocent people die in reprisal, from Ireland, where sudden death is part of life, from Tunis, where an astonished businessman is shot dead for no reason he could possibly understand, from Munich, from Lod, and now from England, where every mailbox is a challenge and every unattended suitcase is a threat.

It is a new kind of crime altogether – the crime for advertisement. It is a new situation in that sorrow and suffering is achieved for the *sake* of sorrow and suffering, as an end in itself, because it gets publicity, and thus groups without actual power commit loud and senseless outrages *only* to get visibility in a world largely indifferent to them and their causes.

The difference between the pub bomber/airplane hijacker and the soldier is that he exploits not his enemy's weakness but his compassion and concern. The use of hostages (which we may well see here soon) simply makes use of the adversary's conscience, obliging everyone to choose between surrender to blackmail or the deaths of innocent people. Conscience is thereby priced very high indeed, and the dumbest terrorist knows it.

Here comes our dilemma – 'our' being what we are reluctantly obliged to call the media, who are complicit in everything. The bombers, the hijackers, the Tupamaros, the PLO, do their work for the coverage they get. Since it is propaganda, the press and the TV become their instruments. At the same time, a propaganda crime is a true happening, in which real people are killed and blinded, which by any standards is news. This is a problem: when someone commits cruel murder to get in the press or on the TV, should he be so indulged? His murder will thereby be rewarded. Yet it cannot conceivably be ignored. My own view is that these truly dirty deeds are counter-productive; this is wholly personal. My trade has obliged me to share in so much organized death that I now have a peculiar loathing of violence, even for – or even especially for – 'patriotic' motives, and the lousiest IRA sneak-killer would argue that he had loyalties; moreover only an imbecile would deny that the Irishmen's cause exists, and indeed may well be right. And every nauseating destruction of the innocents undermines and diminishes that cause, until it is lost in disgust. To my mind, this is a poor victory. We share in the whole process. When the cameras move in on the wrecked pub, or the limp and daggered Arab corpses flung from the kibbutz window, we watch it, because we cannot do otherwise. Thus we help the story unfold, and complete the crime.

To the rest of the world the Irish business is pretty small stuff because it is largely incomprehensible; the outsider's reasonable query is why the hell the Pope doesn't move in and at least *say* something about it: a proper point. Far more immediate to most people is the more spectacular and longer-term violence to the random traveller, which can happen anywhere. In an hour or two from now I shall pass through the airport security control, I shall presumably be searched in a desultory way, inconvenienced and delayed, which would be welcome if in fact it effectively stopped the violence in the air, which manifestly it does not.

The point about this new dimension to peaceful travellers' lives is that it is another corruption of liberty with which we have got to come to terms, presumably for ever, since the search for the publicity crime looks like being with us so long as it pays off in headlines, and so long as no international action exists to deal with it *as a whole*. The obvious body for this sort of anti-violence cooperation would have been the United Nations, and once one could have had hopes of that morally moribund institution. But now the UN publicly acclaims an admitted conspirator and gives its imprimatur to a blackmailing gangster. Since Arafat can win international recognition and respectability by terrorism (with Britain bravely brandishing its equivocations by not daring to vote either way) why should not the IRA be heartily encouraged to do likewise? One day we shall be obliged to treat formally with the IRA, just as ultimately we had to treat with the Mau Mu in Kenya, EOKA in Cyprus and with every anti-colonialist revolution with an arguable case, however repellent the manner of its promotion. One day we shall be obliged to think about that, when once again history has taught that it teaches nothing.

With how much more decorum do the real Mr Bigs of the strong-arm world compose their mutual hates and fears, organizing their arms race into a sort of awful Olympiad – with everything except a referee. What does it matter if Russia and America can stock up enough packaged death to blow the planet up three times, providing they can arrange to do it together. Meanwhile we cross the street when we see a postbox. I do like a nice sense of proportion.

2 December 1974

Honour Blight

It is old stuff now, and the ritual ribaldry is done, but the wound still smarts. The weekend has let the fact sink in that once again – for the fourteenth, the fifteenth, time? – I have been passed over for my peerage. This happens time and again, presumably through some bureaucratic oversight. I may have been petulant in the past, but this time one can only thank God for having been spared. This bunch of jokers, chancers and comic singers ennobled in Wilson's final frivolity established forever that the only honour worth having now is to be left alone.

The thing seems a worse outrage than it did three days ago. I am not acquainted with Harold Wilson (obviously, or I would now be in the queue at Moss Bros for my ermine) so I do not understand his motives. If his considered idea was to bring the establishment of the Lords into ridicule and mockery, he has done it. This in no way bothers me, since I hold it to be a preposterous institution anyway. If he wanted to bring the whole method of the Labour Party into almost irremediable disrepute he has done that too, and that matters a lot more. Sir Harold Wilson, grabbing his own absurd Garter first, has turned out to be a pretty bad joke. Indeed a friend of mine who was himself rash enough to accept a life peerage some years ago was moved sufficiently to make a serious inquiry of the Clerk as to how he could now resign it. He was told that he could not. You can, with some difficulty, relinquish a hereditary handle, but a life peerage is for life. You should, he was told, have thought of that before you took it on. He reflected ruefully on Groucho Marx's old philosophy: 'Any club that would accept me I wouldn't want to join.' Well, he kens noo.

I know very little of these new noblemen, and that is quite enough for me. The only thing in common among them, as far as anyone can see, is that none of them is a socialist, or has done a hand's turn for the cause of the Left – which of course is their prerogative, having mostly eluded the working class some time ago, doubtless with relief. The catalogue of their names startled even the *Times* leader into saying: 'These are the very people whose lives are the

47

contradiction of everything for which the Labour Party stands.' It is hard not to feel now that the same must be said for the former Mr Wilson.

What must have made every Wilsonian writhe in embarrassment was the storm of irony that greeted this new collection of coronets. Old-fashioned lords could be tyrants or dunderheads, they could even, literally, be given the chop, but they were not figurees of fun, they were not millionaire money jugglers or mackintosh manufacturers or escaped vaudevillians, now promoted into senior legislators of the Upper House of Parliament by a bizarre quirk of personal patronage. For that is the point: the nonsense of the titles is of less importance than that this quaint crowd is now potentially part of the machinery of government. I say potentially, for it is unlikely that these Kagans and Delfonts and so on will spare much time from their lucrative activities to become political meteors in that geriatric institution of Westminster, even for £13 a day, the standard lordly wage.

What I am longing to know is, when these new patricians are introduced to the House with all the formal razzamatazz of fur and velvet, who will be their sponsors? Officially they will need a couple each. The casting of this sketch will be a problem. Can it be that we may yet have the delicious spectacle of Lord Bernstein of Granadaland gracefully walking up the aisle with a berobed Lord Grade of ATV-land? Can we look forward to the great double act of Lord Gannex and Lord Burberry? Who will take the arm of my Lord Weidenfeld, unless it be Milady Falkender, from whom all blessings flow? There should be a full House that day, for once, if only for laughs.

A. J. P. Taylor has just made the sensible suggestion that the best way of handling this silly and invidious honours business would be simple to revert to old Lloyd George practice and put the titles up for grabs, that is to say: sell them. The old Liberal Party made quite a good thing out of that in its day. I can find no fault with this. If some rich chancer wants a peerage let him have it, at the going rate. The country can be stuffed with lords for all I care. But that must buy them no right to sit in Parliament. Nobody should have the right to sit in Parliament. That must be elective. Even the future Lord Callaghan would probably agree with that. It is interesting that the two ex-Prime Ministers who have honourably refused to be honoured are Tories: Harold Macmillan and Edward Heath.

There is much to be said for the existence of a second House, a deliberative Chamber of Westminster, in the nature of a Senate, or whatever one wanted to call it. Such a body would have constitutional usefulness, provided the whole hereditary principle were abandoned for the absurdity it is. I would have no objection to the Grand Duke Grade sitting on it, if he got enough people to vote for him. The letters MP have some dignity. So could the initials for a Member of the Upper House – MUH. Except that the printing gremlins in certain quarters would surely get it wrong, and spell it MUG.

31 May 1976

Jock's Trap

New words are the by-product of the time, almost as preposterous as the situations that create them. I never in my life heard tell of an aquifer until the drought brought it out the other day, like the ladybirds, and now I see it everywhere: it seems to be a sort of secret reservoir. Last weekend in Scotland I got another golden newie: undervolution. It means underdeveloped devolution, and it is very modish among the intellectuals, which as you know means everyone in Scotland.

I have a feeling that our jovial Prime Minister will probably get an earful of this when he arrives in Edinburgh tomorrow. His fidelity to the rather dodgy cause of regional whatever-it-is – nationalism, self-interest, local pride – is such that himself is to spend three days among the tartan tea cosies and thistle-shaped haggis holders already being assembled for the festival. It is not often that you find the natives preparing gifts of beads for the visiting missionaries. Moreover it is fitting in these days of the MacBogus that the plastic bannock timer in the likeness of the

49

Rabbi Burns should be made in Hong Kong. Finally our distinguished patron and leader will be able to take a quick butcher's at the biggest souvenir of all, the Royal High School, which will be the seat of the proposed Scottish Assembly, if and when.

I think he will find the Scotch people (and I will resume calling us Scottish when we start calling the Dutch Duttish) in a rare state of confusion, and not just after closing time. They are of course God's own people to a man, but perverse. Those who have been hollering loudest to be rid of what Clifford Hanley calls 'the scunnersome English yoke' imposed by the Treaty of Union in 1707 now see the knot slipping, and in consequence are obliged to find every reason in the world why the process should be opposed. Devolution (a) goes too far or (b) doesn't go far enough. This 'schoolroom Parliament' as they call it, is (a) an unworthy concession to a mighty race or (b) handing over authority to political bairns. The arguments on this matter of identity go on and on and, the Scotch being what they or we are, the conventions of the game insist on a man changing his attitude half a dozen times in a night, so that he can loudly and temporarily espouse the point of view that he senses is the most unpopular. The Scotch have forever taken enormous pains never to be on the winning side.

Doubtless for this reason I detect great changes in recent months. In the days when any sort of national recognition was a very insubstantial mutton-pie-in-the-sky, everyone in the talking pubs (which are distinguished from the others where even the odd word is thought to absorb good drinking time) was fist-thumpingly patriotic, deploring the betrayal of 1707, proclaiming the unchallengeable Caledonian virtues and qualities. Now that even Michael Foot has become part of the Celtic fringe it is obligatory to do a dialectical about-turn, for fear of being caught with your breeks down in the Establishment camp. Therefore, having hitherto argued that Scotland deserves to rule the world, it becomes necessary to argue that it is unfit even to rule itself. This *volte face* comes easily enough. Since every Scotch infant is born into the world in the sure and certain knowledge that he is the salt of the earth, that not only did the Scotch invent everything worth having and write everything worth writing and know everything worth knowing, he can now go into the self-denigration kick well aware that *everybody knows, he doesn't mean it*. Thus in the talking pubs where once the sweet birds of the SNP sang fit to bust, you now hear as follows:

'Parochial by nature, that's us. Folk heroes still Harry Lauder and Andy Stewart, at least if you believe the effing BBC. Bet they wish Billy Connolly never been born, Hogmaneffingay, that's our image.'

'Wait till I tellya. They devolute us, right? So who comes in? Buncha fly-men. Local politicians – all fly-men, chancers. Waiting to be devoluted.'

'Talk about oil? No bother. Yon Westminster will stall and stall till the oil's run out, say eight years. Then they got us over a barrel. Over a *barrel,* geddit? To hell wi' poverty, chuck another pea in the broth.'

'It's a big world, right? Then show me any fella in Scotland's politics who knows about international affairs, or even gives them a thought?'

And so on, into the night, luxuriating in a wallow of abasement, because when the fish 'n' chips are down it's no' true, *they know we don't mean it.* Only when the stranger starts diffidently to agree will the tune change. 'Whaddya mean, inadequate? Who gave you David Hume, who gave you the triple-expansion engine, who gave you effing logarithms, who gave you Jimmy Maxton, who gave you penicillin, who gave you Walter Scott and Rennie Mackintosh and Adam Smith? Who gave you the bluidy television?'

For myself, I long passionately to see the day of freedom dawn. Devolution, nationalism, separatism, whatever. I have seen so many independence ceremonies throughout the late colonial empire – flags coming down, flags going up, royalty-adorned, the despised exalted with the gentlest patronage. I long to see it happen in Scotland too – and for the basest of reasons: curiosity. I cannot wait to see what we'd do with it.

23 August 1976

Nick of Time

If you want to know the time, ask a policeman. He may be preoccupied at that moment pursuing an armed robbery, or a racist demo, or a multiple rape, or a Communist spy, or a bank raid, or any of the contingencies that make a policeman's lot not a happy one, but he will tell you the time if you ask him nicely, respectfully, and in English. That I know. He may look young enough to be your grandson, but that is the way it goes and it is your fault, not his.

Sir David McNee, the Metropolitan Chief Commissioner, is rightly the spokesman and champion of his force. He says in his first annual report that the cops are not getting a square deal. He claims that their job is being made unnecessarily difficult by 'certain restraints of criminal procedure'. He blames 'well-meaning people' and 'libertarians' for making it easier for the crooks and harder for the policemen. By this he means that too many villains are being granted bail, by soft-hearted or pusillanimous magistrates. Too many people aren't in gaol who ought to be. I am sure he is right, though sometimes for different reasons than Sir David's.

'Of 230 people arrested for major crimes by the robbery squad (during 1976–77) 52 were on bail.' This is very bad news. I wholly sympathize with Sir David McNee and those who serve under him. It must be seriously galling to get someone in the nick only to see him released through some pettifogging rule-of-thumb by the Bench. Or as Sir David puts it: 'The unstinted and over-charitable granting of bail to ruthless armed robbers.'

From the policeman's point of view there is much to be said for this argument. The criminal classes are not to be trusted, other than under lock and key, and rarely then. It occurs to me, however, that the fact that a ruthless armed robber can be granted bail must logically mean that he has not yet been convicted of that particular ruthless armed robbery with which he is charged, and cannot therefore be called a ruthless armed robber until he is legally convicted of the ruthless armed robbery in question.

Doubtless every ruthless armed robber remains so forever, and I have acquaintances who would prove that point, but there is this quibbling point that even if he has a dozen convictions he is still technically innocent of this particular ruthless robbery until he is found guilty, however proper the presumptions of the police and however familiar they are with his form. This is one of the absolutes of our doubtless barmy social institutions, whatever you or I or Sir David may say. It is one of the risks we take, to avoid the greater hazards of the KGB.

I trust the British police. I would not say that some of my best friends are policemen but I do not know any who are not. At least I did not think so.

An evening or so ago we were at a delightful and friendly social occasion, and we found ourselves dining with a policeman, a very well-informed man. I will not say what was his rank, his division, nor even town, because I would not wish to prejudice the day when he gets his come-uppance, as he surely will. He was a personally agreeable and cultivated chap, with a sensitive appreciation of good things, and his demeanour impeccable. And I will bet a quid to a penny he is part of the National Front. In the course of a leisured conversation he said that anyone who spoke of rational tolerance for cannabis was talking left wing crap, that all socialists are on grass or vice versa, that the only society that made sense of law and order was the South African society, and that their regime should not be challenged but encouraged. If he had his way, he said thoughtfully. . . . He was in conversation with an Asian lady at the time, but no matter. Proceeding in an easterly direction, that is to say to the right, he offered the opinion that it might have been no bad thing if the German Nazis had won the last war, they at least knew what they were doing; they understood discipline. So said he, who was too young ever to have met a Nazi, unless perhaps among his own acquaintanceship.

It was a rather chilling performance, but not unrevealing. I repeat that he was a respected police officer, educated in the aesthetics, in good standing with his colleagues, with many years to go. And he argued, with quite confident and wholly sober civility, that it might not have been a bad thing to have been occupied by Hitler, that one must stand behind Dr Vorster, and that anyone to the left of Enoch Powell was almost certainly on pot.

But of course he was the exception that proves the rule. I hope.

19 June 1978

53

Tour Force

The question seems to be: do we want the tourists or do we not? Probably only in London, and then only in parts of London, are we aware of them as a pervasive and inescapable presence, locusts, monopolizing the West End, jamming the public transport, disputing in absurd languages, spreading vast maps on the sidewalks; we have tourists like Los Angeles has smog. They drift around with a purposeful aimlessness; they make life exasperating for the natives who inhabit a city that is a penance to live in anyhow. I do not especially mind them, because I keep out of their way. The tourists are said to be an export asset. They contribute to the balance of payments, whatever they are: therefore everyone who is shoved off the pavement into the bus routes of Oxford Street is contributing to the national exchequer. Or so they say.

The other day the playwright John Osborne, once the standard Angry Young Man and apparently fossilized in that ageing role, did a vehemently bitter and I would say rather ill-mannered piece in our local evening paper, recommending us Londoners to go out of our way to make life so disagreeable and unpleasant for the tourists that they will get fed up with us and go away. Snub them, said Mr Osborne, insult them, misdirect them, pretend not to understand their language, overcharge them – treat the tourists, in short, the way British visitors are treated in Paris, just to teach them a lesson not to come back.

That seems to me an overreaction. Tourists get in my hair as much as they do in Mr Osborne's, but I have a residual conscience about them. I have spent so much of my life as a professional alien in almost every country but my own that I feel an intuitive sympathy for anyone brooding over a street map at a troublesome corner, with no proper words to ask the way.

I am fundamentally friendly. When a tourist accosts me at Euston and asks how to take the Tube to, say, Acton Town, I escort him (knowing nothing about it myself) to the Underground map, which is the best geographical diagram yet devised, and show them. I never ask why on earth he should want to go to Acton Town. A curious number of tourists seem to need it: a mystery. There is some arcane attraction there; one day I must investigate it.

I am not always fundamentally friendly. Only a couple of days ago in Portland Place I was tapped on the shoulder in a most peremptory way; naturally I assumed it was the CID catching up with me at last. Not so; it was a German in a tartan jacket.

'Hyde Park,' he said, 'Where is?'

I paused to collect my thoughts as to how you got to Hyde Park from Portland Place, and this seemed to annoy him.

'Hyde Park!' he snapped. 'Is here?' and pointed directly at the BBC's Broadcasting House.

'Correct,' I replied, nettled. 'In there, take the lift to the sixth floor, and there you will find Hyde Park.' John Osborne would have been proud of me.

It will not have escaped eagle-eyed observers of the Kensington and West End scene that the Arabs abound more than ever. Every one is suspected of being enormously rich. This irritates the natives, who resent people being enormously rich, or even having that reputation, and who are tempted into snide comments. The current *New Statesman* carries an angry letter objecting to a Diary paragraph ('Foreigners, happily flogging people for distilling illicit alcohol, are still not used to Western refinements like actually paying for goods . . .'). That, says the writer, could not have been said about Jews or blacks.

Unhappily this is true. I feel the same irrational prejudices when passing the *kuffiehs* thronging the doorsteps of Harley Street or prowling the shops of Brompton Road. Is it the case that we dislike other people's affluence, and that the Arabs now take the place of the Jews of the twenties and thirties?

I must be becoming unpleasantly insular. I grumble at rich Arabs, I also grumble at evidently non-rich and inoffensive young Scandinavians crowding the Undergrounds, bearing vast burdens on their backs, each one occupying as much room as two working commuters. Where, I wonder, do they put up all those tents and sleeping bags and field kitchens that they ceaselessly manipulate round Piccadilly and Bond Street? Do they in fact ever put them up at all? Or are they just the insignia of the new European

Wandervogel forever travelling hopefully, never to arrive? Except, perhaps, at Acton Town.

Or maybe the sixth floor of Broadcasting House.

7 August 1978

High Rise

Let me offer this as a challenge to the Director of Public Prosecutions and Sections 1 and 2 of the Official Secrets Act, 1911: the major communications centre in southeast England, with the codename of PO31, is situated in London W1 at the corner of Cleveland Street and Howland Street – No. 60 Cleveland Street to be exact – and let the DPP make what he likes of it.

This highly elaborate communications centre is vital to all manner of radio and telegraphic systems, some extremely sensitive and some not. It is far from inconspicuous, being indeed visible for a considerable distance. It masquerades as a high-rise eating house, but that cover was blown long ago when vigilant visitors detected an array of dish antennae directed at several strategically important compass points, the dishes having obviously nothing to do with the kitchen. It became evident to the discerning that this was not the innocent phallic symbol it purported to be, an electronic Cleopatra's Needle, but a highly sophisticated instrument of information and transmission. It is colloquially known as the Post Office Tower. Its very size and ostentation is of course an ingenious device for defecting attention from the true centre of activity, which is deep under the booking office of Goodge Street Underground station on the Northern Line, though do not reveal that I told you so.

The above load of rubbish has no reference to any proceedings in the Central Criminal Court, past or present, on which, being *sub judice,* I would not dream of commenting. On the general principle of what is and what is not an Official Secret one could use this as a *reductio ad absurdum.*

Suppose you have – shall we say – 52 communications centres, obviously perfectly well known locally and familiar parts of the environment, which nevertheless a judge rules may not be publicly identified except by numbers on a schedule available to the jury. The twelve good men and true are therefore aware, as who is not, of where these places are. The *Times* newspaper – shall we say – has in any case published an article on the subject seven years ago, which is presumably a cherished but long-forgotten item in the KGB files. The twelve good men and true presumably have families and chums here and there who will happily pass the word around to anyone who can be persuaded to listen to such boring stuff. *We know where the bases are.* See that blurry great mast there? American, innit? On these details the security of the nation depends.

I read the other day that there are American satellites – and I suppose Russian ones too, and probably Mongolian and Albanian and Ruritanian ones too – that have cameras capable not just of identifying single ships on the seas a hundred miles below but of producing recognizable pictures of the individual men on deck. I am not sure that I wholly believe that, though life has taught me to believe almost anything; nevertheless not long ago I was shown a satellite photograph of an American town that clearly showed a traffic intersection. I did not hasten off to Soviet intelligence with this electric news, since I reckoned they would have had the print long ago, and the fact that American towns have traffic jams cannot be especially news to them. With little all-seeing golfballs going round and round up there, who needs spies?

For many years now I have worked on the principle that there are no longer any secrets of any kind not known to those with a specialized interest in finding out. I live on the assumption that all phones are tapped, all rooms are bugged, hidden cameras abound, every bus queue is peopled by secret agents with poisonous umbrellas, that a complete and detailed dossier of one's every move is on record somewhere, probably in some pleasant country house in the Home Counties. This accounts for the wholly blameless and innocent nature of my behaviour: I know before I do it that I shall be found out. That goes for full-frontal espionage to surreptitious amours. Long ago I gave up my undercover work for the Brezhnograd activity when I discovered that my contact, known as Z, was in fact Bill Fotheringay-Maltravers, an old drinking pal whom I had known since childhood and who was moonlighting on the side for KGB, and furthermore was successfully seducing a desirable commercial attaché on whom I had had my eye since the days of Khrushchev. One bares one's soul because one knows that, anyway, it has been docketed and computerized in Hemel Hempstead, or some such.

That is how I can risk letting on about this secret installation at 60 Cleveland Street, because I dare say several people have noticed it already, and if they believe it to be a Post Office Tower, then so be it; they will take no harm and I shall not end up in the Old Bailey. I could go further, and describe in some detail the operations of the complex and secret Agitprop Establishment in Wood Lane, London W12, which works under the cover of Television Centre. This is an ingenious stratagem, since it pretends to be exactly what it really is, therefore one knows it cannot be. There are several such outfits spread all over the country, working under the control of the Brezhnev Bullshit Company, going under the initials BBC. They are quite shameless about this. Or there is the intelligence network that goes under the innocent-sounding name of the Hampstead Debating Society and Gossip Group, centred in a pub on Haverstock Hill. . . .

But soft, we are observed.

18 September 1978

Right of Reply

Dr Edward Norman, Dean of Peterhouse and God's oracle on the BBC, is most obviously a devout and presumably sincere believer, and his marathon Reith Lectures on the radio have left me with the vivid impression that in Mr Norman's view Jesus was evidently no Christian. This is a troubling paradox from a gifted and articulate scholar, a young academic rooted in reaction. His argument (perhaps rather arbitrarily synthesized) is that the churches are wholly wrong in associating themselves with matters of social consequence and secular concern, that contemporary Christianity is horning in on wordly considerations better left to the politicians. This, Dr Norman implies, would not have happened in Christ's time. To me this goes absolutely counter to history – or what passes for history in the very subjective reportages of the time. I think JC should have the right to reply.

Christ preached a heavenly destiny, true, but he did simultaneously concern himself deeply with man's sufferings and inequalities on earth; he was a social reformer; he fervently engaged himself in the Palestinian politics of his time and therefore fell foul of the Establishment, both Roman and Sanhedrin, and was punished by death on the cross. If the confrontation of Jesus and Pilate was not political then I do not understand the word. According to the gospel of Dr Norman – as I read him – Jesus Christ identified himself with the values of his mortal world and thereby betrayed his mission, as does his Church today.

Nobody has ever accused me of being a theologian, so the only charge I can bring against Dr Norman is of being a perilous pedant. Dr Norman is a religious man and I am not: it is therefore an impertinence for me to challenge him on his own ground. Nevertheless in my imperfect eye Dr Norman stands accused of black heresy, and the BBC for providing a forum for didactic revisionism that would have made even the late Sir John Reith flinch.

This newspaper had a guarded editorial criticism the other day of Dr Norman's theme, that the Christian Church is in error in concerning itself in current affairs. In my opinion it was too guarded, as is necessary in *ex cathedra* pronouncements. Dr Norman's argument should not have been criticized; it should have been denounced. Consider some of Dr Norman's theses in his final broadcast. 'The instinct which once prompted holy warfare, rather than diplomatic accommodation, is now rampant in a secularized form; it is let loose in crusades for human rights, or to extinguish what is judged to be racism or economic exploitation.' Implicitly, that is *wrong*. The Dean of Peterhouse implicitly condemns a Christian crusade for human rights and majority rule and against 'what is judged to be racism'. He objects to the modern Church's 'need for theology to be rooted in the day-to-day struggle of people to overcome the conditions that sentence them to poverty and oppression'. In the name of Dr Norman's God, what the hell is wrong with that?

'Now there may be sound enough reasons for men to act in the hope of preventing the sufferings and lessening the injustices of human society. *But. . . .*' Listen to that awful 'but'. I will bet that Jesus Christ wouldn't have put in that smug, self-satisfied 'but'. 'There are no sound reasons for identifying the accompanying politics as themselves true.' What is this prig talking about? If sufferings and injustices are to be remedied how is that to be done other than politically? Will the new Jerusalem emerge from a pulpit in Peterhouse?

'Christ's teaching calls on the loyalty of men with a unique authority, originating outside historical circumstances, upon its deliberate evocation of timelessness. That should make us cautious of identifying the ultimate Purpose with the shifting values of society.' If one can penetrate the pretentious opacity of the prose, one takes this to mean that Christians should not bother about the life today, only the life hereafter. Was this why Jesus had his hands nailed onto a piece of wood?

'There may be sound enough reasons for men to act in the hope of preventing sufferings and lessening the injustices of human society.' Listen to the pious conceit of the man: there *may* be sound enough reasons. Presumably, according to this man's logic, there equally may not. There may be sound enough reasons for men to promote and encourage suffering and injustice; indeed we know that only too often they are. Dr Norman would judiciously evaluate these alternatives in the light of – of what?

I was happy to see that Val Arnold-Foster in her radio column in this paper had a bit of a go at this man too. She was writing about a prize-winning programme from Radio Forth *The Lanthorn*, about an inter-denominational centre in Livingstone used by a variety of congregations as a church, recreation hall, canteen, social circle – all the mundane purposes the Reith lecturer condemned. 'Unlike Dr Norman, many of the Christians expressed themselves in the woolliest of sociological clichés. But, unlike Dr Norman, they sounded kindly, optimistic, and, above all, humble.'

Might almost verge on the political, too, if politics is, as I suspect, about people.

11 December 1978

Spike Action

Since this is the most critical crisis of the decade – nay, of the century, of history, of recorded time – and since the government is (1) making a masterful recovery from the abyss or (2) has made an irrecoverable boob of the whole thing, I am bound to take things seriously. I have to tell you that I am a bit behind the game, rather as was our Mr Callaghan on returning from his sun-kissed hols.

I am sitting in a railway train, which is indeed moving at quite a lick northwards, through what I would take to be northern Siberia did I not know it to be the desolate Midlands. No prospect pleases. All my life I have been anti-winter. Also I have no reason whatever to know that there will be such a train to bring me home again. I hope this does not mean that I shall have to spend the rest of my life in Manchester. But if it comes to that, so be it; there are as many good folk in Manchester as ever came out of it.

I am very equivocal about strikes. I have been a member of my union for pretty nearly forty years, not that anyone noticed. Until quite recently it resembled being a member of the YMCA. Things are different now. I had what must now seem to be a simple-minded understanding of strikes. I believed them to be concerted action by workers with a common theme to pressurize their employers to improve wages and conditions and so on. They said to the bosses: you need us; now we need you. They were not (speaking like the ghost of some Tolpuddle Martyr, I suppose) overt interferences and threats to the lives and economics of total strangers. Commuters are workers too, after all. Who in God's name would be a commuter unless he was?

It seems to me to be quite a new and interesting economic ploy. In a word, the unions now apply the pressure directly, not on the employers but through the intermediary factor of the public who are in no way explicitly involved, except in so far as their own personal lives and jobs are dependent on a solution to the dispute, and who become bitterly impatient, whatever the technical rights and wrongs of the business. Therefore authority *must* surrender to a sustained strike of public services or face an anarchical situation. It is a curious consideration. I regard it without passion, reckoning that I can do without managing directors more easily than I can do without dustmen.

If I were a truck driver I would probably have been on strike, though I am not absolutely sure; or were I a railwayman similarly. I often suddenly long to go on strike myself. The difficulty is I have no one to go on strike against, having no job to reject, no wages to increase or diminish, no differentials to maintain, no security to establish, no pension to lose, no hours to limit, no status to maintain, no concessions to demand, and no one to give a damn whether I go to work tomorrow or not. Except, possibly, me. Nobody is going to require me to clock in tomorrow. Indeed my life could be one long holiday, if I felt like giving up eating and drinking and paying the rent. I read a heart-rending letter to the *Guardian* from Spike Milligan. Seized with an irresistible urge to join in the national frenzy of inactivity, poor Spike has no recourse but a solo strike: from today he will refuse to tell any jokes, and will picket the BBC to stop any other comics doing so. He will have a hard time. There are few jokes being told in the BBC these days.

Many long years ago I was briefly involved in an industrial action on the top of the Andes in South America. The details elude me. For some reason I was working with a film crew on the Altiplano of Bolivia, which is somewhere in the stratosphere at about 15,000 feet, when somehow or other word got through that our technicians were on strike. Exactly why I never discovered. Eagerly we hastened back to suck in a breath or two of oxygen in La Paz, only to find that much the same sort of thing had happened there. The *gastronomicos* union of the hotel was also on strike, and there were no cooks, no lifts, no service, no nothing. How my brothers complained and protested at the denial of their human rights! I must say I showed admirable solidarity with them; it was much more important to have food than to have some nonsensical documentary film. Nevertheless, having no special commitment one way or another, I felt the situation had a certain piquancy; everyone was on strike so nobody got anything. How the thing was resolved, or indeed if it ever was resolved, I have no idea. Nor did it in the least matter: a gang of foreigners sulking in an immobile tourist hotel – what could that matter to the economy of a South American state?

Our affair, surely, is a different matter altogether. Having hotel patrons make their own beds is one thing, closing down hospitals must be another. How free can the collective bargaining be between a hospital deprived of supplies and the patients who must have them to live, and who are not only powerless to affect the issue but who may well be wholly unaware of what the issue is?

New conditions demand new words. Perhaps there should now be a new definition of industrial action which is in effect collective political impatience; not just an assault on those who pay the wages but on all society, whether or not that society can affect the situation one way or another. I cannot help feeling that 'strike' is the wrong word, with its honourable associations of 1926 and all that.

The unions' case may be wholly proper, and I am not going to write a *Telegraph* leader to say it isn't, but the public case is sounder still. I would say that the hapless Mr Callaghan has now been done out of his election chances by his own side, and while I am sorry for him, I am sorrier still for us.

22 January 1979

Untold Riches

A day or two ago I was talking to a rather rich man, which was an invigorating experience for one who usually mixes with his equals. This gentleman was not only most civil and courteous but also ostentatiously modest, if you know what I mean, and he lives in this country not because he has to, like most of us; he came here from choice and remains with enthusiasm. I asked him quite simply why he chose to dwell in a land which, from all I read in the papers, is not only on the brink of ruin but has a lousy climate and raging inflation and mounting unemployment and punitive taxation and all the conditions that clearly lead to imminent catastrophe.

He rebuked me for believing idle gossip. Britain, he told me, is a wonderful place full of people as rich as he is, or even more so. I should mention that much of his prosperity is derived from entertaining these people with extremely expensive food and drink, which they like. Apparently there is no lack of customers – and they are by no means all Arabs – who are happy to pay a hundred nicker a time for a snack and a bottle in exotic surroundings and surrounded by like-minded lovelies. This greatly surprised me, because I now live a sheltered life and was under the impression that all rich people were taxed into penury and dined in Wimpy bars. This is apparently not so. There are places, one of which belongs to my friend, that frequently have to turn away customers clamouring to be relieved of their dough for the transient pleasures that come out of a gramophone and a glass, and when I say dough I mean it. When I saw the bill that someone else was signing I winced so visibly that my friend asked if I was feeling all right. I was not.

I find this phenomenon hard to reconcile with the philosophy of Sir Geoffrey Howe, who is about to set these wastrels an example by cutting public expenditure on such vanities as the National Health and housing and of course unemployment and sickness benefits. As the *Guardian* so properly said the other day – oh upright judge! – to withhold benefits from the out-of-work and the ill for five days instead of three constitutes a public fraud on people who have been paying their insurance contributions for years.

My own case is trivial but not irrelevant. Not long ago I became eligible, as I thought for the pension which a beneficent State offers all who have kept up with their stamps. Instead I got a form asking me if I intended to continue doing any work, and if so how many *hours a week*. I replied, naturally: as many as I damn well could. To which came the jovial answer: in that case, mate, you can whistle for your pension for another five years. I am obliged to conclude, in spite of all the exhortations, that productivity is actively to be discouraged. Perhaps if I had been making engine bolts for the DC-10s it would have been different.

If it is not too late I have a suggestion to offer Chancellor Howe, and that is that there is a good case to be made for putting up the fares on London's Underground railway, occasioned by the soaring cost of chalk. When I went into my modest station a couple of days ago I thought momentarily that I was in a graphics exhibition. One chalked sign said: 'NO phones working.' Another said: 'Lift out of order.' Yet another said: 'Ticket machines not in service.' Finally another said: 'There are NO lavatories.' At that point they must have run out of chalk, because it was left to the out-of-service lift man to tell the customers that there were in any case no trains running from the station because of some unspecified defect on the line. 'Make your way to the next station,' he said, 'they might just be okay there.' Since a station that has no lifts, no tickets, no phones, no lavatories, and especially no trains does not quite fulfil my exacting standards for a station I went home. I was only going to do a job, after all, and that must have seemed to all around a quixotic thing to do. My behaviour would doubtless have met with the hearty approval of the DHSS, but it was not much help to me. I wonder if Sir Geoffrey Howe has ever travelled by Tube?

One month after the New Dawn, or four weeks into the Thatcher Millennium, as you choose to see it, things seem to have moved but hesitantly into the promised glories. I view with alarm the prospect of having to pay two bob to post a letter, and God knows how much for luxuries like a pint of milk and a loaf of bread. I am not consoled by the privilege of being able to vote for a European MP, among candidates whose names I do not even know, since nobody has told me.

Let us hasten off to the disco, where at least you can still get a gin and tonic for under a fiver.

4 June 1979

Comic Cuts

I am a guardedly moderate super-fan of free speech and all that jazz. I would not necessarily rule out free writing, and even free reading, or anyhow free-ish. Allow me therefore to salute a truly horrid little publication that was born last week. It is called *New Nation,* and it is the first authoritative printed gospel of all we hold most un-dear, to wit the National Front. Welcome to Cads' Alley, chaps. Let me go further and rub it in: Shalom, *New Nation*!

I hereby offer free, gratis, and for nothing a commercial for this slimy periodical, which I warmly recommend to all liberals, democrats, wets, and mealy-mouthed mini-Marxists, in the sure and certain knowledge that it will confirm and reinforce their natural distaste for the National Front and all its works, of which *New Nation* is, at least so far, quite the nastiest, and that is saying something. Let me add, if I have tempted you, that you can buy this thing for £5.20 a year from the NF lovenest at 73 Great Eastern Street, London EC2. If you are an African, which God forbid, it will cost you £6.80, and probably a kick up the bottom for your impertinence. Or if you are doubtful you can buy a single issue for 50p from any newsagent daft enough to stock it. Its editor is Richard Verrall, ably assisted by the ubiquitous Martin Webster. Now read on, advised in the lavatory.

Is it possible to be simultaneously comical and vile? Can you conceive of a craftsmanship at the same time evil and ridiculous? Yes, bwana, you can. It is also possible to be simultaneously aggressive and defensive. 'In Britain we have scuttled an Empire, betrayed our kin in Rhodesia, admitted to our overcrowded and impoverished island millions of totally unassimilable racial aliens and . . .' wait for it '. . . been taught to believe that any resistance to these policies is an admission of the monstrous sin of "racism".' Things were every bit as bad in ancient Rome – where, oddly enough, Empire turned out to be not Right but Wrong, since 'there flocked in all the scourings of the Levant and North Africa . . . idle and vicious alien mobs living on welfare and entertainment (*panem et circences*).' Really, Mr Verrall! Using a wog language?

Interesting titbits of history emerge. Remember the sinking of the liner *Lusitania* in the First World War? Well, it was nothing of the kind; it was a put-up job by the late Winston Churchill. The *Lusitania* was a munitions ship disguised as a liner to attract American passengers who were to be the live bait for a German U-boat to nudge Woodrow Wilson ('a muzzy-headed shyster whom the Jews had trained for the Presidency') into the war. Later, of course, Churchill was to compound his crime by waging war on the Nazis, for which the NF has never forgiven him. It is not long, naturally, before our homely people's magazine digs up the hoary old chestnut about the imaginary 'Holocaust' and the so-called 'six million Jews in the gas-chambers', so shrewdly exposed by the fearless Professor Butz some years ago in his Hoax of the Twentieth Century. Not of course to speak of the crude forgery of Anne Frank's *Diary*. It didn't happen, or, *New Nation* implies, if it did so what? I admit I am getting just a bit fed up with this recurrent revelation. The Jews are 'a sub-race'. The blacks are, of course, black. Science confirms the 'biologically determinist view of man and society. . . . The hereditary genetic inequality of human races is now established by a vast wealth of research challenged only by a few Marxist cranks.'

And so on, far into the night. Shall I never tire of headlines like: 'Order, Prosperity, Science, Beauty – The Unique Gifts Of The White Race?' Let us ceaselessly remind ourselves that 'the epoch-making technological and scientific developments on which every society relies is the product not of the teeming millions of Asia nor of the savagery of the African jungle, or of the human ant-hill that is China, but of the family of nations of North Western Europe.' The cinema does not escape. In *Kramer vs. Kramer* 'cool, blonde Joanne (played by the impeccably Nordic Meryl Streep) decides to leave her dwarfish Levantine husband, and one can certainly sympathise with her there'. One could quote forever from this despicable comic. There is a Letters to the Editor page. (One always wonders how a magazine finds readers' letters for its first number.) There is a stern injunction against charity, 'for this or that organisation asking for money to feed poor little Ram Dhamdhirti or Kim Upchuck or M'Bugga M'Bugga'.

You might wonder why I bothered to spend my 50p on this emetic stuff. Well, I didn't. It came through the mail, for free. You might wonder, again, why it is always me who turns up at the receiving end of this peculiar traffic. The answer is not hard to find. It is well known among the NF buddies that I am a Jewish, Negro Liberal married to one of the teeming millions of starving Asian traffic wardens and with a dozen mistresses in the human anthill that is China and occasionally chips in for the little M'Buggas of Oxfam and so forth and I need to be taught a lesson. Well, here endeth the first. I used to worry rather about the National Front; now I have read the revealed word I worry no longer.

15 June 1980

Killer Touch

The lobby is plastered with slogans, repeated on scores of button-hole badges. 'Don't Kill', they say. A curious injunction, one might think, in a big and honourable teaching hospital. People who work in hospitals need no recommendation not to kill; their vocation and their job is very much the reverse. 'Don't Kill', they say, and they mean it quite passionately. It means: Don't Kill Us.

I don't work in London's Westminster Hospital, though I suppose I could be called a sort of regular customer. I have a vested interest in this old cure-and-comfort shop, in which I have spent many a wretchedly pleasant spell. In fact I am writing this piece inside it now, in the intervals between making imaginary love to the nurses, who have no right to be so considerate to us tedious old bores, and pretending to light conversation with surgeons who occasionally slice me into a reasonable shape. I have done it before; it is less amusing than a Bangkok massage parlour, but greatly more useful in the end.

Now this important, and I would say invaluable, institution is obliged to put up posters asking authority to spare its life, and to station a table at the entrance requesting passers-by to sign a petition that the Westminster Medical School be allowed to survive. Tens of thousands of people have already done so. It may make a difference, if anything can make a difference to this impenetrable government's backward path. The report some weeks ago of the working party on teaching resources, chaired by Lord Flowers, diagnosed serious trouble in the University and the Health Service in London, and recommended amputation. Or more accurately a series of transplants, taking bits of several teaching hospitals and grafting one onto another in the hope that something or other will survive. It is the Westminster that must surrender its heart. The operation no longer makes news, except in Horseferry Road.

As anyone can see by walking in the front door, the Westminster Hospital and Medical School is not taking the Flowers Report lying down. They have prepared and printed a detailed refutation of most of the working party's report. They accept the fact that cash is short – except of course for things that go bang and the airfields that house them and the places that make them – and they accept the fact that economies must be made, except of course in defence. (Query: Is a doctor's training not a defence? Not according to Flowers.)

What they do not accept is the Flowers recommendation that London's medical training centres be reduced to six conglomerates, which will mean the virtual disappearance of several of them, including the Westminster. The school 'has the most profound misgivings about the validity of the working party's conclusions' (largely because the working party has not revealed the evidence on which it reached these conclusions) and, not unnaturally, wholly rejects that it should accommodate Lord Flowers by arbitrarily shutting itself down. Lord Annan, Vice-Chancellor of the University, was sufficiently exercised about this draconian proposition to dig out a few academic figures, which is apparently more than the Flowers lot did. He writes: 'If one takes the percentage of students at London medical schools who pass the final degree examinations at first attempt, Westminster Medical School is top of the list with an average of 88.5 per cent passes over the ten years 1970–79. Of the twelve medical schools eight got a similar pass record of over 80 per cent. But Westminster is top of the list.'

This, it seems, was not a factor of much interest to the Flowers people. 'There is no indication,' writes the *Lancet,* 'that the working party examined any data that might have permitted it to contrast the academic achievements of the various London medical schools.' In a word, the Flowers committee was starkly out to save money, let the bones fall where they may.

Learning to be a doctor is pretty hard work, on both sides. The teaching of clinical medicine is quite different from other disciplines in that the load falls mainly on National Health consultants who are also recognized teachers of the University. There has to be a very high staff/student ratio. Many NHS consultants are simultaneously distinguished clinicians, medical researchers, *and* eminent teachers. 'Over the last thirty years,' says Westminster, 'we have witnessed a gradual blurring of the distinction between the roles of NHS and academic staff.' Which cannot but be a good thing for hospitals, doctors, students – and us. It would surely take a council of boneheads to put that situation in jeopardy.

You might wonder, if you can be bothered, why I go on so much about the impending risk to hospitals. I sometimes wonder myself, considering the volume of tomfoolery that goes on in that other Westminster up the road from here, where the surgery largely consists of the insertion of knives in backs. I suppose it must be that the political Westminster is very much an abstraction to me, while the medical Westminster is not.

The one, in the name of freedom and monetarism and conservatism and liberty and the pursuit of affluence, calls: Off With Their Heads. The other, in the name of our survival, and its own, must now put the message on its white coats saying, unbelievably: Don't Kill.

8 July 1980

Feather Boa

If all the Olympics were like the stunning piece of theatre on the terrace that opening day, I could even bring myself to watch them. A shifting sequence of multicoloured patterns, diagrams, pictures, formed themselves from a steep bank of what must be the best-rehearsed crowd in the universe. It was showmanship of a magical order. And how different from the showoffmanship in the arena itself, an essay in effectual childish petulance embarrassing to behold, an exhibition of clumsy hypocrisy, on both sides, that made one sigh for the glory that was Greece.

They say that the Anglo-Saxon vice is humbug. If there were an Olympic prize for that, I believe we would have won a gold before the Games began. If we officially disapprove so properly of the Soviet policies and their exploitation of the Olympiad as a crude cosmetic, why on earth do we go? If we believe on the other hand that the Olympic message of universality and brotherhood transcends the immediacy of passing politics, why on earth do we not go proclaiming that belief, flying the flag and standing up to be counted – instead of slinking in furtively, pretending to be neither here nor there, willing to wound and yet afraid to strike? The spectacle of the hapless and humiliated Dick Palmer, secretary of the British Olympic Association, plodding dismally by himself around the arena behind a board mysteriously describing his native land as 'Boa', pretending unhappily that he was not really in Moscow at all but in some sort of translated East Grinstead, was one to rend the heart for a gesture simultaneously both pitiful and ridiculous. Meanwhile the rest of the Boanese delegation remained most conspicuously out of sight, lurking in their lockfast quarters in the Olympic Village, passing the time and missing all the fun of the only amusing day the Olympics provide.

To be frank, this performance in the 3000-metre Compromise Quibble makes us look fools. Either we are in Moscow, or we are not in Moscow. Either we detest the Russian brutalities in Afghanistan so vigorously that we will not sully our feet by running about on a Russian field, or we don't. Or, more likely, we want to have a go at momentary schoolboy glory, but not while Mr Brezhnev is around.

Spare a thought for poor David Coleman, of the BBC. David Coleman who, I should guess, knows as much about Afghanistan as I know about athletics, was clearly enjoying himself no end but, mindful of his role in the Establishment, felt obliged to remind himself from time to time to leaven the enthusiasm of his commentary with grave criticisms of the ceremony he was observing. 'Terrific!' he said as the costumed crowds performed their brilliant routines (and for once, whether he knew it or not, the word was absolutely right) 'but of course, don't forget the security is tight, the KGB. . . .' Too true. One could have wished the security had been as tight in Munich.

I always agree with the *Guardian* leaders. (Or, as you know, I risk a public flogging in Farringdon Road, where no gentleman wishes to be seen publicly flogged.) But last weekend the leader said it all: 'Moscow will not be a disaster for the Soviet Union, but it will be no triumph either. The Western boycott has produced its predictable result: a mess, a stand-off, a no-score draw.'

Lord Killanin at least stood up to be counted. Lord Killanin, who has achieved the enormous age of sixty-six and is giving up the presidency of the IOC, welcomed everybody, 'especially those who have shown their complete independence to come, despite the pressure placed upon them'. But this tribute, alas, was wasted on the brave Boanese, demonstrating their complete independence from pressure by sticking indoors.

The Olympics will not and cannot make an iota of difference to what is going on in Afghanistan. Does anyone imagine that the Soviet Union is going to deflect its disagreeable course because our Mr Palmer walked round the arena carrying a pole without a flag? How the Russians must have laughed at the Land of Soap and Tory trying to play both ends against the middle on the world's television screens.

It was always improbable that I should be selected to represent my great nation in any Olympic capacity, in Moscow or anywhere for that matter, but had this folly happened, what should I have done? I should have been in quite a dilemma. I bitterly resent the Russian behaviour in Afghanistan. At the same time, I have to remember 1838 (for I have a long memory) and indeed 1878, when it was the British who invaded Afghanistan, for much the same crazy reason that the Russians had: to keep the other bastards out. Neither performance, it seems to me, excuses the other. On balance I should probably not have gone to Moscow, largely because I have always found Moscow as dreary a place as Leningrad is enchanting. At the same time, I should have felt a strong urge to go, if only because Mrs Thatcher told me to stay at home. She, I remind you, who expresses her Afghan horror by demanding a boycott of the Olympics, while presiding over a government whose traders and businessmen have never had it so good in the Soviet Market.

What I should not have done, I think, is to go to the Moscow Olympic Games and pretend I wasn't there. Is there a gold medal for cant?

22 July 1980

Flight of Wasps

One of my horror fantasies is of waking up some grey morning to find myself in bed with the Ayatollah Khomeini. This is improbable. The other is one day emerging from hypnosis as a paid-up member of the Monday Club. This is not exactly likely either, but one must go through life prepared for anything.

Until last week's festival of light in Brighton, I had forgotten that the Monday Club still existed. I am still uncertain of just what it is or how it is recruited, other than from the right-wing fringe of the Tory Party that considers Sir Keith Joseph to be on the wet side, and holds it as an act of faith that Mr Tony Benn has horns and a tail. Its chief ornament is Sir Ronald Bell, Conservative MP for Beaconsfield, than whom none could be dryer, other than Snow White herself – and even she condoned the company of those seven deformed and doubtless racially impure dwarfs.

The other day Sir Ronald Bell told his Mondaymen, not for the first time, that his slogan remains: Send home the blacks. Stopping them coming in is not enough, though desirable. The natural increase of those already here was the big trouble. 'Repatriation has been in the Conservative Party programme since 1964,' he said. 'We put it into the Immigration Act, 1971. Nothing happened.' I think Sir Ronald Bell confuses the word 'repatriation' with 'exportation'. Surely you cannot 'repatriate' someone who has never in his life clapped eyes on the land of his fathers. Thousands of black and brown and khaki people in Britain were born here and have never been anywhere else. The only immigration they ever did was from their mothers' wombs and that as a rule without their consent or approval.

It could be urged by staunch Mondaymen that one way of stabilizing the situation would be forcible sterilization. It will be remembered that this plan did not bring lasting popularity to the late Sanjay Gandhi in India. Moreover his method was not racially discriminatory; all you had to be was poor, and defenceless.

Sir Ronald Bell was not without friends at the conference itself. Mr John Pinniger, representative for, I am sorry to say, Dundee, told the conference that the menace they must recognize 'is that racial integration within one society is a sheer impossibility', and he demanded the abolition of the Commission for Racial Equality 'before it does any more damage'. I should have thought that the Monday Club could usefully have composited these proposals with that of Mr Teddy Taylor, MP for Southend East and a former Conservative minister, whose predilection is for the restoration of capital punishment. Could one not, perhaps, hang people for the offence of being black?

The social philosophy of the new Far Right has long interested me. Having grown up in the Hitler–Streicher–Mosley age, I am a bit more uneasy about it than, for example, are my children who tend to see it as an aberration which will pass as the Beatles passed, and the Flower People, and skateboards, and smallpox. It is pretty evident that this is not happening. The National Front becomes increasingly preposterous, but it doesn't lie down. The Martin Webster-type of clown can still get its audience of vicious nitwits. The so-called British Movement urinates on synagogue doors, and daubs up swastikas – though rather inexpertly; it almost always draws the swastika backwards, pointing paradoxically to the left.

When we moved into this street, we found a scrawl on the wall: 'No Yids.' This seemed ambiguous. Was it a reassurance: there are no Yids here? Or a warning? I phoned the council, and to its credit the sign went that day. But why was it there at all?

We are at least better off than elsewhere. It seems clear that the neo-Nazi infection gestating in Europe is feeding on violence: that Paris synagogue bomb a week ago killed four people; the Munich beer festival explosion killed twelve; the Bologna railway station bomb killed dozens. In America the Ku Klux Klan refuses to disappear; in Germany the Hoffman Sports Military Group openly wears its Nazi uniforms; in France nearly one-quarter of the National Action group is said to be serving policemen.

We have not come to that, not yet. But Sir Ronald Bell was not speaking wholly to himself. I do not think he was speaking for the Prime Minister. Mrs Thatcher has never publicly expressed any racialism, as far as I know. But she did permit her Home Office Minister of State, Mr Timothy Raison, to say at Brighton: 'We have got finally to dispose of the notion that Britain is somehow home for all whose countries we once ruled.' I have never had the pleasure of meeting Mrs Thatcher, who is clearly not given to explosions of unconsidered rhetoric. (Though anyone who could have allowed her scriptwriter at Brighton to get away with things like 'The lady's not for turning' should have had a course of subediting on Comic Cuts. Tory Party jokes are more leaden than Labour Party jokes, and I can't say fairer than that.) Nevertheless Mrs Thatcher allowed, perhaps encouraged, Lord Gowrie, Minister of State for Employment, to tell the Confederation of Indian Organizations: 'Any suggestion that the government was contemplating, or had ever contemplated, forcible repatriation or eviction of an ethnic minority is pure fantasy.'

I am glad to hear that, because otherwise it would have pretty well emptied my household. I do not want to sound even marginally racist myself. Some of my best friends are White Anglo-Saxon Protestants. But not, I am glad to say, all.

14 October 1980

Orange Lemons

Most journalists know that it is either very difficult or very easy to write about matters of which one knows little. I know a bit about one or two things, and repeat myself immoderately, and hardly anything about a great many other things, about which I shut up. It may just have been noticed that one area into which I never venture is Northern Ireland. It must be about ten years or so ago that I was asked by an American newspaper to go and look for a while at some sort of minor unrest that seemed to be developing in Ulster. It was not especially grave or important, but there was the notion that possibly – just possibly – there might be something in it, and nobody reported anything from that dreary part of the world.

I do not go in much for premonitions, but I had an oddly vivid one then. I knew hardly anything about Ulster. Years and years before I had been briefly to Belfast to have a ride round the TT Ards Circuit in the Guinness Bentley, and it struck me as a place of meagre attraction. For some reason I had a powerful feeling that Ulster had the makings of more than a little local difficulty. I had had about twenty years of little local difficulties that grew up – like Korea and Vietnam, and I was fed up and tired, and I felt that anyone who got mixed up in Northern Ireland might well be in for a long ride. I think it was the first assignment I ever turned down.

This surely entitles me now to sound off about the place at least as much as those who opine about Bonnie Prince Charlie's phone calls without having heard them, or analyse the motives of the late Bobby Sands, when they would not know a martyr from a maverick.

Apparently there are more international reporters in Ulster now than ever before, waiting, as Bernadette McAliskey is reported as saying, 'for the starter's orders for the civil war'. It is an accepted and fairly reasonable comment that, as always, their presence will be self-fulfilling, encouraging the tensions they demand. This is marginally unfair to the trade. Nobody has yet suggested that the pop press is paying Ulstermen to murder each other, though in the current climate after the Sutcliffe business, it may not be long before somebody tries.

The spectacle of Belfast children – who in their lives have known no other fun than throwing stones, capering, and showing off to the TV cameras – is deeply depressing: how will they ever come to terms with a dull situation like peace? The Brit soldiers, only just older than the kids, play cowboys and strike attitudes with their guns, accepting the morbid melodrama. Stocking masks and hoods are standard make-up for the baddies, riot shields for the goodies; the thing is a sickening charade.

It sometimes seems to me that my generation of correspondents spent its time covering successive chapters of imperial disintegration, as it were watching a newsreel endlessly and obstinately replayed. The sequence varied hardly a jot: India, Malaya, Kenya, Cyprus, the scenario was the same. Whitehall replied to the independence demands by insisting that it could *never* – a famous word – surrender its responsibilities; imposing emergency laws; gaoling the Gandhis and Nkrumahs and Kenyattas and Makarioses and Mugabes; calling in the Army; failing in the end to prevent the result that had been inevitable from the start; and sending over some unfortunate minor royal to pretend we had meant it all along.

Ireland has taken a few centuries longer than the rest; there is no other difference. Except one: the people of Ulster do not want independence; it is one side or the other. But the white rednecks of Rhodesia did not really want it either; they got it just the same. And Ian Paisley will be at one with the dreary Ian Smith, sulking in his tent. To find oneself vigorously on the side of Mr Enoch Powell is a most eerie feeling. What can have gone wrong? Nothing has gone wrong; Mr Powell has gone right, if that be possible. Enoch calls Paisley 'a bully and a coward'. His reasons, however, are not quite what they seem. To Enoch Powell's oblique and ingenious reasoning, Paisley is a fifth columnist. 'Is he not the secret weapon of those who want to send Ulster the way of white Rhodesia?' Well, blow me down. And to think we never guessed.

Mr Paisley is just about the meanest and coarsest public figure in the land, not to speak of being a truly outstandingly unattractive boor. It has been worked out that Mr Paisley has never publicly uttered a word of generosity about anyone except himself, and an occasional favourable reference to Jesus Christ, whom he refers to as his Maker, which I should have thought was a pretty poor testimonial. Can it be, as Mr Powell suggests, that all this is an act to discredit the Loyalists and make the pro-Brits look fools? Yes and no, says Mr Powell. 'He is afraid for his own skin, afraid of the fringe men of violence on whose backs he would fain ride, provided he can distance himself from them when serious trouble looms.'

You could have fooled me. But I am more easily fooled than Enoch Powell. Or could this just be the double-double-cross of all time? That, to nobody's surprise, is the Irish Question.

12 May 1981

Sinking Feeling

In any political system in the world other than ours it would surely be impossible for all three parties simultaneously and publicly to make charlies of themselves and parade their confusions as virtually to entreat the electorate to join the ranks of the Don't cares – and at the same time give the impression of having noticed nothing. Mrs Thatcher's Tories have gone through the process of drying out, which I suppose is how you define the eliminating of the Wets, with Mr Prior's rather abject surrender into becoming a Damp, and taking the Northern Ireland job he said he wouldn't, simply to keep his foot in the door of Denis Thatcher's business address. The Liberals celebrate the very first day of their betrothal to the Socidems by publicly splitting over disarmament, and then instantly forgetting all about it. Labour provides its own form of fission under the gnomish enchantment of Mr Benn. More and more I am relieved to be involved in no kind of party politics. Blessed are the Eskimos, who have none. It is a bit ignoble; sorry.

It must have been a puzzling experience for Mr Brezhnev last week to meet the top men of the British Labour Party, Mr Foot and his deputy Mr Healey, the only politician able to challenge Mr Brezhnev in the all-European eyebrow stakes. They went to talk about European nuclear policy. The leader of the opposition, Mr Foot, is a proclaimed nuclear disarmer; Mr Healey supports the NATO decision to accept American nuclear installations in Britain.

What sort of an opposition party is this, Mr Brezhnev may well wonder, which sends as its delegation its two leading men who publicly disagree on such a wholly basic principle? They appear to get on well enough personally, he reflects, and presumably they must be accepted as an alternative British government. This, Mr Brezhnev must have pondered, would never do for the Kremlin. To Moscow the promotion of dissidents to the rank of national representatives must mean, Mr Brezhnev may well conclude, that the British parliamentary system is as nutty as he had always supposed.

This, naturally, did not prevent Moscow announcing, through the loyal Tass of the Durables, in its time-honoured opaque phrase that the talks had been 'constructive' and conducted 'in a friendly fashion'. This probably compensated for Mr Brezhnev's turning down Michael's scarcely veiled hint that he would sooner have had a vodka. We are of course never told what exactly goes on in these cryptic, cordial and constructive conversations. Even in my time there must have been hundreds of them, mostly ending in much bogus backslapping, signifying nothing. There was, I recall, one nice variant at the 1960 Summit in Paris, timed with exquisite accuracy to coincide with the exposure over the American U2 spy plane in Russia, which ended with Mr Khrushchev walking out in wild sardonic laughter and President Eisenhower slinking away in pitiable humiliation. That did for Summits for a long time.

Last week's in-and-outer in Moscow could hardly be called a Summit, or even a foothill, but I dare say it did everyone a world of good. Did they discuss the New Jerusalem that even at that moment was being born in Llandudno? I sometimes wonder if Mr Brezhnev has even given thought to the Liberal Party, let alone the Social Democrats. It is true, when you come to think of it, that 'Steel' when turned into Russian becomes 'Stalin'. It seems to be somewhat inappropriate to our couthy wee David whose manners are so much better than anyone else's. He gave a resounding envoi to his party conference, sounding as ever like an inspired prefect of a decent Border school, and got a rapturous reception from a meeting who had just disavowed his vote. It must be said about the Liberals that they would give a standing ovation to anyone reading out the telephone book, if it were read in terms of decent moderation. They are a wonderful lot. Perhaps I should have been a Liberal. Perhaps indeed I am. But I could not possibly say so now, not after David Steel's warning about last-minuters climbing onto his bandwagon. Actually he called it a 'lifeboat', which is not quite the same thing.

Long years ago, when I shared Mr Steel's homeland, I did in fact have to be rescued by a lifeboat, in the North Sea off the Firth of Tay. The freighter I was in caught fire. We took to the boats. Mine sank. Ever thereafter my image of disillusion has been symbolized in the concept of a leaky lifeboat. So what, you may ask, happened to us? Well, we climbed back abjectly into the burning ship. The fire had gone out.

This of course is not a parable; just a silly story.

22 September 1981

Mr Foot's Soft-Shoe Shuffle

To the families of Mrs Thatcher's Brave Boys who have already left their bones in the South Atlantic to fulfil her vain purpose, and of all the others who will do so by and by, I send the one thing that cannot help now: our deep, sincerest sympathy. I have never lost a son in war, though too many colleagues and friends; and it is perhaps impertinent to be sorrowful now when before I was only bitter. But I am sorrowful, as I well knew that soon I would have to be, and that would be reason enough to close the subject, as I dearly wish I could.

The measure of the Argentine war is that we were sick of it, in the truest sense, before it even began. I find that sadder than anger. By now I should know better. But even now I find it hard to accept that we have been edged into a war, almost imperceptibly, manoeuvred into a conflict with God knows what implications, rather as though it were the accepted conclusion of a remote debate, the arguments of which we have never been completely told. The UN Secretary-General, who is evidently a concerned and reasonable man, has soft-keyed the debate in an emollient way that I simultaneously admire and hate. Nevertheless he did make an eleventh-hour proposition to which nobody seems to have paid much public heed. Our Tory government brushed it off, giving no reasons except to itself. The Labour opposition, which seems to me to be behaving inexplicably unless, as I cannot believe, the explanation is ignoble – has hauled down the flag. The patriotic emotion was well understandable on that first extraordinary day . . . but even now? Mr Michael Foot says: 'Our concern must be for the troops' safety.'

Is there anyone in the country whose concern is not for their safety? Is there anyone who does not wince at the news of every casualty? Every ship sunk, every airplane destroyed? Is it inhuman or thoughtless to ask, with every moderation, who put them in jeopardy in the first place? HM government and HM opposition. And now Mr Foot has sacked three members of his team – John Tiley, Andrew Faulds and Tam Dalyell – who alone on the opposition front bench demanded a vote against the war. Can it really be imagined in any fantasy that opposition to the war implies any conceivable support for the appalling regime in Buenos Aires? The fact that it officially became an odious, fascist regime only a few weeks ago is an historical accident; that our soldiers and airmen are being killed by our weapons merely shows that the armaments industry lies outside the boundaries of politics, morality, or even sense.

'The reality of war,' said the *Guardian* leader last week, 'remains, and the concomitant hope that this war – uniquely – will prove swift, successful, without pain or self-reproach.' It will not. So far from being swift, no war ever had such an interminable prologue. Successful it may be, if success is judged on the first round. Without pain or self-reproach – no; the first has already begun and the second is on the way.

The furtive conduct of the operation until now – the strange officialdom that implored the media to applaud its size and strength while helping in no way to provide facilities for doing so – is wanting everything both ways. Either the British expeditionary force is doing something that has honourably to be done, or it is doing something of which it is ashamed. Mrs Thatcher tells the Tories in Perth: 'How thrilling! How exciting!' I wish Mrs Thatcher a long and happy life, but I wish she could know what it is like to be on a landing craft, getting her thrills first-hand.

What worries me – and I worry pretty easily – is how incidental the whole thing has become, how accepted, how unquestioned, how readily forgotten. For thirty years we have been solemnly proclaiming: the next war will be the last. It is upon us now, and it seems of less consequence than a good riot at a football match. I am terribly conscious of being an interminable bore about this thing; I pray it will not last for too long. Of course it will, for years. People are already asking what happens when the shooting stops? When enough decent men have been killed to preserve sovereignty over a colony which we have been trying to get rid of for years. Do we keep the ships and soldiers there forever, or until Galtieri dies, or until Argentina suddenly becomes the democracy it has never been for a generation? Now that it has started, I want to see us win. Rather I want to see the Argentines lose. A military triumph of that indefensible regime would be a disaster for South America. Diplomatically there can be no triumph for anyone.

My colleague Peter Jenkins put it more neatly than I, describing the Falklands as 'a besieged Antarctic Berlin, without importance or meaning'. In fact Berlin in its crisis time had a far greater meaning than the Falklands, being not only in the same continent as ourselves, but twenty times as populous. I spent that year there, very conscious of the fact that I was round the corner from my homeland, and the Russians just round the corner from theirs. I admit that is a mean and wholly practical reason, but let us be cruelly candid.

It is not I alone who was never especially caring or even aware of the Falklands until the other week; neither were you, neither was Mrs Thatcher, neither were the five hundred or so men who three weeks ago were alive, and are now no longer alive. In theory, I love and respect every one of the eighteen hundred Falklanders, and wish them safety and survival and freedom in the days to come. I would grant them the inalienable right to live in their own country, even if they have not yet the legal right to live in ours. But of one thing I am pretty sure: by and by we shall be saying the sad old words: the operation was a complete success, but the patient died.

25 May 1982

Right Mindedness

The Falklands fighting is over for the time being at least, but the malady lingers on. The bosses refuse to let it lie down. In my view – and I am sure no view is more derided in Downing Street – this is foolish of them; they are unwise to keep reviving and parading this wanton and costly episode as a God-given triumph of the righteous over the sinners. It was nothing of the kind, as is even now becoming apparent, and will certainly become more so still if Lord Franks' committee is allowed to do an honest job.

Already the ironies appear. A day or two ago government whips in the Commons blocked a Labour member's bill to give four hundred Falkland Islanders British citizenship. What sort of cheap lawyers' quibble is this? What was all that kith and kin Mrs Thatcher was endlessly droning out in her Boadicea act? Did those 255 British soldiers die 8000 miles from home to protect the integrity of a community that she will not now acknowledge as countrymen? Was all that money spent, those ships and aircraft lost, the hardships on the field and the heartache at home solely to teach the Argies a lesson not to be impertinent, and not to pre-empt a piece of imaginary Thatcherland which, without much doubt, they will shortly inherit anyway?

I should suppose that Mrs Thatcher would deny, at least publicly, running her imperial affairs on a racial basis. It would not be easy to sustain, but she would try. With the standard catch in the voice and the moist eye. Let her therefore try this one: there are about a thousand Falkland Islanders who can claim legal privilege because they have a parent or grandparent born in the UK. There are four hundred others who cannot. It was not made apparent during the recent hostilities that the British forces were on the side of the Us, not the non-Us. It is apparent now. The government whips established that there are four hundred Falklanders who have no citizens' rights at all, and for whom we take no responsibility even now. Perhaps somebody might have told them.They could then have arranged to have their grandparents born in East Cheam. It is a bit late to try now.

I cannot in honesty claim to grieve too deeply about the mis-fortunes of the Falklanders. There are colonial societies far more in need of sympathy, like the unlucky people of Diego Garcia in the Indian Ocean, who were summarily thrown out not long ago at the behest of the Americans, who wanted their home for an air base; the Diego Garcians, unlike the Falklanders, still mourn in exile without redress.

It may possibly be deduced by now that my political affection for Mrs Margaret Thatcher is something less than fanatical. I dare say she would feel the same about me if she had ever heard of me, which she has no earthly reason to do. On the other hand I don't run her country, but she runs mine. Last week in Cheltenham – where else? – she told her congregation: 'Britain's Empire once ruled a quarter of the world. Britain now will not look back from her victory.' This drove the current *New Statesman* to wonder, quite seriously, if Prime Minister Thatcher was still technically in her right mind. Of course, she *is:* that *is* her right mind. And it grows righter and righter the more the sycophants applaud, as well they might. In good time the worms will surely turn, but not while the bandwagon rolls. Let us face it; in an election tomorrow she would sail back in. God, or whoever is on her side. Already in fickle headline terms the remote Falklands fantasy is overtaken by the greater physical melodrama of the Middle East, where the body-count far transcends the South Atlantic, and the architectural destruction is so much more photogenic. Moreover, as Mrs Thatcher knew, the Falklands never threatened a serious international involvement, while the Middle East did, and does, and will. Very soon now Mrs Thatcher's moment of glory in the Falklands will be overwhelmed by strife in the Levant and strikes at home. She cannot keep the *Canberra* coming home every day.

This month, however, comes the state service in St Paul's Cathedral 'to give thanks for the conclusion of the Falklands conflict'. And now, as they say, a word from our Sponsor. . . .

13 July 1982

Plumb Censorship

The outlook is stormy, particularly in teacups. For some reason the air has become thick with trivialities blown up into major issues – thus, of course, becoming major issues in fact. Like our current Defender of the Face, Mr Michael Heseltine.

Turning to a more wholesome subject: the Editor of the *Guardian*, who has lost a battle but not, one hopes, the war. One is supposed to respect one's Editor, not sympathize with him. I do both with enthusiasm, especially since the other day when the Court of Appeal snagged the *Guardian* on a legal quibble and obliged it to surrender a government document – not because it was compromising or dangerous, simply because it was, well, embarrassing. It was a legal quibble because it played about with the wording of an Act, and distorted its meaning. The *Guardian* was in honour obliged to conform because the newspaper has always argued that one must obey the law, or get it changed.

Many readers will already know what it was all about: a zealous mole leaked a letter from Michael Heseltine to Mrs Thatcher, ruminating on how to get a good press – or at least a less bad one – for the arrival of the American missiles at Greenham Common, and especially on how to clobber Heseltine's arch-hate, the CND.

The whole thing is legalistically tangled to the point of absurdity. To begin with, it was a nonsense to classify as 'secret' a demure billet-doux from one blond to another, discussing a matter of mutual concern: how to screw up the damned newspapers. Can national security be endangered by publication of a memo on publications, impediments to, and aggravation of? The only revelation was that Mr Heseltine is a clumsier and more *naif* youngster than even we believed, and that at least one of his minions dislikes him enough to risk his job to make that fact clear. That at the same time it gave the arrival date of the cruises seems of very much less importance, because it was already on the point of being made public anyhow. The one odd thing to me is that at the time Mr Heseltine appeared not to be on speaking terms with his political mistress. Or does the government always communicate by memoranda among the people who meet each other every day? Or does Mr Heseltine know his phone is bugged? Like, I have long supposed, most people's.

The *Guardian*'s case was based on Section 10 of the 1981 Contempt of Court Act, which for the first time gave newspapers a legal right to protect their sources. But this, it now seems, works only for the murmured confidences in the famous lobby, the parliamentary old-boy network of the Establishment, both political and press. It does not work for anything on paper. This week's *Observer* newspaper, which broadly shares the *Guardian*'s view on this matter, if not on everything, editorialized: 'We are back with our iniquitous system of nudges and leaks, where "official" information – about what is being done on our behalf at our expense – is parcelled out in small bits to favoured journalists in a form and at a time that suits the convenience of the politicians in power. Government by news management breeds opposition by leak. . . .'

Nobody mentions the word 'censorship', though that in essence is what it is all about. The Editor of the *Guardian* will not go to gaol, I am happy to say, but the civil servant who provided the Heseltine letter, if he is ever identified, as he possibly may be through photocopy techniques, will almost certainly rue the day; which is precisely why the newspaper was reluctant to surrender the document, and why the whole principle of confidentiality is so dangerously at stake.

Actual 'censorship', however, came into the news coincidentally in the same week as the *Guardian* furore. The study group chaired by General Sir Hugh Beach, which is studying the protection of military information in time of war, declared that not only would the press be censored, but would demand to be. Leaving aside the curious assumption that after the next world war newspapers will be needed, or even exist, the whole Beach Committee's report is, like all military brooding, strangely nostalgic and other-worldly: 'Public interest would be served by some inhibition on freedom to publish.' Such as, possibly, the sudden disappearance of printing presses and/or newspapermen.

The subject has long intrigued me, and for once the word 'intrigue' is specific. I have worked through censors in many countries; some, like the Israelis, most diligent and efficient; some, like the Chinese, lackadaisical and humorous; and the harshest and silliest, in my experience, was that of the British Army in Cyprus during the Suez campaign. I did not very much approve of that war, but I was not allowed to say so, even in a hint. By and by I found it impossible to file anything at all. The use of the word 'war' was forbidden, though the military themselves rarely spoke of anything else.

The current *Guardian* case is quite different. All it has done is threaten the whole *modus vivendi* of public figures and journalists, whereby important confidences are exchanged every day with mutual trust, to the advantage of both. As the late John Bunyan wrote some three hundred years ago: 'One leak will sink a ship, and one sin will destroy a sinner.' The *Times* newspaper put it last week in a graceful leader, very *Times*-ishly entitled '*Caveat Talpa*'; 'Let the mole beware.'

So don't bother with me, Mr Heseltine. I don't know nothing.

20 December 1983

Grime Warp

It has been a long and tiresome time for Arthur Scargill and me, though at least he got his name in the papers. Dear Diary tells me that I went out of business at exactly the same time as did the miners. That makes it more than half a year in which the nation has had to get on without the miners and me. Guess which was noticed. And lo! Whom do I have to ask to lead me back? The *same* miners.

Last week the past jumped up and hit me. My memory did a somersault at the mention of a name I hadn't heard for nearly forty years.

Grimethorpe. It is a cliché now, but it was far from that in the high summer of 1947. It was high drama then. And part, indeed, of my education. Grimethorpe! It couldn't possibly be a real place. It must have been a sort of Dickensian invention to illustrate the deathbed of industrial England; clearly a symbol, not a place. Of course it was both. And still is. All 1948 I had been on the trot: Asia and Africa, back through a mysterious central Europe. I got home exactly in time for what is famously known as the 'miners' stint strike'. It was coalmining theatre of a vivid kind, and its setting was . . . Grimethorpe, Yorkshire.

The stint strike was exactly what it said. The Coal Board had decided that 140 coalface workers should increase by 2 feet the amount of coal they must cut per shift. The difference sounded academic . . . to everyone except the miners. Work stopped. The day I got there Mitchall Main and Bentley, Houghton and Thorne came out. Frickley and Hatfield were already out. All because of Grimethorpe. At Barnborough Main two thousand men went home, because of Grimethorpe. Fourteen thousand men were idle – resentfully, reluctantly, triumphantly – because of Grimethorpe. Across the great Yorkshire coalfields, fifty thousand more men were wavering and waiting and arguing on the edge of a strike that would make a folly of everyone's good intent. Because of Grimethorpe.

Somewhere in the north there was a schoolboy called Arthur Scargill, of whom no one had ever heard. Is this, in 1984, where we came in?

It is an eerie feeling to read again after all these years what I was writing about the mysterious 'Grimethorpe'. I have been lent the cutting from the *Daily Express,* from which I quote and to which I am greatly obliged, feeling uneasily that I really did it all yesterday.

At Grimethorpe here the men sit pointlessly along the street, while the women wait querulously or patiently at home.

The situation makes fools of us all. It gives strength to the hands of the wrong people, and reduces all argument to vanity. But before we turn the heat on the miners – those of us who never cut a ton of coal in our lives – let us see what it is all about. There are two sides to this bitter question, and both of them are wrong.

One by one the other pits follow Grimethorpe. The increase which was to have boosted output by 500 tons a week, is losing it at the rate of 10,000 tons a day. . . . [Remember that only fairly recently had the miners been nationalized. The whole situation was so new that I could get away with this.]

This is no longer the miners' business. The whole excuse for my nosing into a strictly personal dispute is that I own Grimethorpe Colliery. It belongs to me, as it does to you, and to Mr Shinwell, and to the 2,000 Yorkshiremen who used to work in it and who now refuse to do so.

I want to know what we have done [a mysterious 'we'] to be humiliated in our belief and deprived of our right. Do not believe for a moment that Grimethorpe has not a case. Why pick on us for the extra stint? We have been averaging 13½ tons a shift from a 3 foot 9 inch seam. We have been sending up 20,000 tons of coal a week with only one shaft: very rare.

That was the miners' case. After so many years it may make sense or not.

Now we all know that we are politically on the road to the miners' millennium. Thousands of us who are not miners rejoiced when their day came. What, then, are they up to now?

Except for archangels, digging coal is just as filthy and dangerous a job for the National Coal Board, as it was for the Marquis of Grab.

Besides, many miners do not believe in the famous crisis. The pits which have produced some of the most politically alert men in the land, also produced great numbers who can only be described as distressingly human, with a cussedness all their own.

After a craft of men have been shoved and kicked around for generations, absorbing every kind of resistance to society, you cannot expect them to grow haloes at a nod. Think of the pits. Think of the indescribable, hideous villages. Think of a place actually called 'Grimethorpe'. . . .

I do not think that I have ever repeated old, old words of mine with anything other than embarrassment. But I could gladly have done that lot yesterday. And then consider that on the very week the two thousand Grimethorpe miners were called on to vote on the strike: six hundred turned up, only twelve voted.

How sad it is, said a colleague in Yorkshire that very week, when the wrong people turn out to be right. How much, much worse when the right men turn out to be wrong. Beware nostalgia. It never forecast anything correctly.

23 October 1984

O, America!

Primary Class

It always seems, and indeed it is the case, that the Americans take longer to elect a headman than anyone else on earth. On and on they go, seemingly forever; a sort of elephantine pregnancy. Except that it is indeed only too human; from start to finish it takes the American nation just about nine months to bring forth and be delivered of a President, though the seeding must take place not once or twice, but over and over, in what they call the Primaries, as well they might.

Those of us who still read the papers could get the impression that from now on all Americans spend their time hurrying from one voting booth to another – New Hampshire to Florida, Florida to Illinois: what are these places where candidates win with 30 per cent of the votes, on issues that probably will be long forgotten by November, when that great political obstetrician in the sky wearily announces, as he must, that it's a boy?

These endless Primaries are somewhat baffling to us, who have no such system of eliminating heats for the big final. It is arguable that this gives much more democratic participation in the choice of candidates. It could also be said to be a costly and time-consuming charade, culminating in the two-ring circus of the summer conventions, when you can possibly get your head democratically stove in, as has nearly happened to me from time to time.

In a sort of peripheral way I have been around most of these four-yearly presidential rituals ever since Harry Truman made every one of us look silly by winning in 1948. Some were low comedy: some were high drama. I still treasure my 1964 badge which says, if you can believe it: 'On the staff of Barry Goldwater.' For some reason everyone trooped down to Arizona for this most resounding non-election day; Mr Goldwater had taken over for the scene of his wake a very posh hotel outside Phoenix, so posh that it was, as they say, 'restricted', the euphemism that meant it did not willingly admit Jews. However, it seemed at the time that at least 70 per cent of the New York and Washington press corps were as Jewish as could be, and one of my happier memories is of the speechless resignation with which the desk clerk watched the signing-in of all us Goldbergs and Finkelsteins. And even more so when they celebrated poor Mr Goldwater's crushing defeat by dancing the Hebrew *horah* round the swimming pool. It was naughty, but nice.

Not so funny was the famous Battle of Chicago of '68, when the indomitable Studs Terkel and I (and if you don't know who he is you should) held off the advancing hordes of Mayor Daley's armoured police in Lincoln Park with their gas and their clubs – that is, for about 20 seconds when we were obliged to run for our lives, hopefully to fight another day, which never came.

It cannot be just the onset of middle-aged regret that makes it seem that the glory has departed from that political scene, the characters grow more commonplace, faded and grey, the issues blurred, the clarion calls muted, the choice every time grows more banal and the result more unimportant. The Presidency of the United States is probably the most significant and potent office in the world. Does any ordinary American *really* care (any more than I fear that by and by when our time comes we shall care here) who gets the job? It seems frighteningly clear that after the appalling trauma of Nixon nobody of genuine quality or stature would even *risk* inheriting the White House. Perhaps Jeremy Thorpe was right in saying that we were partly to blame by 'dissecting and destroying the already tarnished image of politics as an honourable profession'. Perhaps at this very moment I am guilty too.

The Americans are very precise, not to say pedantic, on their constitutional detail, less so on the values that inform it. The voters poll 'on the First Tuesday after the First Monday in November of the year preceding the year in which the presidential term expires'. The State Electors meet 'on the First Monday after the Second Wednesday of the December following'. The President is inaugurated on 'the subsequent 20th of January'. Nothing could be more certain, secure, solid. It would seem that God, who apparently took a week to create the world, was in far too great a hurry.

It will be Mr Ford, Mr Carter, Mr Jackson, or Mr Humphrey. For what we are about to receive, good Ford, make us truly thankful.

15 March 1976

Telling Time

Chicago. Now the dust has settled and the post-election hangovers have somewhat subsided let us now praise famous men. First let's try to find some. It's hard to come to terms with a great nation whose President-elect, having a matchless first name, insists on being called Jimmy. When they do it to me I flinch, but it makes Carter beam, and that as we all know is a Grand Canyon of a beam. I find myself warming to Mr Carter; victory becomes him, even victory with the most fragile majority since Woodrow Wilson's sixty years ago. Jimmy Carter isn't yet a famous man, but I have the feeling he may one day just become one; he might even be the man to rescue the US Presidency from emptiness and decay. It will be a hell of a job, but it just could happen to a political innocent like our peanut man, whom I mistrusted all the way, until now.

For me there is no more exciting place to be than the United States in presidential week, and I have attended the ritual many times. Yet by now, with the whole thing history, I am so saturated with politics that I am almost driven to reading the sports pages, but one consideration seems to have escaped attention. The President of the United States, who in January will be James Earl Carter, chief executive of the most powerful country in the world, head of state of a vast democracy, commander in chief and button pusher of his and our destiny, is being cast as a decent, well-intentioned simpleton only marginally less silly than the luckless Ford. I believe this is not the case. Our Jimmy is crazy like a fox.

The thirty-ninth President is going to exploit naïveté for all it's worth, and it's worth a great deal today. Jimmy Carter readily admits to knowing nothing about Federal administration, and indeed that will be his big asset. There is at least no vestige of a link with intrigues that have befouled American politics, not even a ghost of a connection with Congress, itself now riddled with scandals. It is true that he has the nerve to talk openly of questionable matters like trust and compassion and love. But in his election eve television commercial he came out clean, whereas Gerald Ford produced a nauseating promotion about how kind he had been to his wife during her treatment for breast cancer.

The American air has been throbbing with post-electoral punditry, which in this country is even more leaden than ours. Carter, the theory goes, was elected in spite of himself, because he was a Southerner and a Democrat and because eight years of Republican crookery and recession were too much for Ford to beat. Carter blended the votes: just enough Southerners voting for their religion and just enough Northerners voting against the status quo to squeak him in, they say. Jimmy was prettier than Gerry, Jimmy had a Southern Comfort accent, Jimmy had a nice wife and a hot line to God. All this is doubtless true but none of the pundits has even yet said the obvious thing: that Jimmy Carter was elected by the poor people. The Georgian farmer got in by the vote of the dispossessed and the anxious people, the blacks of the Mississippi delta, the Chicanos of Texas, simply because he was something new and uncommitted and because, rightly or wrongly, they believed that for the first time since Franklin Roosevelt there was a Democratic candidate who might actually do something about them.

Whether he does or not is another story, but that is what the apotheosis of this quite commonplace American is all about. The making of every President is 50 per cent mythology, of course; the image of the simple peanut farmer will now give way to the reality of the big businessman in the peanut business, who will have to learn about Washington and above all about international affairs from the ground up; in the meantime the new President will symbolize the hope of experiment.

That is naturally too simplistic a proposition for the television gurus. When Walter Cronkite closes his spot by saying ' . . . and that's the way it is tonight' 20 million people think he means it, while all he means is that that's the way Walter Cronkite's script writers see fit to shut the show. Yet that is the received wisdom of the day. When Cronkite tells us we stay told. Presidents come and go but the prophets endure, wise after the event to the bitter end.

8 November 1976

Line to the Sky

When Martin Luther King was murdered in Tennessee just ten years and a week ago I heard of it in a strange and unsettling way. I was in, of all places, Hong Kong, and two things arrived in the hotel room together: a cable from Dr King confirming a date we had made for Chicago that month, and the daily paper with the news that the date would never be kept. There was no reason for the coincidence, and no significance in it, but it oppressed me as though it were some king of omen. It was of course nothing of the kind. Yet every encounter I had with Martin Luther King seemed invested with some oddity that had nothing to do with the civil rights campaign that we endlessly discussed. The last time I saw him had been just as I was leaving for Asia. 'Maybe I ought to come along,' he said, 'understand they're a little short on democracy there too.' He grinned and said: 'Be seeing you.' But he never did.

We met in London, in New York, in Montgomery, above all in Washington. There in that steaming summer of 1963 America had gathered in its hundreds of thousands on what the faithful believed was to be the biggest symbolic Grand Canyon of social change since the Civil War; the civil rights protest was advancing on Washington in what could not fail to be the most enormous public demonstration ever known: the Great Freedom March. For a year and more it had been disordered and sporadic – Mississipi, Alabama, Tennessee; the groping, humiliating contests over schools and States' rights. Not it had suddenly become national, universal, inescapable.

On that August day some 19 million semi-citizens were formally to insist, through their 200,000 physical invaders of the capital, that in the future they must have the vote where now they had not, and the right to work where now they had not, and the right to send their children to school where now they had not, and that this future should not be years away, but tomorrow – or even sooner. And in the van of this vast affair was Martin Luther King. At least two thousand newspapermen were baying at the barricades, with sixty-eight radio circuits and twenty-seven television hookups, involving that Old Crock of the space age, the infant Telstar. And this is where it is rooted in my memory, since never before, nor since, have these things entered my life.

I was trying my prentice hand at TV reporting. As I imperfectly recall the situation, the communication satellite of those days did not hang around permanently overhead, available on demand; the thing whizzed round and round the planet in a tremendous hurry and could be used only for the very few minutes between appearing over one horizon and vanishing over the other. For these few minutes the TV people paid huge sums of money. I never felt less in control of a situation in my life.

The freedom march was tremendous, but short – the simple mile between Washington Monument and the Lincoln Memorial. Nevertheless it took hours. I was up at the Memorial, from which Dr King was to speak. There was no sign of him. The satellite thing would be overhead in half an hour. In fifteen minutes. In eight minutes. Five minutes later it would be gone forever.

The vanguard of the freedom march appeared. Luther King climbed slowly up the steps, pausing to chat convivially on the way. The TV producer gave me signals of a mad and terrible desperation; without doubt we were going to miss the goddam boat. The cameras turned. Martin Luther King made what seemed to be interminable acknowledgements of the vast applause. His words were totally inaudible. The producer screamed: 'We have eleven seconds to go.' Luther King continued to wave, at his leisure.

And then there came to pass a thing that proves how valuable it is to be working with someone with a hot line to Heaven. Precisely at the moment when the signal went to show that our electrical colleague had arrived up there and was in business, so then did Martin Luther King hold up his arms to quell the applause and spoke the first of those words that forevermore are part of his memorial.

'I have a dream,' cried Dr King, 'I have a dream, that one day. . . .'

Moses had spoken from the mount and we had it on tape. By the time he had finished our space-box was probably somewhere over the Persian Gulf, but I didn't mind; I was too busy being sick under a rose bush.

That was fifteen years ago. Five years later I had to hear in Hong

Kong that someone – who, one wonders still? – had shot King dead on a balcony of the Lorraine Motel in Memphis. What a waste.

10 April 1978

Fill Your Thimbles

I think this is the first four-yearly American spasm that has not found me busying myself somewhere in the US watching Them, the People, doing their presidential ritual. I ought to be regretful, even nostalgic; this used to be the one element of continuity in an antic life. Every four years on the dot – if you can call the dot a timing so eccentric: a public vote on the first Tuesday after the first Monday of the November of the year preceding that in which the Presidency expires, with the States Electors voting on the first Monday after the second Wednesday of the following month. Very American semantics, defining so tortuously something so simple.

I should as I say be rueful that I am not there, but I am not. I am already bored, and I do not bore easily. Watching the Carter–Reagan TV debate last week, I felt sympathy for a great nation faced with such a dispiriting choice. And here we saw only the 'highlights'. Highlights! What can have been the substance of what was edited out? So I am not, as of yore, watching the box with drowsily carousing colleagues in Chicago, but with my drowsily carousing self 4000 miles away, and heigh ho for that.

That Debate of the Decade from Cleveland was a strange, shifty, awkward vaudeville. It revealed little of Carter behind the dead and mournful eyes, at the same time uneasy and reproachful; or of Reagan behind the professional projection, the practised smile, the glossy unreal young-man hair above the snakeskin face. Were they, we asked, from the insulation of neutrality, contending for the leadership of half the power in the world?

Very well, this is the way the world goes. It is inartistic that the bang should be preceded by the whimper, but doubtless that is how we can contemplate the bang. Just as it was destined that absolutes should be determined by mediocrities. It was a measure of this bitter acceptance that the Republicans paraded their despairing slogan: 'Why not a cowboy for President? We have had four years of a clown.' This truly chills the blood.

We are told that every American-born child grows up in the knowledge that he – or now possibly even she – can grow up to be President. It is an indispensable part of a proper democracy. It is also true that the trail from Log Cabin to White House is not much trodden now, though Ronald Reagan did it on a bronco. From the Georgian peanut farm is not especially more romantic than from the California movie studio, nor is one more ignoble than the other. Yet watching the competitors jousting so lamely in Cleveland, I thought back to another depression, to a Roosevelt. They have been a pretty puny lot since then. Yes, even the well-intentioned Eisenhower, the overrated Kennedy, the extrovert LBJ, the dreadful Nixon and Ford, the almost-human. Could it be that the great Oval Office has over the years become so equivocal and beset that Americans of stature, intellect, genius, and humour dare not stand for the office, lest they should win it?

How arrogant it is for an inhabitant of a now trifling nation to be so glib about the dilemmas of a master race faced with the recurrent democratic problem that becomes the more tormenting the more seriously one takes it. We are impertinent enough to heckle from the sidelines because, resent it as we may, it is our election too. The cold war paranoia, however indirectly, has haunted every statement in this election, as now it does everything. I would say that, broadly speaking, it is the source of most economic and human misfortunes today, far beyond the Carter-Reagan frontier.

A nation as strong and vital and creative – and indeed kind – as America should not drive its symbolic gladiators into the presidential arena insisting: I am a tougher all-American patriotic anti-Communist than you. Especially it does not have the right to build its whole political posture on the assumption that all people that on earth do dwell are haunted by the same myth of the Russian bear. Because it does; without it, its myth would have no meaning. It forgets, I am sure, that while Europe vigorously rejects the Soviet-style Communist solution, it does not regard social democracy as the first stage to disaster, nor the welfare state as a step towards the darkness. American politics cannot bring itself to understand that most of us reject the dreary sterility of Kremlinism and the cynicism of free-for-all capitalism; that we do not choose between Marx and Milton Friedman; and that when both putative Presidents claim to be bastions of the free world, they do not necessarily speak for you or me.

Since I cannot go to the election, my wife is in Chicago to see fair play. An hour ago she rang me from our long-standing host, the incomparable broadcaster and wit, Studs Terkel, famous in song and story. This weekend he is quoted in *Time* magazine: 'If I had a thimble and poured into it the difference between Jimmy Carter and Ronald Reagan, I would still have room for a double Martini.' In fact that is not supposed to be funny.

Forgive one more quotation. Exactly 200 years ago, an election speech by Edmund Burke: 'Applaud us when we run; console us when we fall; cheer us when we recover; but let us pass on – for God's sake, let us pass on!'

I wonder who's saying that now.

4 November 1980

Yanked Around

This is, after all, what used professionally to be called the Silly Season, for the paradoxical reason that Parliament was out of business and politicians on holiday, which most of us would have thought de-sillified it quite a lot. However that may be, it justifies the telling of bad dreams.

The TV *Dallas* is a soap opera; the real Dallas was a soap tragedy. It was days ago but it haunts me yet, and will haunt us all for a couple of months, maybe even years. The US Republican convention marked the beginning of the end of presidential politics, if not the end itself. In retrospect even the Olympic Games was a scene of intellectual dignity; the Miss World contest an exercise of meaningful decorum, the miners' strike an interlude of grace and hope. Yet Dallas–Reagansville must be accounted a part of serious political history. And the only people in the wide, wide world outside the State of Texas who must have felt enriched and encouraged by the farce were surely the handful of Russians who were allowed to see it, and possibly the praesidium of the USSR. The heart of the Free World sank.

If I had been running Russia, which God forbid, I would have played TV tapes of the *Ron-and-Nancy Show* day in and day out, to demonstrate to the cheerless Reds that what they are up against is not a peril but a pantomime. That too would of course have been foolish, since the real rulers of America are far from fools. It must be quite a new aspect of confrontational propaganda to present yourself to your enemy as a society of hysterical halfwits, led by an ageing ham forever rooted in a B-movie past, while in reality you are a very different kettle of gefilte-fish. Perhaps they did not deceive the Russians. But they certainly fooled us.

As my respected colleague Alex Brummer (who was there, after all) put it: had this unanimity of nomination happened behind the Iron Curtain the Reaganites would have called it a Soviet-style fake. The awesome thing was that in Dallas it was not a fake, any more than *Guys and Dolls* is a fake. It was scripted, it was performed, and it was applauded. It does not matter that it was badly scripted, absurdly performed, and applauded on cue. It got the ratings. And it will virtually certainly get the votes.

Neither you nor I have the slightest political or moral right to deride or deplore the fashion in which the Americans conduct their electoral vaudeville – except that in the circumstances of today it must have its meaning for us. If our patron and closest ally acclaims a coming government *because* that government threatens future war and mayhem and because of, or in spite of, the candidate's making offhand and off-colour jokes on camera about bombing Russia, then we are inescapably involved in that future, and one of these days we may have reason to dread the light-hearted and even merry way our closest ally gambols towards the brink with its balloons and bonnets, singing 'Happy Days Are Here Again'. When I go to whatever is rashly called my Maker I do not want to be holding hands with Bob Hope.

I have often advanced the theory that the reason why successive US presidential candidates diminish in stature and quality with every four-yearly election – and take a look at everyone since Roosevelt – is that any American of intellect and value is scared to stand in case he should get in, and thus join the catalogue of no-goods or nonentities who have inhabited the White House in our time. The late Adlai Stevenson, last of the political intellects, once told me: 'I am standing for election knowing that it may be the last independent decision I ever make, and not a very smart one at that.'

I have attended several presidential elections since my first in 1948, when the faceless little Harry Truman astonished the world by getting in. It was perhaps the last occasion in which the American people licked the political machine. Presidential elections were not always sad. But Dallas was sad. There must be something super-thespian in a politician who is actually televised watching himself on television, with cutaways of his wife watching him watching himself. I believe that in all my life I have never seen a situation that so triumphantly set out to parody itself. I deeply hope that Mrs Thatcher, studying this charade from her cosy telly in Switzerland, did not get ideas of emulation. It will not matter; say what you like about the British electorate, our politics are potty, but rarely puerile. Besides, we have not half as many flags to wave, nor reason to wave them.

One can reject Communism, or dislike it, without feeling the obsessive need, as Reagan does, to shout one's disapproval aloud at every breath. Indeed I have heard the psychologists' theory that the loudest-screaming anti-Commics are akin to the uneasy queers who must forever denounce homosexuals.

This is far too deep water for the Silly Season.

I am frightened of contemporary America, and even more so of the America to come. Yet to say 'Some of my best friends are American' is a patronizing and insulting truism. At least two of my best friends *are* American, and our families belong to each other. At a difficult time they stood by me when many did not, and they are not just good American friends, they are the best people there are, and we shall be loyal to one another if Reagan lives to be a hundred and Mrs Thatcher moves into Buckingham Palace.

O, America!

And my friends have other friends, and a kind of thoughtful liberal American takes a lot of beating. Sometimes needs it, too.

28 August 1984

The Last Shalom

Phantom of Revenge

The Children of Israel produce outstanding soldiers, excellent companions, fine musicians, remarkable scientists, magnificent farmers. They produced men and women who brought green life to the desert, who defended a country technically defenceless, who assimilated scores of disparate societies into one, whose courage and ingenuity are beyond question. The one thing they never learned to produce in thirty years of independence was an internationally accepted image of helpfulness and compassion. Where those qualities exist – as they do, in good measure – they are overwhelmed by boneheaded pride and arrogant impatience. It is no pleasure to say it.

Last week's truly brutal Israeli attack on the South Lebanese villages around Tyre was – coming at this time, and to put it at its most cynical – the most mindless act of anti-public relations that even an enemy could have devised. There is just no getting out of that. The accounts of PLO provocation are almost certainly true, but the deed exceeded both pity and reason. An army that could mount such a pinpoint precision selective operation at Entebbe did not, surely, have to subdue a guerrilla camp by killing up to a hundred civilians all around. Are Israel's Phantom pilots so much more casual and wanton than her commandos? If so, they handed propaganda to the PLO on a plate. Mr Begin must be supernaturally sure of himself, and if so, I wonder why?

I have to declare interest, and with some feeling, because I am that increasingly unpopular thing, a friend of Israel. I was there when the State came into being, nearly thirty years ago, and I cannot count the times I have since returned. I shared in all but one of Israel's four wars. I have endless ties and bonds with its affectionate and exasperating people. I do not think there can be one responsible Israeli who has no confidence in my goodwill, which may indeed occasionally have been a bit irrational. I feel that last week's crass and impulsive demonstration on the non-combatants of Azziyah and Nabatiyeh make the advocate's task very hard indeed.

I know every Israeli argument; indeed I have been making their case for many years: a small and vulnerable and neurotic country only now recovering from the trauma of the Holocaust, surrounded on three sides by thirty times as many enemies who until the other day denounced their very existence and vowed to drive them into the sea. Everyone knows the argument. Everyone accepts the bizarre and tormenting circumstances in which Israel had to fight for survival, and will probably have to again. I have been writing about it for years. I know that for two decades the Arabs refused even to negotiate with what they defined as a usurping non-existence. I know all this, and from experience; it still does not justify killing children in Lebanon.

'They wish to drive us into the sea, and now they say compromise. What do they want, that they should drive half of us into the sea? Or that half of us should go into the sea halfway, tell me.'

'They say they have to preserve their national identity, so they drop bombs on babies; what is all this?'

It is perhaps terrible to be strong. I was with the Israeli Army in the Six-Day War of 1967; in Sinai it was obvious that it was all over. The Egyptians were defeated and demoralized, fleeing home over the desert without transport or even water. I sought out an extremely senior official and I said: 'Could you, or your UN man, make an announcement to this simple effect: "We have won a total military victory; our enemies are in flight; we are the victors. But nobody in the world knows more about dispossession, homelessness and despair than we, who have known it for two thousand years. We shall not impose that even on our foes; tomorrow we shall drop water and food on them, to see them home and to prove that we are men." '

I was impertinent enough to say that this was a magic moment; once in a thousand years does the morally right thing coincide with political expedience. You would, I said, have international opinion rolling on its back: a persecuted people now magnanimous in victory. He said – and I can understand him – 'We didn't ask them to come; let them find their own way home.'

It was then my fears began, and that was ten years ago, I am still unshaken in my hopes that the Israeli State will survive, and prosper, and one day maybe lend its expertise to the regeneration of the Middle East, as in all sense it should. But last week's work does not help. A nation that has basically had the world's sympathy for a generation, and now needs it more than ever, could hardly have gone more out of its way to alienate the goodwill of those who wish it well. The Lebanon raid has probably lost more friends than thirty years have acquired. What a pity this is, and how we shall all so soon live to rue it.

14 November 1977

Steps Back

For zealots, sentimentalists, patriots, humbugs and fanatics of all persuasions the Middle East right now is a fine and fruitful place to be; for people of reasonable goodwill and hope it is more of a depressant than it has been for years. I got back last week after a month in Israel; for the first time in thirty years of such visits I was relieved to get away. This is nobody's fault in particular; just that hope deferred maketh the heart sick. I was last there less than a year ago. In the meantime Sadat's gesture of going to Jerusalem made the heart leap, and I truly believe on both sides; the breakthrough was on the way. And then the open door led into a labyrinth.

I have resisted the consideration for as long as I can, but it can hardly be denied now that Middle Eastern affairs have achieved a total self-destructive bloody-mindedness, a death-wish that seems to transcend all optimism, sustaining itself with the tensions it has endured for a generation and now seems unable to live without. The place is peopled, as was once said in another context, by those who have difficulties for every solution. The Egyptian President's visit to Jerusalem, acclaimed as history at the time, has in fact already receded into history. The euphoria of last year has given place to a resigned disenchantment: we are not just no further on, we are several steps back.

Egyptian deviousness meets Israeli obstinacy. Arab confusions and obfuscations meet Israel's dogmatism. It is as though, having blundered so magically to the edge of peace, both sides flinch from it as from some dangerously unknown quality that nobody understands, as though hostility and fear had been everyone's *raison d'être* for so long that we cannot contemplate a future without it.

For twenty years I have been, and remain, what is rather pretentiously called a 'friend of Israel'. It does not, as is often implied, mean being a non-friend of Palestine; very much on the contrary. But for thirty years Israel to me was the most stimulating and courageous of places, which is why today I am saddened by its sadness and troubled by its inflexibility and distressed by its increasing international unpopularity. It is fair to say, yet once again, that Israel seems capable of anything, except presenting an imaginative and reasonable image of itself to others. Official spokesmen, conformist to a man, provide the clichés of righteousness, many of which have a generation's truth. The intelligent non-politicals, of whom I suppose there are still a handful in this country of critics, are in a state of exasperation not far from despair. That the first chance of peace for thirty years should founder in a sea of semantics seems perverse to the point of lunacy. To the outsider, however understanding of the dilemma, many of the issues seem both trivial and tiresome.

They are very much not so to the people involved, which makes it hard to argue. You, they will say, do not live here. They are right, though I was in Israel years before three-quarters of its population, since I was there when the State was born. Maybe that is the trouble; for many years I felt that a nation born of a sort of idealism should be ideal. So did many of us. We asked more than any people could give.

Shimon Peres, chairman of the opposition Labour Party, argues that President Sadat turned the proper scenario back to front, offering the world the happy ending at the beginning, and leaving the complications to be unravelled thereafter. He complains that the script was faulty from the start, with all the concessions made in public and all the bitter detail behind closed doors. All is complicated by the public intervention of President Carter of the US, who is generally held to be as wise and perceptive about the Middle East as most Georgian peanut farmers. Nevertheless the leaders flock to him.

By now the argufiers of both sides are so committed to their several causes that they no longer seek rational conclusions but only to present the propriety of old and deep convictions, in both cases offered as the word of God. The shorthand for that is 'defensible borders' on the one hand, and the 'Palestine cause' on the other. The Palestine cause is now so intrinsically part of the Arab mythology, and so manifestly nothing to do with the wellbeing of the Palestine people, that no move can now be made unless hallowed by anti-Zionism.

What is certain is that Israel's stance on the Palestine issue will not be tenable much longer, and that sooner or later she will have to withdraw from the West Bank – or, as it is now known, Judea and Samaria. While Israel's ten-year-old occupation endures there is bound to be increasing resistance from a people whose urge for escape from Jewish colonization is no less than was that of the Palestine Jews in 1948 – and who, realizing that they are now the very eye of the storm, will increasingly exploit that. Israel will be obliged, despite herself, to react with more apparent oppression. The moral appeal of her case will diminish. Even now the horrors of the Nazi Holocaust are a fading memory.

Meanwhile there are not domestic troubles to seek in the land I have just left. Inflation in Israel makes ours seem to be in its infancy. Prices soar by the week, by the day, almost by the hour. Emigration from the Promised Land almost exactly equates now with immigration; as many leave as arrive. The controversial Israeli settlements in the Sinai have divided the government – especially the provocative one at Shiloh, which was preposterously disguised as an archaeological expedition; the current gag in the cafés now is: 'My son, the archaeologist.'

Could there be another war? It is openly and seriously being said in the Israeli press that Israel could expect eight thousand dead in a three-day war. Who could have thought, after last year's jubilation in Jerusalem, the kisses exchanged between Anwar Sadat and Golda Meir, that this could be contemplated even as an abstract consideration?

In a couple of months it will be exactly thirty years since the State of Israel came into being in Rothschild Boulevard in Tel Aviv. The celebrations are being prepared – with the eye, as ever, on the clock.

6 March 1978

The Good Soldier

The news of General Moshe Dayan's death in Tel Aviv is three days old, but until now I had no opportunity to say I was sorry. He was one of the first Israelis I ever came to know. Indeed when I met the man who did so much to build the State he was not yet an Israeli, for there was no Israel then.

It was a paradox that the man who made his name as the ruthless commander of the toughest-ever army went to his death proclaiming the absolute need for reconciliation as the only way of escaping from the Palestine impasse. General Dayan was in fact on the edge of being derided as a dove, which is not a good thing to be if you want to get on with Prime Minister Begin. Moshe Dayan did not particularly want to get on with Mr Begin, from whose government he resigned in 1979, retreating into a home-made, political wilderness. It is brutally ironic that the ailing and invalid Prime Minister Begin, who has been on his public deathbed for years, has outlived Dayan.

Moshe had been a soldier since he was fourteen, when he joined the Haganah, the illegal Jewish guerrilla force fighting against the Arab activists and the British, roughly in that order. In 1939 the British put him in gaol for ten years, for illicit military training, and two years later whipped him out of gaol to make use of his illicit military skills on the OK side – i.e. against the Vichy French. Moshe Dayan was perfectly happy to fight anyone if that got him out of gaol and he did not have to shoot Jews. It was on that operation, in Syria, that a bullet hit the telescope he was using and put out his left eye. The resulting black patch was his symbol and trademark ever after. Fairly simple cosmetic surgery could have eliminated it, but: 'Without the old patch, who would know me?'

Occasionally he took me to his home for a family occasion with his then wife Ruth. There was also the celebrated and attractive daughter Yael, writer of books. Yael will not be gratified to be reminded that from time to time I gave her a bath. She was, to be sure, about a year old at the time, but one has to start somewhere.

Moshe Dayan had a standard joke for introductions, 'Here is my

friend Chaim' – he sometimes called me Chaim, to my annoyance –
'Chaim used to be the *shabbas goy* of the Haganah.' I need hardly
explain that a *shabbas goy* is a non-Jew employed by Jews to do the
jobs on the Sabbath that the orthodox may not do themselves, a
very smart piece of Hebrew casuistry. I would deny this vigorously,
and he would give his curious lop-sided smile and say: 'You must
learn to tek a choke.'

In 1966 he came to London, on his way out to the Far East. As
though he did not get enough conflict in his own backyard he was
going to write some articles on the Vietnam War for the *Sunday
Telegraph*. He had never been to the region, which I knew fairly
well. He had conceived a strong wish to see not only the south of
Vietnam but also the north, which at the time was an uncommonly
difficult place to get into. I had been there not long before, and
Dayan wanted to know if I could make use of my very tenuous
acquaintanceship with its Premier, Pham Van Dong, to put in a
word for him. Since he was perhaps the best-known of all Israelis
this seemed to me a silly operation. Nevertheless I sent off two
long cables to the Premier and to Ho Chi Minh. Nobody ever
replied, naturally. The Hanoi people disliked wasting money on
courtesies. So Moshe Dayan never got to North Vietnam, but he
wrote some good articles on the war, as seen by a soldier. The
following year he was up to his neck in his own spectacular Six-Day
War, when Israel swiftly overwhelmed Sinai, rubbing out the far
stronger Egyptian Army, then the Jordanians, then the Syrians.
Dayan seemed to be on every front at every minute. I think neither
he nor I saw a proper bed for a week. After it all Dayan gave a press
conference at which I was told he was bright as a button; I was fast
asleep.

From that time on the shadows closed in. Many people had
thought that he would follow old Mrs Golda Meir as Israel's Prime
Minister, but that dream was destroyed by the catastrophic performance of the Army in the early days of the 1973 war with Egypt.
The Army quickly redeemed itself, but too late for Moshe Dayan's
record. Now it was downhill all the way.

This was a pity; in my opinion the warmaker Dayan could have
done more for peace and brotherhood in the Middle East than the
embittered politico Menachem Begin. Dayan always remembered,
and talked continuously about, his childhood in Kibbutz Degania,
the first of the kibbutzim founded by his Russian immigrant father,
where Jewish and Arab children played and coexisted happily
together in hopeful days of six decades ago.

'It can be again,' he told me in the middle of the Six-Day War. 'I don't know how, but it can.'

His death puts the clock back.

20 October 1981

Cruel Paradoxes

For his column in this week's *Observer* its distinguished Irish ex-Editor Conor Cruise O'Brien milks a pailful from the *Guardian*. I propose now to siphon him back again, thus developing the chicken-and-egg situation known as Courteous Cannibalism, or who-does-what-to-whom.

The subject – as inescapable now as was the Falklands the other day – was of course the fighting in Lebanon and poor little Israel's new role as the Bully of the Levant. Dr O'Brien cites a *Guardian* headline, 'Why the Israelis have become their own worst enemies', and quotes a reader's letter: 'If the ideas of Ayatollah Begin continue to determine Israel's policies and actions, the day will come when an increasing number of non Jews in Europe and America will say that perhaps Hitler had a point.'

For thirty-four years it has been difficult to be open-minded about the Israel situation, and now it is impossible. The Hitler–Begin analogy is horrible enough to be appealing, especially to people who were probably crypto-Nazis anyway and who can now come crawling from under their stones. And of course cynics can quite properly say that the Israelis have asked for it – or rather, their implacable leader, whom the satirists call Ayatollah Begin; who grows more daunting as he becomes more infirm; and of whom one is sad to say that nothing will more become his stay on earth than his leaving of it. These are cruel words for a cruel time, especially when Israel's ambassador in London lies gravely wounded by a would-be assassin's bullet.

Making abstract judgements on remote conflicts can lead to embarrassing paradoxes, as when opponents of the Falklands foray were made to appear to defend Argentina's indefensible junta. Today to flinch from the Operation Carnage in Tyre and Sidon is to be accused of siding with the unlovely Yasser Arafat. Yet many of us who have wished Israel well for a generation find themselves winning from the crude and arrogant General Ariel ('No mercy') Sharon, Israel's Minister of Defence. (Why is it that Ministers of Defence, including ours, spend all their time on the attack?)

The *Observer* quotes another *Guardian* letter: ' . . . every Jew must accept some responsibility for the Israeli Army's attempted genocide of the Palestinian people.' This is manifest rubbish. Nevertheless the question could legitimately be asked: why does the Israeli opposition keep so mum? The obvious answer is that the Israeli opposition behaved precisely and exactly as did the British opposition at the onset of the Falklands affair, and closed ranks with the government so as not to appear unpatriotic – or worse still, wet. Political expediency was more important than moral principle.

And just as our Labour opposition has somewhat recovered its critical nerve, so have the opposing voices in Israel. Last week's *Ha'olam Ha'zeh* had a piece by the courageous maverick, Uri Avneri, called 'Labour's smallest hour'. It said: 'The man who cut the most pathetic figure was Shimon Peres. He looked like a fly sitting on the head of an ox announcing, "We are ploughing!"' It was Peres who promised, in Begin's name, that the campaign had no aim beyond the 40-km protection strip. It was Peres who promised that Israel had no intention of taking Beirut, while Ariel Sharon's planes were preparing for the conquest. It was Peres who promised that Israel would observe the ceasefire, while Sharon was denying it. 'The leaders of the Labour Party, Peres, Rabin and the rest, look like wretched shadows of the Likud. They proved conclusively that their place was in the dustbin of history. They are just the groupies of Ariel Sharon.'

Other voices are beginning to speak out. The other day a press conference was held in Jerusalem by Professors Yeshayahu Leibowitz and Assa Kesher. Despite hesitations, Leibowitz said, he was forced to describe Begin's policy as 'Judeo–Nazification'. That was a terrible thing to say, and clearly it wounded Leibowitz to say it. Kesher claimed that Begin was dragging up every atrocity committed by the Allies in the Second World War to justify his actions. The Allies had been right to go to war, 'but Nagasaki and Dresden were not justifiable'. He said the campaign was a criminal act, but when he added, 'like the attack on our ambassador', he was interrupted by Leibowitz. 'I remind you that our foreign minister murdered Count Bernadotte.'

This is dreadful stuff, this dredging up of all the old ghosts. Yet this is the stuff of Israel's argument today, and I am glad I am not there to hear it. Once upon a time I might have been tempted to join in. Even now my mind irresistibly goes back to that day in the Tel Aviv Museum Hall, and the transformed David Ben Gurion speaking in the names of Joshua and David and Nehemiah, of the fugitives from the Crusaders and Saladin, the survivors of Dachau and Ravensbrück, of the immigrant bus drivers and waiters in the cafés of Dizengoff Square, and the hundreds of thousands yet to come. He proclaimed the Jewish nation, to be called Medinat Yisrael, with the call: 'We offer only peace and friendship to all neighbouring peoples. . . .' And they, for their part, offered hatred and war.

That was on the Sabbath eve of 14 May 1948, which, as I surely have no need to say, was the fifth day, or Ayar 5708. It seems a very long time ago.

29 June 1982

In Time of Tragedy

Four weeks off the treadmill is a penance. If I had hoped for a tranquil month untroubled by deadlines and datelines, I made a big mistake; I merely shared everyone else's. News is a drug as difficult to shake off as (I suppose) heroin – indeed worse; there are treatments for chemical addiction, but as far as I know none for mine. What the papers say is all I know.

The dominant story of the month was, and remains, and I greatly fear will continue to be, the tragedy of the Lebanon. I say 'tragedy' not as the usual easy word meaning sad, or unfortunate; tragedy has to have a certain inevitability about it, created by the human fallibility of people either good or bad, whose motives are irreconcilable and whose destiny is disaster. All the true classic tragedies have been inescapable conflicts, generally rooted in misunderstanding; the Middle East is the eternal example. I have worked a great deal in the Middle East, which I have greatly disliked because its behaviour and politics are informed, as far as I could ever see, by malice and jealousy and revenge, and very little else. This is the kind of absurd generalization into which the region drives one. There were, and are, exceptions, but very few today.

Of all the artificial and divided parts of the world, created arbitrarily after the Second World War by the Turks, and the French, and indeed us, I suppose I came to know Israel best – largely because I was there to watch its birth; I watched two of its major wars; I shared the common enthusiasm for its creation because, almost certainly, I shared some of the Western guilt for the unholy Holocaust of which Zion was, we believed, the redemption. Most Anglo-Saxon Arabists chided me for sentimentality, or innocence, or over-compensation. It made no difference; I went on for twenty years watching, with a sort of pride, Israel at last making the desert bloom. I never let Israel down; Israel let me down.

When I wrote that some weeks ago, and indeed forecast months ago what has happened now, the sides changed; I was now the turncoat, the false friend. There are now many like me, berated for saying that the really false friends of dignified Jewry now are the embittered gang whom Israel has chosen to lead it into the shadows. Virtually overnight almost the whole of articulate world opinion changed course. Never in my experience was a switch so simultaneous. In most cases there was regret and sorrow; in others, a hint of relief. It suddenly became acceptable to be anti-Israel, or at least, understandably, anti-Begin.

There is an English magazine called *Voice of the Arab World,* published in London by Claud Morris, a journalist and very old friend of mine with whom, nevertheless, I have had understandable differences of opinion over Middle Eastern affairs. The current edition is a bonanza. No fewer than seven pages are close-packed with quotations from Anglo–American publications of impeccable respectability, expressing unanimous shock over the events in the Lebanon.

From the *New York Times*: 'In Lebanon's ruins Israel's obviously formidable military machine has claimed a very important casualty: the faith that Arabs and Jews have something else to offer one another beyond mutual hate and destruction. And we are all – Arabs, Israelis, and others – that much the poorer for it. Mr Begin can claim for himself a great victory: he has helped perpetuate the only world he knew.' *Time* magazine: 'A Western ambassador in Beirut remarked sadly: "I ask myself what has happened to those Jews who were filled with spirit and light, who gave us hope and inspiration? Have they all gone? I am sick at heart." ' Patrick Seale in the *Observer*: 'Mr Begin is waging an implacable war of attrition against any form, anywhere, of organised Palestinian military or political activity. . . . Mr Begin has a positive interest in preventing a moderate Palestinian leadership from emerging.' Leader in our own *Guardian*: 'Middle America and Europe, hunched over the evening news, do not care whether five, ten, or fifteen thousand are allegedly dead. Their screens have been filled for weeks with bodies laid end to end. For them it is not a matter of how many, but how many more?' Pierre Mendès France, French elder statesman and former premier, himself a Jew, in the *Nouvel Observateur*: 'Mr Begin can be described as a "mad fanatic".' And so on for nearly sixty entries from serious, considerable, uncommitted and valuable newspapers, all shocked with grief and not a dissenting word.

The Dag Hammarskjold Centre for the Study of Violence and Peace publishes in London a journal called *Chronicle*. There, fairly, appears an explanation from the London correspondent of Kol Israel, the Israel radio service: 'What was Israel to do in the face of such provocation? No state could afford to let such a situation develop on its borders, let alone a state like Israel, permanently threatened with destruction. The PLO threat and provocation was the final cause of the war in Lebanon.'

And now Beirut is Berlinified. Beirut had no special history, no noticeable moral values, it was inhabited by fairly civilized cynics whose only intent throughout the whole conflict was to be left alone to make a good thing out of all the neighbouring strife. It was not a specially noble aim; nevertheless it was the only Middle Eastern capital with any attempt at grace and culture, and now it is the biggest shambles of them all.

There is a moral there somewhere. I do not know quite what it is, unless it be: never use this word 'tragedy' too lightly: one day it may catch you up.

5 October 1982

Mideast in Aspic

It is sometimes useful to look at the present through the eyes of the past. Let me be bumptious with an old quotation:

I'm impatient and troubled and anxious and fed up, as most people are, about this political folk-dance on the Middle East peace talks – even though it is presumptuous to be irritated over other people's life and death.

The fact is it's no longer a middle-eastern thing, this Israeli-Arab business; it's everybody's thing, and that's why I have the impertinence to intrude on it. . . . Because I was personally mixed up in all the Israeli–Arab wars, I had hoped to get mixed up, however marginally, in the Israeli–Arab peace. I still hope so, though I must say with vanishing confidence. . . .

Nothing very special about that; the ordinary run-of-the-mill pious moralizing. Except that I broadcast it *sixteen years ago*. I blundered on the old script yesterday, while looking for something completely different. It is dated 1967, which must put it soon after the brief melodrama of the Six-Day War. The only point of bringing it up now is its alarming and ominous timelessness. It was said in 1967; it could just as well have been said yesterday, or today, or indeed tomorrow and tomorrow and tomorrow. Israel at that time was nineteen years old; it is now thirty-five and what has changed?

For the better: nothing. For the worse: a very great deal, because the stakes are higher and the global context more threatening. But the fundamental resemblance between what we were saying in 1967 and what we are still saying, even more desperately, shows the really frightening fact that the Middle East has learned absolutely nothing.

Back to 1967, and a trace of unexpected prescience:

Taking sides racially is a preposterous position. In any case we know perfectly well that, even if any accommodation were made or forced upon the Jews and the Arabs it still leaves hanging in the air the biggest factor of all: the Palestinians themselves, who aren't represented at any peace talks and who not only have the biggest personal stake in the argument, since they argue it's their land we're arguing about, but who also could gain huge international understanding, if they were not so crude and opportunist in their methods. . . . I assure you it's a great error to assume that there aren't multitudes of Israelis who understand the Palestinian dilemma: they'd be fools if they didn't.

There are I am sure Arabs who comprehend the dilemma of the Jews. But to solve one dilemma, as things are now, you must negate the other. We live in a crazy world of bogus absolutes.

Sixteen long years after that, the absolutes are even more bogus and the world crazier.

Israel's Foreign Minister at the time was Abba Eban, whom I knew. Abba Eban was an intellectual, sensitive and highly articulate in several languages – exactly the things that in a statesman make people uneasy, and why he is not Foreign Minister today and never will be while Menachem Begin runs the shop. I heard him at that time make a television broadcast of a straightforward simplicity quite unheard of in the Middle East of that period, and even less so now.

What you can't understand, he told his people – he did tend to be patronizing – is that if there is ever to be a peace conference, it has primarily to be about peace. Boundaries, yes; aspects of sovereignty, yes; security, yes; dignity yes. But these are things of which peace is made; peace isn't just a by-product of its own conditions. That is to say, the means for once are not more important than the ends, though if you listen to folk around here you may well believe they are. What *are* we supposed to be talking about, said Abba Eban: geography or peace?

It is a remarkable thing how one can build up a kind of nostalgic folklore in one generation. In the middle of all that trauma of 1967, when men of both goodwill and bad were wrangling about how to stop fighting without losing face, I vividly remember thinking that it had been just twenty-two years earlier, on the island of Rhodes, that we had been doing the same thing, going through exactly the same motions, negotiating the first armistice after the Palestine fighting. As now, everyone was being dragged struggling out of dreamland into reality, with the Israelis and the Arabs vigorously pretending that they were not consulting with each other at all, which was of course total bunk. We would all like to think that the same sort of face-saving melodrama is going on now.

The difference today is that neither of the two sides is solid. The Syria–Yasser Arafat schism, which has been latent for years, is now in the open. In Israel it seems clear that Mr Begin has finally managed to achieve what he seems to have been working at for years: the worst public relations image of anyone even in the Middle East. He is a gravely ill man and recently had a personal tragedy in the death of his wife, but even that cannot save him much longer. Finally, his long-time ally, Shlomo Argov, has deserted him. Shlomo Arbov was his last ambassador in London; last year he was shot, nearly mortally, in an assassination attempt in Park Lane: he will never walk again. I was lunching with Mr Argov only two days earlier, and his loyalty to Mr Begin was steadfast. It was the attack on him that precipitated – at least formally – the Israeli attack on Lebanon. Now it seems that even Mr Argov is critical of that adventure, and has allowed this to be quoted publicly. This is, I well know, not a thing he would have lightly done.

Forgive this accidental essay into journalistic nostalgia. I won't do it again. I just felt: how short a time is sixteen years, and if I did it once, I might chance it again.

As we always say at the end of Ramadan; and Shalom to you too.

12 July 1983

India

It Isn't Allahabad

I have a very valuable picture – to me only, that is; it is worth about 5p, I suppose, or possibly a bob or two more since it is signed by one of the half-dozen great statesmen of the century – which was taken about twenty years ago in the garden of the Indian Prime Minister's house in New Delhi. It shows the Prime Minister, Jawaharlal Nehru, with his daughter Indira and her small son Rajiv. The little boy is scratching his ear, his mother is smiling down on him; her father is looking broodingly at the ground, as though at the shadows that were soon to overwhelm him, his country – and now his daughter and inheritor of his enormous office: Mrs Indira Gandhi, that willowy young woman in my picture, Prime Minister now in her father's place, and now convicted of political malpractices and corruption to maintain that place. If it is possible to be shocked and not surprised, that is what I am.

For a Prime Minister to be indicted in a High Court of her own country for offences so grave would surely be a startling thing even if her nation were not, as it is, by far and away the biggest parliamentary democracy on earth. In twenty-eight years of independence nothing has been so damaging. The case against Mrs Gandhi is under appeal, and consequently I suppose *sub judice* still in some way, but in any case I did not propose to comment on the Allahabad court processes, which I do not wholly understand and which are not particularly meaningful. This is a time of bitter regret for India, with which I am so involved, and for the Nehru family, who are at least a partial cause of that involvement.

Mrs Indira Gandhi has been convicted on three charges of corrupt malpractices in connection with the elections in Uttar Pradesh four years ago. If these are upheld on appeal she must cease to be Prime Minister and will be debarred from holding public office for six years, which effectively means that she will be disgraced forever. In the meantime she proposes to stay in office, which suggests either a lot of courage or a lot of brass neck. It will be a very tense few months in the Indian Parliament, I should imagine. I am glad this is not going to be one of my Indian Summers. (And what a punctuation mark for International Women's Year.)

A day or two ago I was asked by Thames Television to discuss this matter with a charming Oxford student called Zareer Masani, who had the consummate bad luck to publish his biography of Mrs Gandhi on the very day of this catastrophe. It turned out to be a derisory two or three minutes, to accommodate an item about child motorcyclists. It seemed an indifferent way to mark the twilight of the most important woman politician in the world, but again not surprising.

It would be an impertinence to claim to know Mrs Gandhi, but her father was I think comparably the greatest man I ever met, and the Nehru family showed me much kindness and consideration in the days of their eminence. Pandit Nehru was a big influence in my life. The legend had already faded before last week's debacle to his daughter, and the last days of Nehru's rule were clouded with equivocations and futilities, but I remember the days during and after the torment of Independence when he was very kind to me. He was the most complex of men, afflicted as one could see even then with the strangely incompatible attributes of compassion and vanity, of which his daughter and successor inherited only one.

I recall the young Indira Gandhi of those days, her father's chatelaine and protector, herself compensating for a lost marriage by watchfully guarding her father's brief moments of privacy and rest. My old photograph in the Prime Minister's garden tells a lot about the Nehru dynasty. The fact that it became a dynasty is in itself a sad thing; republican dynasties are to me intrinsically wrong whether they be Kennedys or Nehrus. It was inescapable that this one should be undermined by the banal issue of corruption. Indian corruption is almost as leaden a cliché as Indian poverty. There is no way of assessing its extent. I can say this without contempt or patronage, since my own family roots are now shared equally between our countries. I once wrote: 'In India corruption, public or private venality, is sanctified by the oldest of traditions; it is denied by nobody; indeed the totality and pervasiveness of Indian corruption is almost a matter of national pride: just as India's droughts are the driest, her famines the most cruel, the overpopulation the most uncontrollable, so are all aspects of Indian's corruption and bribery the most wholly widespread and spectacular. Many Indians resented this: 'It is unfair and unkind,' they said, 'to challenge us with what cannot be denied.'

Mrs Indira Gandhi, Prime Minister of 500 million people, has now been formally convicted of what is acceptably a way of life, of doing in high office what everybody does in low office. This is in no sense to excuse it – nor will it for a minute be excused by her enemies, who are legion, and who have prospered by malpractices infinitely worse than hers, but who endlessly denounce 'that woman' because she professes socialist principles, and who have now caught her flat-footed in exactly the sort of fiddle that has always been their own way of life. It is as though a head of government should go to the block for a parking ticket.

Throughout its entire twenty-eight years of independence India has been governed by one party, the Congress Party. It is now fragmented, but *plus ça change,* and so on. Congress has been sustained by corruption forever, by the black money from the wealthy business houses, who as quid pro quo have been tacitly allowed to run their own parallel economy for their personal enrichment, and for the growing impoverishment of the people. This was the case even in Pandit Nehru's day; it was no secret that this honest man in his final weariness was well aware of the sycophancy and corruption that surrounded him, and remained silent while it flourished, because he was too vain to acknowledge it and too weak to fight it. For years it has been a lifestyle, the acceptance that every official can be bribed, every commodity can be adulterated, every scarcity exploited, every privilege bought. The true irony is that the Prime Minister, Mrs Gandhi, has now been caught on a procedural point of order that is routine a dozen times a day to her detractors.

Mrs Gandhi is convicted of using the machinery of government to win her election in Rai Bareli in 1971. Every incumbent head of government in every country uses that advantage. Mrs Gandhi was clumsy enough to let her opponent get a toe in the door, which was either excessively foolish of her or uncommonly smart of her opponent. It is interesting that he was not a representative of the moneybags groups, or of the extreme right-wing Hindu set, but allegedly a socialist. This is where Mrs Gandhi now finds herself in a quasi-Wilson situation, denounced by those she claims, with diminishing conviction, to represent.

The tragedy of the Nehrus has been on an almost classic pattern: they proclaimed and believed in the principles of social democracy and sustained and promoted their party through the nastiest aspects of unbridled and dishonest capitalism. Pandit Nehru was a sincere and skilful demagoguc, too intelligent not to know of the crookery around him but too sensitive, or too vain, to admit it, and too busy or too weak to challenge it. His daughter, born and bred in the devious Congress tradition, doubtless believes in what her father believed, but she is too harsh and abrasive a personality to exercise charm, and arrogant enough to think that power was a permanent substitute for skill.

This is a strange misjudgement, in a woman who in her own person is both charming and skilful. For a politician with these attributes it was a stunning folly, for example, to provide her young son Sanjay with an official licence to build India's only mini-car – at a time when India was crying for food not mini-cars. Or, for that matter, to indulge in the lunatic extravagance of a nuclear explosion in Rajasthan – a gesture that would have made her father flinch with horror.

This Allahabad court case was no surprise to any literate Indian; it had after all been on the cards for four years. Yet let it be said for India that it did take place; it is doubtful whether any other Asian country would have thus arraigned its Prime Minister so publicly and humiliatingly. This is a very considerable plus for a country so haunted with minuses.

It is improbable that Mrs Gandhi will resign; the appeal may not be heard for a long time, almost certainly not before another general election. She is still very strong, and still carries immense resources of patronage. The Indian people are volatile and emotional, but they are not like the Irish: they have a limitless capacity for forgetfulness. Mrs Indira Gandhi will survive, a tarnished but durable decoration on a sad and eternal civilization.

16 June 1975

India Goes Back to Sleep

For two weeks reproaches have been falling on my head from all sides for writing here that Mrs Indira Gandhi was just possibly not the holy mother of the people's peace, and that the great and enduring nation of India was slipping into a sad and perilous confusion, that the high hopes of the vastest Asian democracy were changing to regret, and doubt, and even fear. This was, it seemed, Anglo-Saxon arrogance, neo-imperialism, and the personal expression of a humbug and indeed a traitor. It may well have seemed so at the time.

The Prime Minister of India had then only been convicted of admittedly technical charges of political corruption, and perhaps it upset me more than it should have done: that such a lady of such a lineage in such an office over such a nation would even casually ignore the rules that applied to Caesar's wife. I can understand that this seemed priggish, and Mrs Gandhi would be the first to tell me so. It gives the least possible satisfaction to be proved right, when one had all along hoped to be proved wrong. Perhaps even tomorrow I may have to apologize for a misjudgement. I would like to think so, but I know in my heart it won't come to pass.

Last week the biggest parliamentary democracy in the world was turned into something indistinguishable from, say, Brazil, since overcoming political opponents by imprisoning them is the step before the last. A technical state of emergency is easy enough to impose, and terribly difficult to reverse, since by its very existence it denies contest or argument. The emergency, in any case, was Mrs Gandhi's alone. Now she has enveloped all India in the crisis of her own embitterment. It is a frightening thing to see a constitution, however fragile, destroyed out of pique. It is a melancholy experience to have seen it coming.

'What is it about India that arouses the venom of the Western writer?' Thus one of my disillusioned Indian correspondents. 'What is the spark that sets the Anglo-Saxon [and the Pict and the Scot and the Celt] searching for the mote in the Indian eye? What gives Cameron the right to be sententious about a Prime Minister who has done well by her country?' That was last week. There were many such letters, some written even more in sorrow than anger, but even more the other way round. And it is a serious, not a frivolous, question. What is it about India that arouses such complex emotions in Western writers, whether they know anything about it or not? Is it quite impossible to be objective about India?

It is certainly very difficult. A country so highly charged with its own emotions, so bizarre in its extremes of grace and wretchedness, imposes all manner of jumpy responses from the Westerner, Indophiles and Indophobes alike. The worst betrayal is that of the critical friend, or the captious lover, the one who resents having to defend what he should only admire. I have known India for nearly thirty years. Even before I ever set foot in the subcontinent, I tried to know it, working in the old India League with the late, irascible, demanding Krishna Menon, himself embodying all his country-men's paradoxes, inspiring both impatience and affection. By the time I finally saw the country, in the neurotic days when Sir Stafford Cripps was the despairing midwife at the birth of a nation, I believed that the creation of an independent India was the most important thing in all politics, and to this day I still believe that it was.

In the years to come I learned and unlearned a good deal, that is to say one day I knew it all and the next I knew nothing, a common enough experience among Europeans in Asia, especially those who tend, as I did, to be smug. I had the incomparable advantage of an acquaintance with Jawaharlal Nehru, whose daughter is now the dictator he would have flinched from being. I admired Mrs Indira Gandhi almost, though not quite, as much as she admires herself. I defended the anomalies of Congress government, until they became indefensible.

I am married to an Indian and I have an Indian family. I believe I am as committed to India's right to the pursuit of happiness as a stranger, perhaps impertinently, can claim to be. I find it strange to be charged with Anglo-Saxon venom.

It is ironic that Mrs Gandhi justified her draconian decisions almost in the same words used by President Nixon when he too was at bay. 'It is not important that I remain Prime Minister, but the institution itself is important.' She spoke of 'a widespread con-spiracy' without defining it; she accused 'certain people' of inciting mutiny without naming them; she invoked the rule of 'law and order' without acknowledging that this is precisely what has been overruled, or that it was the honourable imposition of the law by the Allahabad Court that convicted her that has brought India to this desperate pass.

It has very properly been said that India dramatically demonstrated her democracy by the fact that her Prime Minister exposed herself to the action of the law and the verdict of the courts. This indeed could hardly have happened in Mao's China or Brezhnev's Russia – or, for that matter, in Wilson's England. It was an honourable event and a courageous one, and, as it turned out, too great a risk. Within days nearly seven hundred of Mrs Gandhi's political opponents were hauled from their beds and imprisoned, including the old and ailing Jaya Prakash Narayan, the veteran Gandhist – how paradoxical the word sounds in this context – who is perhaps the most revered and scrupulous figure in India, whose crime against the law was his demand that the law be upheld. The equally ageing Morarji Desai was taken too; one does not have to admire his politics to say that his prime offence was to have opposed Mrs Gandhi, and his ultimate indictment to have competed with her.

How can anyone explain this extraordinary situation? Hardly even on the grounds of straight party expediency: Morarji Desai, Jyoti Basu, Samar Guha and Charan Singh come from every variety of political background and principle from Communist to the far Hindu Right; the only common factor detectable is that each in his own way challenges Mrs Gandhi personally. The only analogy could be if Mr Wilson in a highly uncharacteristic fit of fantasy were to lock up Enoch Powell and Tony Benn and Hugh Scanlon and the Rev. Lord Soper and Bernard Levin.

The infinitely more important question is: can Indian democracy possibly survive this body blow? Or, more troubling still, did it ever factually exist? Statistically it is the case that, until now, India sent more voters to the polls in free elections than anywhere else on earth. If democracy were computable in numbers India would be unrivalled. But is it possible to mould a democracy in the party political sense (which was what India aimed to do) from a community of 500 millions, speaking sixteen languages, 70 per cent of whom cannot read or write? Is it pedantic to wonder whether such an electorate, with every good will and the most honourable intentions, yet with no possible resources of communication beyond the village level, can ever be much more than ballot fodder for a central power in New Delhi? And if the topmost level of the Establishment has been proved corrupt, is it not inevitable, inescapable, and even reasonable that the pattern should be fulfilled down to the smallest bureaucrat with an ounce of patronage at his disposal?

This can be, and doubtless will be, called intolerant and cruel; let

131

it then be said on whom the blame must largely fall, which is not Congress, not Mrs Gandhi, not 'certain people', but ourselves. After a century and a half of dominating India to our own advantage the British abandoned India without that least paternal legacy, an educational system. The Raj gave them no schools. Instead we gave them universities, assembly lines for the production of a babu elite; we left the masses to do as best they could, because that suited our purpose and was also cheaper. And now we – or I – have the insolence to comment on their backwardness.

'We made a tryst with destiny,' said the huge small voice of Mrs Gandhi's father in that hot night of 1948, echoing over a continent. 'At the midnight hour, while the world sleeps, India will awake to life and freedom.' And so it did, and me with it. Perhaps by and by it will again. For the moment it is put in durance. The daughter of that frail, indomitable gentleman, the first Prime Minister, has accomplished by decree what her father did with a kind of angry love. How well I can understand that kind of angry love.

I must be forgiven for returning again to this Indian mystery – for the last time, I promise you. I love India, perversely, as much as I love anywhere; I once lived there and I nearly died there; I claim the self-indulgence of regret. My wife, who is a patriot and a very discerning one, says to me: 'We must be thought of as a special case. There aren't any absolutes. Economically the miners here were accepted as a special case; politically and democratically India is a special case; our society is unique and without precedent and not necessarily to be judged by your rules; give us time.'

For the moment there is no choice. Congress rule in India has been venal and elusive; Mrs Indira Gandhi is collecting hostages to fortune. Yet nobody, from any part of the tormented Indian spectrum, yet offers anything better. Maybe this sorrowful climax to the tryst with destiny will, somehow, evolve the alternative.

There was a phrase, long forgotten, in the Indian struggle against ourselves, which spelled out the meaning of Indian dignity, and let me recall it now: *Jai Hind*.

30 June 1975

Crow's Nest

In the compound of the room in which we have been living is the big tamarind tree where the crows live crowing and quarrelling and contending all day long with raucous and ill-mannered argument, competing for each other's place on the branch, flapping off in a huff, returning to jump angrily up and down. Nothing happens, except noise and birdshit. As though India did not have enough of both. To me the crow colony is the government, the Indian government; their behaviour is almost indistinguishable. We down below are the powerless people. The difference is that we expect little from the crows; we hoped for so much from democracy. We had waited so long for what has come to so little.

I use this impertinent 'we' because I have a stake in India, and as much as anyone identified joyfully in the electoral miracle seventeen months ago that blew Mrs Gandhi's dictatorship out of power and aimed for the skies. Now at last, we said, we shall abolish the tyranny of emergency laws, of political imprisonment of censorship and oppression and malice; now at last will prevail the considerations of social justice and progress. Everyone knew that the new Janata government was an ad hoc coalition of rival parties united only in its opposition to Indira Gandhi; nevertheless it was to be the redemption of a confused and frightened nation, the second biggest in the world.

Now after almost a year and a half of the brave new world it has turned bitterly sour, the disenchantment has become almost tangible. Tyranny has been replaced by absurdity. The government of India did indeed re-establish the rule of law and the freedom of the individual – and then instantly abandoned every national consideration to personal in-fighting and the pursuit of individual ambition. It is as though the apostles had begun by ferociously jostling each other out of the pulpit. Maybe they did, but not as publicly as this, nor with such humiliating results.

In March 1977 Janata was sent to power, overthrowing Indira Gandhi. The eighty-year-old Morarji Desai was made Prime Minister. Two other people badly wanted the job, called Charan Singh

133

and Raj Narain. There was also one Jagjivan Ram, a high-powered defector from Indira's Congress; he wanted it even more. They all set to work to destroy their own leader. It was put about that the Prime Minister's son, Kanti Desai, had corruptly used his father's position for personal and corrupt gain. (This seems to be standard practice; it is the long-standing charge against the awful Sanjay, Mrs Gandhi's son.) The Prime Minister gives the impression of trying to shield him; one up for the opposition. Nobody knows whether this is just or unjust, since nobody wants to risk public investigation. Now the rivals themselves are in contest. The Charan Singh lot are gunning for Jagjivan Ram, but they can find nothing special against *his* son except some amorous adventures illustrated by some tasty nude photographs. What a way to run a band of brothers!

These are terrible words to write about a place in which one has been so deeply involved for so long, but India seems to be insoluble. These are not my words, but those of the *Business Standard* of Calcutta, only the other day: 'Corruption in public life has been a matter of deep concern since long before Jawaharlal Nehru died . . . for over a decade government have permitted colossal evasion of tax payments, smuggling and black market, a far-reaching withering of morals. . . . There is almost nothing and nobody now that money cannot buy.'

Obviously Mrs Gandhi and her rump party are laughing. They have to do nothing but stand by and wait for their initially well-intentioned opponents to destroy themselves. The Prime Minister, Morarji Desai, is an octogenarian with deep commitments to the Hindu philosophy of detachment; he is still bright as a button in everything, I am afraid, except politics. The socio-economic system of thirty years of Congress remains as it was: the rich are indulged and the poor are forgotten, or at least get useless sympathy, while the political leaders scratch each other's eyes out. How very sad; it is a great and wonderful country, run by time-serving buffoons.

We, it seems, are to be spared an immediate election. The Indians may be less fortunate; many an economic-political crisis is on the way. An enormous and increasingly politically conscious lot of voters may be faced with no choice except to give another chance to the dreaded Mrs Gandhi, or the Communists. The trouble here is that there are *two* Communist Parties in India (as there probably are in most places), one more orthodox than the other. The one that calls itself 'Marxist' got 23 seats in the 1977 poll, and apparently gains ground every day – among the literate intelligentsia. But no way will it win.

I believe that the only answer to the awful dilemma of India is a

Chinese form of socialism. I also believe that the rock upon which Communism must break must be Hinduism – a new philosophy based on an egalitarian principle cannot overcome the ageless Hindu principle of caste, the hierarchical thing that is logically indefensible but which will take a lot of changing. Nobody, not even Mahatma Gandhi, ever managed it.

I got home yesterday; the crows continued to squabble in the tamarind tree. And why not? Everyone else does.

11 September 1978

Reddy Steddy?

Less than three weeks to go before the momentous general election of what we still call the world's biggest democracy – the 350 million potential voters of the Indian Republic – and nobody outside seems especially to care, except Peter Niesewand and me. Peter Niesewand covers this lunatic mosaic for the *Guardian* with a dedication that must sometimes drive him nuts. I nowadays am stuck with a simple emotional association over the years; I did that job in the hopeful days, before this enormous nation fell somehow into the hands of elderly frauds and personal time-servers. The description is unkind, but the words are those of loyal and anxious Indian friends who seriously wonder how such a vast and varied electorate can operate in such circumstances of vile jealousies and sectarian manipulation.

The Indian President, Sanjiva Reddy, had a national broadcast the other day, pleading rather desperately for a sense of responsibility during the election time, reminding Indians that the eyes of the world were on them. President Reddy was kidding himself; the eyes of the world have never been on India, except momentarily in times of tumult and natural catastrophes and the occasional war. America has always been basically uninterested in India's domestic affairs, since they never achieved any real political involvement in a society whose intricate social confusions defeated them. Western Europe is the same, since the French and Portuguese colonial associations vanished long ago. The Soviet Union keeps a paternal eye on India's geographical usefulness, irrespective of who runs the place. Britain, having got out in 1947, passed the buck with a certain dignity and charm, but especially relief.

After a couple of centuries of dependence on a remote but on the whole fairly reasonable Raj the Republic of India is now truly on its own. Its traditions and history deserve no less than that. And within thirty-two years one of the great nations of the world has collapsed into the hands of scheming and jealous old men and one eternally ambitious woman. It did not deserve that. But I am afraid it asked for it.

The millions of powerless and hungry Indians will, come the election, do as they are told. Or, more likely, do nothing. The predictions are that it will be a derisory small vote, which really will be tragic, since it will mean that the democracy that astonished itself and the world in 1977 by throwing out Mrs Gandhi, will have abdicated, in apathy or despair, and it will be hard to blame anyone else for that.

Everyone who saw the last episode of Mike Grigsby's Indian TV programme *Before the Monsoon* could not have escaped the theme of almost total public disillusionment, not just with those who so buoyantly replaced the defeated Mrs Gandhi but with the whole political scene, the whole institution of government. They saw bureaucratic oppression of the poor, from whatever side, as an inescapable fact of life, as inevitable as the monsoon itself – indeed more so; monsoons have been known to fail, but injustice and hardship never. So why vote for anyone?

The irony is that never were there more candidates to choose from. Something over 6700 have filed their papers for just over 500 parliamentary seats – as Peter Niesewand says, men, women, and a eunuch. This famous eunuch, called Lakhan Matho, is by a paradox standing for the Muzaffarpur constituency against the most improbable opponent: George Fernandez, a former Minister for Industry, and a more un-eunuch-like personality you could hardly meet. Mr Fernandez is a young and vigorous socialist who was cast into one of Mrs Gandhi's gaols during the emergency and one of the few non-geriatrics in the political hierarchy. Mr/Ms Matho, on the other hand, is one of a strange Indian society who are neutered in infancy so that they may later earn their transvestite livings as entertainers. He campaigns in women's clothes. I would not give much for his chances against George.

There are ominous signs of growing confidence in the Indira Gandhi camp. She is standing in the huge State of Uttar Pradesh, as is Charan Singh, the caretaker Prime Minister who took over the governing coalition from the moribund Morarji Desai. Mr Singh, it seems, is more or less written off. The current talk is that the whole thing will be between Mrs Gandhi (whose son, the dreaded Sanjay, is also a candidate, albeit still on criminal charges) and that other old veteran, Jagjivan Ram, who has the dubious advantage of being a *harijan* or, as we used to say, untouchable. The advantage is dubious because while untouchability is said to turn the caste Hindus off, it is hoped to turn the *harijans* on. And there are an awful lot of them, despite today being constitutionally non-existent. Of such dotty paradoxes are Indian politics made.

To return to the nation's President, Sanjiva Reddy. He may have been wrong about the eyes of the world, but not in his final hope. 'If we complete the election process in the same manner as we conducted the last six general elections, we shall remain a shining example to the world as a people firmly wedded to the principles of democracy.'

Mr Reddy has been right before; he may yet be again.

18 December 1979

Number Cruncher

Once again I go nameless and unrecorded in the nation's archives. However many there are of you in the census you must include me out, for I was not here. In all my life I have stood up to be counted in my homeland only once; for all other censuses I have been elsewhere. It has made little difference to the nation or to me.

The other day, however, I was in on another and somewhat vaster showing of hands and counting of heads, when thousands of distraught officials undertook the heroic and nigh impossible task of determining, or more likely approximating, the number of souls who inhabit the Republic of India. That census, you may well imagine, was no job for the faint-hearted. It turned up a numbing total of 683,810,051. Ask not how they came to reach a figure of such finesse as to include that final convincing One, when as everyone knows the Indian nation's population increases by several thousand every *minute,* and the enumerators well knew that by the time they had totted up the total it was already wildly short of reality. As one Indian newspaper wrily said, it must have made the ghost of Robert Malthus smile.

In just one decade India has increased by 135 million people. That is to say, almost one Japan plus two Australias. The Indians are now substantially more numerous than the combined populations of the Soviet Union, the United States and Indonesia, countries which themselves rate as the third, fourth and fifth most populous nations on the planet. One single Indian state, Uttar Pradesh, which crams in some 110 million, has more people than all but a handful of other countries. Pause for contemplation.

This, for me unusual, sally into statistics was inspired by the circumstances in which I read the figures. There was I, myself in India, in the midst of this grossly overcrowded land, surrounded by these 683,810,051 teeming multitudes, and all I could ask myself is: Where the hell is everybody?

Most beaches on the Indian Ocean claim to be the biggest, longest, hottest, most golden and tranquil, and this one is probably all these things, or at least as much so as the others. I can even name it – Kovalum, in Kerala, in the very Deep Indian South, because it is so remote and expensive to reach, and it is one of the few Indian regions that I never knew before nor shall see again. It was here, with hardly a soul in sight, that I studied the census, which made it clear that, despite all the evidence, I was inhabiting one of the most congested and overpopulated lands on earth. In this lovely desert they could have fooled a stranger. India has been fooling strangers for centuries.

For most of the day this huge beach held no one, except for the raucous and conceited crows whom nobody likes, except me. The Indian crow is the true proletarian, despising everyone. Very early in the morning the fishermen assembled, maybe a couple of dozen. One is obliged to call them fishermen, in the sense that catching fish was their business, but if they resembled anything it was a coterie of rather uncertain demonstrators. Occasionally they uttered plangent cries of what sounded like bitter and organized grief, but which evidently were expressions of mutual encouragement. By and by everyone went home.

In the ferment of Bombay, in the horrors of Calcutta one is only too conscious of the grim problems of a nation's terrible fecundity, of the governmental dread that in most of India there will one day be standing room only. On this beautiful and seemingly limitless coast among the coconut trees it would be hard to believe, did one not know it so well to be true.

In the days when I first knew India one was oppressed by the presence of uncountable people, unmanageable poverty. We did not know what we were talking about. Since Independence the population has *doubled.* Today the statisticians are horrified by the fair certainty of the population doubling yet again in twenty years. This is a hard arithmetical projection based on the current rate of growth: it is not fanciful to foresee 1,400 million Indians by the century's end. Much as I love them, enough is enough . . . not for our sake, but for theirs.

There was once a demographer's parable to the effect that if you obliged the entire population of China to march past a given spot four abreast the procession would never come to an end, since the birth rate at one end would always exceed the death rate at the other. Years ago I was in Peking for the fourth anniversary of the Revolution, and as during an entire day I watched the enormous cavalcade of millions passing through Tien An Men Square I was seized of a terrible dread that this was exactly what was going to happen, and that we would be there, applauding, until doomsday.

Years later, in Delhi at Nehru's funeral, I had the same feeling about India. I am very troubled by multitudes. That is why I liked the empty beach at Kovalum; it allowed me to forget Calcutta. Does this then exonerate the late Sanjay Gandhi and his violent birth control campaign? I think not. His methods were brutal and misconceived (this is not intended as a bad joke) but his ends were proper. But without a realistic strategy of family planning, colossal task though it is, one greatly fears the future for a great nation to whom nature, and Independence, has brought too much too soon.

14 April 1981

A Case of Hydera Phobia

I did not put in a bid for the invaluable trinkets left by the late Nizam of Hyderabad, largely because diamonds do not become me, and also because I almost always have difficulty raising £15 millions at short notice. In any case the Indian government has said I could not take them home even if I bought them, so what? But still, the thought of this dreadful old man's loot brings a nostalgic pang, since I once shared the same roof with these enormously costly and I am told extravagantly vulgar gems. That is to say in a manner of speaking. I was once or twice a guest of His Exalted Highness, as he alone among the kinglets was entitled to be called. That again is a half-truth; I never met the old miser in my life, and I stayed not in the palace but at the guesthouse down the road, for which one was charged so much a day, since the Nizam was not only reputedly the richest man in all the world but indisputably and notoriously the meanest.

These were very stirring times. India had just become

independent. Hyderabad wanted none of this republican nonsense, and declared a sort of UDI. Not that it had to; it had always been by far and away the biggest Princely State of the subcontinent; it had existed for generations on its own, separate from British India, in many ways better run, in other ways madly anomalous, with first-class electric light and about as much democracy as Caligula's Rome. There was a curious analogy with the other huge Princely State of Kashmir. They were mirror images of each other. Kashmir was a Muslim state ruled by a minute Hindu family; Hyderabad was a Hindu society governed by a small and powerful Muslim clique. Both had petulantly refused to join independent India. Kashmir had already paid the price; the Indian Army had marched in. Hyderabad's turn was to come.

Now the allegedly richest man in the world, poor soul, sat in his enormous, seedy palace waiting for something to turn up. In the even seedier guesthouse so did I; that was why I was there. I was also quite keen to encounter an individual whose annual income was estimated at around £10 millions and who lived a life of parsimonious frugality that even his faithful counsellors felt irksome. His opponents accused His Exalted Highness of many things, but never of laying down a rupee where an anna would do.

It was not to be, however. It seemed that many years before the ruler had been rash enough to meet an American journalist, who had sent back to his paper not, as expected, a well-documented treatise on the State's economics, but a terse description of His Exalted Highness's laundry, which he claimed to have seen strung up on the palace roof by HEH's own fair hand. This had so shocked the old gentleman that now the very word 'reporter' sent him quivering to bed with the ague. That was not to say one was short of copy. Daily came a procession of emissaries and propagandists, very conscious of the fact that while the Nizam resolutely refused to accede to India, the vastness of India was closing in irresistibly, cutting off Hyderabad from the rest of the world. They endlessly pointed out that the Nizam (whose ancestors had shrewdly picked the right side in the Indian Mutiny) had the official title of 'England's Faithful Ally', so what about it? Would I kindly arrange for a British Expeditionary Force to come to his aid in the hour of need?

Look around you, they cried, this is not one of your tiresome constitutional monarchies. Every public sign proclaimed it: His Exalted Highness's Gasworks, His Exalted Highness's Post Office, By Permission of His Exalted Highness to operate in His Exalted Highness's Dominions. And everywhere the quaint device that symbolized the Nizam as the crown symbolizes monarchies elsewhere: a curious hat like a mitre, worn only by the Hyderabadi Muslem top crust. The hat was the boss. And uneasy lay the head that wore the hat.

He was called for short HEH Asaf Jah Muzzafarl-Mulk Wal Mumalik Nizam-al-Mulk Nizan-al-Daula Nawab Mir Sir Osman Ali Khan Bahadur Fateh Jung. He had what I was later told was the most elaborate collection of Rolls Royces and Daimlers probably in the world, and was occasionally to be seen driving through the genuflecting city in the oldest and cheapest Ford in Asia, to save petrol.

As the time approached for the inevitable showdown I was persecuted by Mr Fernandosa, who had written an unpublished book called *The Hyderabadi Rulers In History*; he would pop up at unexpected moments and relentlessly read selections from this unbelievably fulsome and boring work. There was no escape from him; he had as much right in the guesthouse as I. If I saw him coming I would retreat to the lavatory and lock the door; to no avail – Mr Fernandosa would stand outside and intone the more awful passages in a penetrating voice: 'We now come to Anwaruddin, Nawad of Arcot, famous in song and story, who was the Nizam's deputy in the Carnatic. . . .'

It was Mr Fernandosa who drove me out. By and by the Indian Army invaded Hyderabad, sailed through it and occupied it and embodied it into the Indian nation, where of course, it should have been all along. But by that time, as usual, I had gone home.

Pity about that jewellery, though. Right now I could do with a 200 carat emerald on a diamond chain.

24 September 1979

Gandhi

After three decades in the shadows of history the man M. K. Gandhi, almost certainly the most celebrated Indian who ever lived, after the Buddha, returns again. He has two simultaneous reincarnations: the re-emergence of the disciple Louis Fischer's thirty-year-old biography of the man, which inspired Richard Attenborough to make his *Gandhi* film which has finally emerged after a lifetime of effort and frustration. Wherever he is now the old man, the old rebel, the old saint, must be laughing up the sleeve he never wore.

In the Hindu manner Mohandas Karamchand Gandhi was doubtless reborn at exactly six minutes past six on the evening of 25 January 1948, the precise moment when the Hindu fanatic's bullets struck him and he surrendered his ghost, the latest of what the faithful believed were uncounted reincarnations, and they may be right.

Mr Gandhi, dead these thirty-four years, defied definition in his life, and even more so now. In a multi-racial, multi-faith, multi-political society, growing by millions every year, he was unique in that he was almost certainly the only individual Indian who claimed to speak for them all. Even, at times, for his opponents the British, whom he challenged continually and from whom he could not shake off his reluctant respect and sometimes even, perversely, affection. The British responded by alternately consoling him, consulting him, throwing him into gaol, letting him out, mocking one day and saluting the next. The British were used to rebels, but to Gandhi's dying day they never knew what to make of such a good bad man. Anyhow, Gandhi outlasted them. Though only just.

Gandhi's life was deliberate and calculated simplicity – almost, it might be said, a simplicity of intricate complication – which surrounded itself with paradox. He spent most of a lifetime seeking and working and fasting for the independence of his nation. When at long last that Independence celebration came, M. K. Gandhi was not there. Freedom had come as he had wished; after all those years the plan had gone wrong. It had come to a divided nation, to a quarrelling Congress, to a land he had striven to unite that had broken asunder, when the top half had turned into a schism called Pakistan.

When the great day came in Delhi in August 1947 and *swaraj*, Independence, was declared, and Jawaharlal Nehru told the crowds in his thin emotional voice: 'At the midnight hour, while the world sleeps, India awakes to life and freedom,' the father of the nation was hundreds of miles away, striving to soothe the civil conflict that same freedom had brought about.

It is repetitive, even banal, to keep using this word 'unique'. Yet Gandhi – without trying or affectation, yet with a keen and calculated sense of theatre – was *sui generis*. No revolutionary of the past had ever so exploited the power of powerlessness, and discovered how passive resistance could flummox an imperialism built on physical force, that was accustomed to being attacked, but not suborned. How does an army deal with 'passive resistance'? How does it subdue an unarmed opposition? How does a railway operate when men invite the trains to run over silent people prostrate on the line? There was no way. And that was how Gandhi won the war he never fought.

To declare interest: I have myself been closely concerned with India for nearly forty years. 'Concerned' is an arrogant word; I feel involved. I first saw the country in the late 1940s, when I was sent to report what was called the Cabinet Mission, led by Sir Stafford Cripps finally to negotiate the Independence that had been argued over for generations: years of casuistry punctuated by bitterness. There was no longer any time left; this time it had to work. It was, of course, and had we known it, the beginning of the end of the British Empire. Those months were accidentally to hook me to India, an unknown land, as I could not ever have foreseen.

In those days to the political world outside the word 'India' equated almost automatically with the word 'Gandhi', which had gone almost into folklore. 'Mahatma' was an honorific existing nowhere else; it roughly means 'great soul', but it has no formal standing, cannot be conferred or really defined. Gandhi never asked for it, but he could never reject it. It is true that he occasionally deprecated it, with befitting modesty, while greatly enjoying the deprecation. Somebody once used the phrase: 'The man of towering modesty.' Only after all these years I dare admit that it was mine.

For years Gandhiji remained a legend, not a man. (The suffix 'ji' is again untranslatable; it equates respect plus affection.) It was my early ambition, in common with that of every journalist in Asia, to meet the Mahatma, and I was young and brash enough to suppose that would be easy. I was very wrong. Gandhi was shrewd and wordly-wise enough to realize very well that you best achieved publicity for your cause by avoiding it in your person. I did in fact meet him in the end, several times. Everything comes to pass in India, in the end. That is usually a very long time.

Gandhi was born in 1868, in the tiny western state of Porbandar in the Kathiawar peninsula. He was born into the Vaisya caste: third down in the complex Hindu caste scale, after the Number 1 Brahmins and the Number 2 Kshatriya, the warrior rank. The Vaisyas just manage to outrank the Sudras, the working class. The word 'Gandhi' means 'grocer', something that the present Prime Minister of India rarely emphasizes. (Mrs Gandhi is no relative whatever; it is a fairly common name. In any case Mrs G. was married to a Parsi.)

To write anything about Mahatma Gandhi today is daunting, to write anything new impossible, after the accepted hundreds of thousands of words of biography, appreciation, analysis and conjecture, not to speak of the huge autobiographical *Experiment with Truth*, which in great detail tells everything about what the man thought, and hardly anything of what the man did. What he did was turn the whole philosophy of India upside down. For generations the Hindu culture had disliked the foreigner, but tolerated him – Muslem, Turk or Christian – simply because the Hindu system was too inward-looking and caste-divisive to be capable of united action. It was tried once, in the Mutiny, and came to nothing. Thereafter the process was adaptation. British merchants exploited Bengal; very well, Bengal would exploit the exploiters. Hinduism was accomplished at adapting to intruders. They found a prophet in a now-forgotten man called Ram Monan Roy, an intellectual Brahmin who served the British, made a fortune out of them, and devoted his life to undermining them in the pursuit of reason.

A century later his inheritor was M. K. Gandhi, a lawyer of forty-nine newly returned from South Africa where he had learned the principles of opposition by passive resistance. Gandhi promoted the *hartal,* a protest by public stopping of all activity, a spiritual strike. This came to its inevitable head in April 1919 in Amritsar in the Punjab, where the British General Dyer broke up a meeting by firing on it without warning, killing 379 Indians and wounding another thousand or so. The British thought they had saved India from revolution. What in fact they had achieved was to ensure, before too long, the dissolution of the British Empire.

It was the punctuation mark of Gandhi's career. He who had

advocated cooperation with the British now said that 'cooperation in any shape or form with this satanic government is sinful'. There ensued the political technique unique to India – civil disobedience, passive resistance, the war without battles, the fighting without force, the ultimately irresistible power of the negative. A chronology of the Mahatma Gandhi freedom fight would be tedious and repetitive – the enormous meetings, the near-adulation, the near-diffident imprisonments by the baffled British who could never understand a political opponent more tranquil and intelligent than they, the fasts unto death that always stopped just in time, the 'naked fakir', as Winston Churchill called him, conferring in his *dhoti* with viceroys and statesmen; all that is on a hundred records.

My personal share in this bit of history was a minute and unimportant factor in the last act: when the die was cast, when the British Cabinet Mission, already conceding the principle of Independence, were merely wrangling as to how to bring it about. The culmination was in the Himalayan hill station of Simla, on which the British insisted to avoid the intolerable heat of the Delhi plains. I met Gandhi on the train, in the famous third-class carriage on which he ritually insisted – as in Delhi he insisted on inhabiting a sweepers' quarter, the slum prepared for his symbolic use by the expensive introduction of bathwater and electric light. (As Gandhi's disciple, the politician-poetess Sarojini Naidu, forever said: 'If Gandhi only knew what it cost us for him to live the simple life!') I had hoped for a few minutes of the eternal verities; all I got was valuable instruction on how to eat a mango without drowning oneself in the juice: 'Be patient, young man; how can I tell what is in store for us? Now you cut it thus, and thus.'

Simla was a lovely place, reeking of the Raj. Permit me a final quote from a dispatch of the time:

The magical moment of the day was dawn. I would crawl out into the pearly haze at five in the morning, collect my horse [in those days Simla allowed no wheeled traffic] and ride out to see Gandhi, sometimes with Jawaharlal Nehru, but he was usually earlier than I. Gandhi lived at the end of a five-mile track in a rather commonplace bungalow called, of all things, Chadwick. There, as the sun touched the spine of the hills, the High Command of the All India Congress would meet, and plan the day's strategy, and consider, and meditate.

It was a strange scene. On the verandah would be Nehru, shrugging into his brown achkan against the early chill, the swathed figure of the enigmatic Vallanbhbhai Patel, the mountainous biblical bulk of Khan Abdul Ghaffar Khan, the Muslem from the Frontier like an Assyrian warrior, and curled up almost invisibly amongst them the little brown Mahatma.

They are all, with varying success, reproduced in the Attenborough film, which I salute for its fidelity, and especially for Gandhi and Nehru.

They would walk up and down communicating, it seemed, through a sort of empathy. It was an Old Testament spectacle. At a certain moment the spell would break; they would fold hands to each other and leave; for a while Gandhi would sit alone, until his noiseless white-clad acolytes would glide around and bear him away to his bath, his food, his massage, his interminable writings.

That was how I saw it at the time, and that is how it remains for me.

I once went to see him in his room; pale wood, bare linoleum, the bleak decor of any furnished room anywhere. I had prepared a few of the solemn-sounding meaningless questions journalists are supposed to ask famous people, a formal gesture, an excuse for personal contact. He answered, patiently, restlessly.

'Surely you must appreciate by now that my belief in *satyagraha*, non-violence, is an active thing, a militant thing in its way. It is possible for a violent man to become a non-violent man, but never for a coward. The political question is nearing its end; let us see a little further. All life implies some sort of violence; we must select the path involving the least. But there again you must go a little deeper. . . .'

All the time the stooping, self-effacing girls in white saris moved soundlessly in and out; they brought nothing and they carried nothing away; they seemed only to fulfil some need within them to circle in the presence, to justify their discipleship. After a while Gandhi would slip his feet into his chapals, extricate himself with some gentle donnish old man's joke; his eyes wrinkled with some secret pleasure and then lost all contact with the moment, peering around for a secretary. . . . I found myself drinking orange juice from a cracked teacup. . . .

That to me, in my fairly innocent simplicity, was Gandhi the man. We now know that the politician Gandhi's triumph was to unite the masses and the classes into the national movement. The masses would follow the classes because Gandhi was held to be a good Hindu, the 'Great Soul'; the classes accepted his primitivism and Hinduism because they knew the vegetarianism, the *dhoti* loincloth, the hand spinning, were his passport to the people. Most important of all they knew that Gandhi could outclass the British in debate, in tactics, and above all in making them feel uneasy in morality. So the big battalions lost out to the naked fakir. And then when the final triumph of Independence came it was empty. It was not one Free India, it was two: a partitioned Pakistan was his final sadness. Mohandas Gandhi did not attend the celebration of his life's desire, because there was bloodshed in Bengal, and where there was conflict the pacifist had to be.

There is a legend that everyone in the world remembers exactly where he or she was when the news came of the assassination of President Kennedy. It is true for me: I heard a radio in a house in Chelsea at 9 p.m.; just ten hours later I was in Houston, Texas in time to see Oswald die.

When Mahatma Gandhi was shot I was no longer in India. I had come off a railway train at Sherborne in Dorset, where I was taking a son to school. Sherborne is a very, very long way from New Delhi and the house of Mr Birla, the last place Gandhi ever saw. At the barrier the Dorset collector took my ticket. He said he had heard the news on the BBC radio.

'They made quite an item of it. He must have been an important old geezer. I wonder who he was.'

4 December 1982

Thoughts on the Trade

Tribal Eye

If one is to believe the splendid wildlife films one sees on the box (and they are about the only ones I do believe), then it would seem that when one elephant in the herd begins to flag, or falls sick, or grows too infirm to stumble on with the mob, then all the other elephants gather around in a way most touching in its solicitude, giving the ailing one encouraging grunts and nudges and evincing every sign of tribal distress. Some of the fitter elephants even try to lever the old soul on to its feet. By and by it rolls over, and the caravan moves on. As far as I know this phenomenon is found in no other animal than the African elephant – except among the analagous Fleet Street pachyderms, a species with similar conditioned responses. When one of their number falls by the wayside and makes piteous gestures, its fellows assemble with lowing sounds of futile sympathy. Some even make half-hearted moves to help, soon abandoned. Others hang impatiently around reflecting on the extra share of fodder there will be when the loved one slings his hook. How sorry everyone was for the *Observer*!

Over the last weeks it has been absorbing to watch the behaviour pattern of the elephants of the newspaper jungle before the travails of their troubled brother. Good old *Observer*; a decent institution if ever there was one, never did anyone any harm, occasionally admonishing things but not denouncing them, neither strident nor effusive; jolly good value on a good day, wouldn't you say, Harry? Not that we actually take it; enough to read with all the others.

I was greatly moved by the emotion that welled up in the newspaper trade at the plight of the *Observer*. This was quite proper, according to my wildlife films; the elephants gathering in mournful curiosity around the sick brother in the herd, some of them mooing ruefully, others unconcealedly licking their chops. On the whole goodwill abounded. One had grown used to a sort of *de mortuis* attitude to the *Observer*. Now all we wondered was what would be the blood group of the transfusion. I could have done with

151

a little of that same herd solidarity sixteen years ago when the old *News Chronicle* bit the dust. But then the *News Chronicle* did not perish of a public wasting disease, but before a firing squad, or so it seemed to us.

I dare say there will be some tut-tutting now about our venerable institution the *Observer* being absorbed into the public relations system of a rich American industry. It gives me no special pang. In the days of the Cadbury *News Chronicle,* we were known as the cocoa press; doubtless the *Observer* will now become the oil press, which sounds like something rather charming in a Greek olive grove.

From all accounts this Robert Anderson is the most philanthropic thing that happened to the oil business since Rockefeller. I must say that if I were Mr Astor I would sooner be taken over by him than by you-know-who, since it is probable that a busy tycoon like Mr Anderson will never see the *Observer* again as long as he lives, if indeed he has seen it yet. If anyone complains that he is American, then so what; Fleet Street has a tradition of expatriate landlords. Both Beaverbrook and Thomson were Canadians, Rupert Murdoch is Australian; the Harmsworth family is, I am assured, Hungarian, if not by blood then by tendency, since no one ever met a failed Hungarian.

So long live the newly lubricated *Observer*! Some forty years ago it missed a great opportunity. Long before I dared set my foot in Fleet Street my father, who knew his way around, took me to see the late great J. L. Garvin, then god of the *Observer*. 'Show respect,' said my father, 'if not indeed awe. For no living man can say less in four solid columns that this great editor.'

I presented myself, and rising from my knees offered my humble duty and asked for a job. 'Where are you from?' asked his Eminence, not unkindly.

'Dundee,' said I, as inaudibly as I could, but he heard.

He said 'Pshaw!' – the only time I ever heard this fine word actually uttered. 'We shall talk again in some years.' But we never did.

I wish the intervening generation had made me as rich as Mr Robert Anderson or Arco, so that I could have bought up the *Observer*. Then the great ghost of Garvin would again stalk the land, thousand words after thousand words, out-Levining Bernard, out-Perrying Worsthorne, out-Reesing Mogg. You have probably never seen a J. L. Garvin article of the old days. It was like the uncharted surface of the moon, of limitless horizons, mystic, wonderful, but of course nothing whatever growing there. But it sure passed the time, for a day or two.

Where are you now, Robert Anderson, when we need you?

29 November 1976

Virgo Intacta?

The lamentations for, and by, the *Times* newspaper are sad indeed; they remind me of the Shakespearian climaxes where the hero intones his own obituary for many a pitiful passage until comes the end, with a bare bodkin, by which time most people have forgotten what the wake was all about.

I observe from afar the mournful scene, now turning into hopeful tight-lipped smiles, with a personal detachment and a tradesman's regret. It is as though some hard-nosed property developer had been given permission to turn Buckingham Palace into a supermarket. I would feel no special aesthetic sorrow, but an institutional loss. It is a heresy to say so, but I feel rather as I did when they pulled down the Holborn Empire music hall: I rarely went, but I liked to think it was there.

Those of us to whom the *Times* was always by far the world's second-best newspaper have been enthralled by its recent professional strip-tease act, so uncharacteristic of demure and reticent Aunty. Last Friday, the day of judgement, by my calculations the *Times* devoted to an analysis of its own misfortunes no less than 163 column inches, an acreage of introspection that one would have thought that great newspaper would have saved at least for the Second Coming. One's heart went out to this noble soul *in extremis*; it was as though one were to make a running commentary on one's own execution. I carry on as though the *Times* were dead, which by all accounts is not so, or not certainly yet. This is the reverse of what we are always told about corporeal death, that the body perishes but the soul lives on. Here, I think, we shall see the reverse process: where the body survives but the soul inevitably slips away.

I am deeply sentimental about newspapers. This is probably because in all my life I never knew any other trade, nor especially wanted to. In my fantasies I have occasionally thought of being a property millionaire, or better still of arranging to inherit a wealthy dukedom, but somehow or other these things never came to pass, doubtless because of fascist conspiracies; anyhow that is the way it is, and that is how we all know in our hearts that the dismal fate of the *Times* diminishes us all.

Mr Rupert Murdoch and the *Times* are improbable bedfellows, but Mr Murdoch has publicly undertaken not to put nudes on the front page, and I believe him implicitly, at least for a while. This is probably (excuse my hobbyhorse) because a half-tone block of a nude in the *Times* would resemble a deep-sea diver seen through a glass darkly, like everything else.

In these austere *Guardian* columns we have no right to speak for our distinguished colleagues on the *Times,* and I apologize for the impertinence. When the die is cast and the commercial deal done there was an effusive leader in the Thunderer defining Mr Murdoch as 'an international publisher who operates successfully in highly competitive markets; his interests . . . do not seem likely to be in any way embarrassing.' Have they ever *read* the *Sun* or the *New York Post*? I am sure they have. These interests are not likely to be embarrassing. . . . But let us quietly wait, not for tomorrow or the next day. Does a sharp operator like Mr Murdoch want the *Times* in order to preserve it on the same sad course that loses it an annual fortune? Naow, cobber. I do not say the *Tit-Times* is upon us yet, but we shall not weary for waiting.

My God, what a prig I can be when I try. A vagrant and misspent youth washed me up on many journalistic shores, but only two took me to their bosom, the late *Picture Post* and the *News Chronicle,* and it is significant that they are both good and dead. I had a kind of frivolous flirtation with others over the years before I found my haven here – but never the *Times*. This was not as odd as it sounds: as the raddled old virgin told her confessor: nobody ever asked me.

I admit interest: I never met Mr Murdoch, but many years ago I worked for him for a week or two. I was asked down to Australia to help in the setting up of a new paper, the *Sunday Australian,* which was to resemble an antipodean version of the *Sunday Times* – you know, they said, like literary book reviews and things. Within reason of course. But Australia was not ready for this very modest overkill of culture and very soon the paper slid into the decent oblivion where it had always doubtless belonged, confirming Mr Murdoch in his intuitive knowledge that you cannot woo peasants with posh.

One's heart goes out to the *Times* as the dramatic day approaches, revealing its emotions editorially like the demure demoiselle awaiting the embrace of the daemon lover, eager and fearful. 'As we covered the news, the news covered us; it has been like playing chess in a hurricane. . . . He [Mr Murdoch] has a reputation for toughness, and no doubt there will be occasions in the future when that toughness will be turned on some of the practices of the *Times*, perhaps uncomfortably. But. . . .'

'But' . . . the lifebelt word of all newspaper editorialists. How one appreciates the pang of that writer.

But . . . 'If Mr Murdoch can make the *Times* a commercially viable newspaper he will have done us the greatest possible service.'

And so – without irony – say all of us.

27 June 1981

Censor Nonsense

I am naturally chagrined that I appear to be the only working journalist in the realm who has not been offered a job on Sir James Goldsmith's news magazine *Now* (sorry, *NOW!*) at the standard rate which, I am told, starts at about £150,000 a year, plus company Rolls. Sir Goldenballs could have bought me for half that, but he did not even try.

I cannot understand it. I am not a boy wonder but I am marginally younger than Manny Shinwell. I did my bit to ingratiate myself with Sir James's business interests by plugging his Marmite! in this newspaper a week or two ago. ('Irresistibly delicious with peanut butter.' Ad.) I do not work for *Private Eye*. (Except, I believe, I did once get into Pseud's Corner, a rare distinction.) I do not know why I am despised and rejected and refused my £150,000 a year for writing interminable paeans on the Pope.

The only possible conclusion is that it is a conspiracy. This was indeed suggested at the Labour Party conference when Mr Bill Keys, general secretary of the printers' union SOGAT, said that if a few rich men and multi-national companies were allowed to continue controlling the press a truly democratic society would never be achieved here. Thus one rich James takes £150,000 worth of bread from a poor James's mouth. Shame, really.

This time-worn theme is taken out for walkies at almost every Labour Party conference. 'Once and for all,' said Mr Keys, warming to his work, 'we have to destroy the myth that we have a free press, because the press we have today is censored by the proprietors who own it.'

For all I know this may well be so, but the curious thing is that it has never markedly oppressed me, and I have worked for some of the most obstinate managements in the business. I do not put it about more than I have to, but I toiled for a time with Lord Beaverbrook, covering the Independence negotiations in India. Since I saw his newspapers but once in a blue moon I was wholly unaware that the Lord – taking his cue in this, as in all things, from Winston Churchill – was bitterly hostile to the whole idea of anyone's Independence, while I was enthusiastically in favour.

Nevertheless he continued to print my eulogistic stuff about Nehru (whom he loathed, simply because Nehru liked Mountbatten, who was no pal of the Lord's). It is true he sometimes put a strapline over the story saying that the piece didn't represent editorial policy, but he printed it just the same. I only learned about this quixotic deal much later. It may have been barmy, but it wasn't what Mr Keys nor I, would define as 'censorship'.

I may have been lucky. I have been mercilessly, and rightly, subedited (and having spent years in the woeful trade I know how it brings tears to the eyes of these great and good men to cut a comma), but I cannot recall ever having had the substance of anything thrown out by a terrible top-hatted tyrant. Indeed when I wrote a column for the late lamented *News Chronicle* (run by the dreaded capitalist Cadbury) I felt that in moments of desperation I could slip in a page of the telephone directory and nobody would notice.

I can see what Mr Bill Keys means when I read the *Telegraph's* description of the Brighton conference as 'the sight of men and women driving by negativity and hostility, diminished as human beings, possessed by that manic infantility . . . the psychic state whose collective ego-demands are taken for reality . . . the need for antagonism and hatred. . . .' I would have thought that was not far from manic infantility itself. We should stick to the *Guardian*: we may be a funny old thing but we are not paranoid.

The mood of the Labour Party conference seemed to be that it would be not a bad idea to set up a national daily newspaper in the interests of the Labour Party. I can think of no madder idea, given the contemporary state of the market, but let them dream. I wonder if it would be unfair to remind them, and us, that there was once exactly such a newspaper set up for exactly such a purpose, in 1912. It was called the *Daily Herald,* and its first editor was the late George Lansbury, on behalf of the TUC. In 1929 the TUC agreed that Odhams should take over as publishers, Congress retaining 49 per cent of the shareholding. This was to be the first national press voice of the Labour movement, and it was most highly thought of. Its contributors included H. G. Wells, Hannen Swaffer, Edgar Wallace, Bertrand Russell, and in its dying days such lesser satellites as Clement Freud, Tom Baistow, and me.

The trades unionists and the Labour Party extolled it, and revered it, and praised it, and consecrated it – and went every day and bought and read the *Express* and the *Mirror*. So in the autumn of 1964 the old *Daily Herald* faded away, and changed its name to the *Sun,* and by and by it was taken over by Rupert Murdoch and turned into the great organ of public exposure it now is.

There is a moral there somewhere. Or perhaps you could call it an immoral.

9 October 1979

Thanks a Million

Some of us ageing journalists who still treasure our days of the quill pen and the carrier pigeon can still recall the time when people bought newspapers for the curious purpose of reading them. Some, indeed, could decipher letters less than an inch high. Our researchers tell us, in strict confidence, that this quaint custom is still followed by patrons of the *Guardian* newspaper, many of whom have been able to read and write since childhood. They are also, it is whispered, not easily bribed.

However, *autre temps, autre moeurs* (you see what I mean: culture) and we are in an industry that is no longer in the business of selling newspapers, but buying people. And people, it seems, do not come cheap. For the last few days the pop papers by a curious coincidence have been leading the front pages with headlines proclaiming their selfless urge to give away a million pounds. The word is of course a cliché now; a 'million' is now the accepted monetary unit, like the ha'penny was in Lord Northcliffe's day and, with Daniel Defoe, the groat. Could you insult a *Sun* man by offering less?

Even in the few weeks I have been away the trade has had a metamorphosis. (Let the *Sun* get that into a front page 72-point.) I can't be bothered to start again, but I watch in wonder. I have been in newspapers all my working life, largely because I enjoyed the trade but mostly because I knew no other. As I recall it, you hoped that people would buy your paper rather than another either because you had more news or you presented it better – which did not necessarily mean bigger.

You were in the business of selling words, for good or ill, and in my day we charged twopence a time for the lot. Very few of us talked about 'millions', because we didn't exactly understand the word. Astronomers talked about millions, which was fantasy; newspaper managements did not talk about millions, or at least not in front of the servants, like us. I don't think they truly knew much more about them than we did. Even now I would vaguely guess that the Editor of the *Times* makes about as much in a year as his proprietor does in a weekend. If you want to make a fortune, don't work on a newspaper: own it. There is absolutely no obligation to read it, even if you can.

It is not that the newspaper business has diminished, or deteriorated – it has just become something totally different. (And you must understand that I mean 'it', not 'us') I do not denounce it, nor complain, nor moralize; it is just that I no longer want to know. I would sooner be a correspondent than a croupier; I prefer copypaper to computers, and I would prefer to work on a newspaper than on a lottery ticket.

Still: all good luck to the Maxwells and Murdochs and so on, say I; the more they prosper the more my mates will get their pay packets, and if it pleases these faceless financiers to call the retailing of newsprint 'journalism' then it is no more ersatz than most of the other bogus stuff they sell.

The measure of these miserable millionaires, self-elevated to Press Puffins, is the wild paradox that they can make even the late and monstrous Lord Beaverbrook seem in retrospect almost benign, and at least professional. I worked for a while for that brutal and oft beguiling being, until he provoked me into the Fleet Street Fight of all time years ago, and dispatched me for a while to professional outer space. Looking back from these wealthy nondescripts of today the base Beaverbrook was an almost saintly proprietor, because he not only read newspapers and adored them but actively worked on them. The *Express* people lived in daily dread that the alarming old demon might walk into the office at any time of day or night, seize the page proofs and demand that the Editor replace the leader page because some editorial contained a sentence of more than five words, the permitted maximum for emphatic Beaverbrook prose. I suppose Beaverbrook must have been as rich as Murdoch – here I get out of my league – but he was not obsessed with money; he cast it liberally about but he never went on and on about it forever like these boring printmongers do today; to dangle the words 'million' as a front-page come-on was probably the one thing in the world he would have found tasteless.

Things in our trade must have reached a pretty pass when I find myself writing affectionately about Lord Beaverbrook. They have indeed reached a pretty pass if you can bring yourself to call the *Sun–Star–Express* etc. pretty. We are fortunate indeed who can work in the columns we do. I have been in this goddam trade so long I value the smallest of mercies, and compared to others this is not small.

Let us not deride the Maxwell–Murdochs etc. Their motives are wholly philanthropic: they want to give people millions of pounds; could one ask more? I never had a million pounds in my life. 'Can you get me this Robert Maxwell on the phone? . . . Hi Bob; remember me? About that million pounds. . . . No, I can't actually read. . . .'

20 August 1984

The Bomb

Rules of the Game

So the International Society for the Promotion of Kind and Compassionate Wars is on the job again. Those decent diplomats down there by the lake are to spend the next couple of months revising the Geneva Convention, if you please. The Conventions, or ground rules, work on the notion that warfare can be made an occupation for gentlemen, and every so often the Red Cross International in Geneva takes them down and dusts them off, to see if they fall short of new progressive military developments, like there is surely an acceptable charitable way of napalming villages or throwing people out of helicopters. It is quite touching, every time they think up a new rule for an old sin, and I suppose it keeps some folk out of worse mischief.

The Geneva Convention has been on the go more or less since 1864, starting with the theme of assuring the neutrality of ambulances, hospitals, chaplains and the like. There was nothing much going on at the time; the Americans were having a civil war and the Prussians invaded Schleswig-Holstein; small stuff. You could at least talk about rules.

From time to time, as now, when they can find a slack moment between major wars, the Committee has another look at them, in the light of experience, or perhaps the eye of faith, and every time it does so the process gets dafter and more fancifully unreal. The Geneva Convention for Cleaning Up Conflict is the biggest humbug produced even by that sterile city and the delegates, doubtless well-intentioned as they are, would do better to save their breath to cool their porridge.

The notion that the war game is susceptible to *rules* is quite hilarious, for those who get their fun from man's despair. My memory is dim about how they went about things in 1864 ('Pray permit General Sherman's musketeers to fire first') but the idea that chivalry could survive the aeroplane and the gas chamber is sad and silly and hypocrisy to boot, because it fosters the illusion that you can somehow disinfect fighting by protocol. Ask the villagers of My Lai. Ask the inhabitants of Dresden or Hiroshima. Ask the people of Phnom Penh, if you can find any. Ask them in the pubs of Belfast.

This Geneva Conference has started off by dividing armed conflicts into two categories: international and non-international. This is absurd for a start; there are no more non-international wars, nor can be so long as the industrial nations in their economic fix encourage and promote the arms trade, protesting only when the other side gets in first. Was Angola civil war, or was it a calculated act of Big Power policy? When the Middle East goes to war again, who will be the sponsors? What about the Lebanon? Nobody knows; they have agreed not to discuss little local difficulties. What is the Geneva Convention attitude to the H-Bomb? It hasn't one. But it is very strict about the protection of regimental padres.

There are established commissions of inquiry into breaches of the Geneva Convention. They must be busy people. The Geneva rules for humanitarian conduct in time of strife are breached every day. Everyone who has seen a contemporary war knows that this is logically inevitable. War, once you have it, is not amenable to any law. Peace, on the other hand, is a perfectly definable condition: peace is government and world peace, if we ever get the hang of it, will quite simply be world government, appalling though that sounds to Mr Solzhenitsyn.

It might not be a bad idea, therefore, for Geneva to stop wasting time on playing about with humanizing war with a sort of international Boxing Board of Control and kidding themselves that we played Queensberry rules in Vietnam and bending its minds to stopping the whole thing. It is, I agree, not exactly a new idea.

I remember years and years ago General MacArthur testifying to the US Senate that in his view war should be outlawed, and because General MacArthur was a virtuoso and no mean hand at the business himself this moved many Senators to tears. They were not too well up on their facts, since legally and officially war has been outlawed for fifty-seven years and indeed many times. It was outlawed in 1919 in the Covenant of the League of Nations. It was outlawed again in the Kellogg-Briand pact of 1928. It was abolished again in the Atlantic Charter of 1941. (There was a pretty drastic war going on at the time; war was to be abolished when it finished.) It was again abolished at the Moscow Conference of 1943. Finally we got rid of war for good and all on 26 June 1945 in the Charter of the United Nations. For half a century we have been outlawing the hell out of war and look where it got us.

The catch was, of course, that all these nations that outlawed war agreed only on condition that it didn't impede *their* plans. This was known as the 'sovereign equality of the signatory Powers', and this was rubbed in every time war was abolished. However, the formal outlawing of war was no doubt of consolation to the Koreans and the Vietnamese and Cypriots and will surely be a source of strength to the Rhodesians when their time comes, since whatever happens will not be legal, and they can always complain to the Geneva Convention.

26 April 1976

Power Complex

'We shall overcome,' we used to sing on the long Easter marches, 'we shall overcome some day.' We never did and we never shall.

The nuclear controversy which caused such a surge of passion in the sixties breaks out again, but crystallized now into academic debate among the scientists, which concerns itself not with the great doomsday issues of our day but with the flat techniques of energy sources and power houses. This is most important, to be sure, but it lacks sorrow. The wrangles among the professors are doubtless vital, but they have not got the drama of the Aldermaston March. I suppose that sooner or later one gets used to anything.

I felt this fairly poignantly, though not unbearably, when I watched the TV *Open Door* programme set up by CND. It was a valiant try, considering the meagre resources and the BBC's emasculation of the opening, but goodness, how sad. Every bitter argument, every point made, was exactly as valid as it was ten years ago; the inescapable reasoning against the Bomb was in no way diminished by time. But to every uncommitted person it must have seemed irrelevant, or even quaint. What is still probably the greatest international moral dilemma of our time, had lost the edge of horror that once distinguished it from everything else. It was like denouncing cancer for being wrong, not like denouncing mankind for being vile.

The argument has wholly switched now from the use of the atom in war, which is generally held to be undesirable, to the perils of using it in peace, i.e. when the boffins decide that the MAJOR source of our industrial and domestic power supply shall come from nuclear sources. As ever, the doctors disagree on all points except one: that heavy radioactive pollution is a highly possible consequence of this notion, and that if it occurs its effects are not only imponderable but irreversible. This seems to me to be a consideration not wholly confined to the professors. After all, it is only last week that Pennsylvania collected a noticeable dose of fallout from a Chinese test on the other side of the world. At least that is where they said it came from.

As far as we are concerned, we are told that to provide the energy for our industrial machine we shall need some eighty or so fast-breeder reactors round our coasts. (The physicists use the terms as if it were a hutchful of rabbits.) We are assured, nervously, that the high-level radioactive waste can be safely disposed of – which is a thing I flatly and unequivocally refuse to believe until it is proven to me, and by the nature of the half-life of this stuff this cannot be established for thousands of years, by which time quite a few of us may have inhaled a lethal whiff or two without knowing it.

What worries me is the rarefied, not to say casual, way in which the whole question trickles out, as though it were a simple question of shifting from steam trains to diesels.

It has been clear for almost a generation that thermonuclear explosions (which include a few dozen simultaneous power house disasters, not to speak of the odd bomb test that the experimental nations are bound to touch off from time to time) could in a few years make the world uninhabitable. We have been told so often that there are enough H-bombs stockpiled around the earth to overkill every human being ten times.

Leaving war out of it (and we'd better) consider peace, detente, the occasional test bomb, and the fast-breeders lending their dubious contribution to a happy world. The likelihood that something will go amiss in that scene is in my view a good deal greater than the likelihood of nuclear war. I remember about twenty years ago hearing Professor Oppenheimer, the great physicist who probably knew more about this creepy business than anyone, asked on Ed Murrow's television show whether he was worried about what his scientific endeavours would later do to the world's future, even ignoring the chance of a war, Oppenheimer answered that he was 'not unworried'. Coming from such a usually articulate man, this was eerily cagey.

Like all conscientious scientists he was badly torn two ways: by the impulse to add something to knowledge, no matter what the cost, and by the wish to make the world a better place. Nuclear scientists must be inescapably schizoid: on the one hand they must create bigger and better bombs, more impressive and perilous power stations; on the other hand they must fear they are working for death; a pretty tense dilemma. Dr Oppenheimer used a curious phrase: he said we live 'at the edge of mystery'.

We can hardly say we do so now. Mankind has had a knack of blundering out of many blind alleys, but not this. This one won't allow us the leeway we have always had, will not allow it again the years of mistakes and recoveries. Not when one day we shall find ourselves in the room with more radioactivity around than we can stand, especially if there is a foetus in the house. This troubles the thoughts of those like me, who know so little. It gravely troubled Dr Oppenheimer, and left him 'not unworried'.

We are now twenty years deeper into the plutonium age, and I'm not unworried either.

11 October 1976

167

The Laser Cowboy

The thought haunts me: a perverse god who in his infinite wisdom arranged for someone to invent the wheel, and then sent him back to the drawing board to make it square.

That would seem to be the case with us. It took the Almighty several thousand generations to people an agreeable world with reasonable folk in a manageable terrestrial environment, on the whole sympathetic to the human kind – and then capriciously to introduce into this decent place something like the current President of the United States.

Can I be growing into a believer? I have never been one in the metaphysical sense, but I am coming to feel that it must have taken a singularly vengeful God to have invented a Mr Reagan, so that one obsessed ex-cowboy could spend the evening of his days ensuring that he would have no successors. That would be of no moment, except that it equally ensures that we shall have none either.

I always tried to be quite jealous of the future of the next generation. It would be bound to do better than ours, given a chance, because it could hardly do worse. And then four or five days ago this President Reagan scrapes back from his atomic attic the old relics of Manhattan Project, the scientists who built the first atom bomb, the nuclear cap pistol they tried out at Hiroshima, and requires from them what his ad-men call the Space Age Super Bomb.

The Space Age Super Bomb is all that I really need.

Let us examine the brief that was given to these distinguished men. It is interesting not for its message but because, in its bureaucratic terms, it says exactly and precisely the opposite of what it means.

Reagan: 'I call upon the scientific community in this country, those who gave us nuclear weapons to turn their great talents now to the cause of mankind and world peace, to give us the means of rendering these nuclear weapons impotent and obsolete.'

In a word: we spent a generation creating the Bomb, another generation perfecting it; we knew not what we did – nor what it would cost – and now, dear God, allow us to do the impossible: un-invent an obscenity and get back to simple humane things, like the broadsword and napalm.

Not so. Not in the least so. Indeed, wholly otherwise.

Reagan: 'I am directing a comprehensive and intensive effort to define a long-term research and development programme to begin to achieve our ultimate goal of eliminating the threat posed by strategic nuclear missiles.'

This is a very worthy and proper objective. But of course he can never eliminate the threat; he can only out-threaten it. Even that could be acceptable, except that two powerful sides out-threatening each other over the years are absolutely *certain* to stumble over the edge, either later or sooner.

'To eliminate the nuclear threat. . . .' It is a pious objective. Yet one must ask: Who invented the threat? Who first baptized the world with the Bomb?

If the Russians could have been first with the Bomb they would have been. If the British could have been first with the Bomb, they would have been. So indeed would Hitler have been. We can leave the eternal moralities out of this. President Reagan is not talking in terms of reducing the conflict; only in terms of seeing that he wins it, with his new lasers, microwave devices, particle and projectile beams; the technology of the TV thriller – which, they say, is even in its fantasies trailing behind reality.

'I am directing a comprehensive and intensive effort . . .' to make quite sure that when the balloon goes up, it is our balloon. Mr Andropov is doubtless saying exactly the same thing, but he is shrewd enough not to shout it so loudly.

It seems quite manifest now that President Ronald Reagan has the marginal political intellect to realize that his (I hope) brief term of office can be made memorable in no positive way at all – economically, aesthetically, socially – other than as in his B-movie days: growling and waving a gun. His Sancho Panza, our female Prime Minister, smiles and applauds and elocutes, and offers no apology to the 50-odd million of us, her employers, for taking us along ('Rejoice!') into her proud and personal suicide pact with the great White House Ham.

Reagan: 'My plan could change the course of human history.' He can say that again. If he has time.

I have boringly to mention for the hundredth time that – unlike Mr Reagan or Mrs Thatcher or the Blond Bombshell Heseltine, or, I am pretty sure, Comrade Andropov – I have in fact seen some Bombs, or Devices, and watched them go off, and seen what they did to a city like Hiroshima, a desert like Woomera, an island like Christmas. This gives me no right to argue, but the experience to get the wind up.

This is a terrible fuss to make about something that even under Reagan cannot be fully operational for many years, but we all increasingly know how swiftly time goes by. How long ago was Hiroshima? How long ago was Agincourt?

If I might have a quick word with our leading man, Mr Reagan. You wrote the lines. You direct the show. Let us be sure it works, for this time, Ron, depend on it: there will be no take two.

29 March 1983

The Nuclear Age

Every now and again a moment of splendidly commonplace reality intrudes even into Parliament. In the Upper House a day or two ago the Under Secretary for the Armed Forces was asked by one Lord Bishopston a simple question: assuming the situation requiring the launching of an English-based American cruise missile arrives when (a) the Prime Minister is, as so often, at the hairdresser's having herself coiffed, and (b) the President of the US is, again as so often, sharpening up his intellect at a baseball game. In such a circumstance who orders the button pushing?

Answer, of course, came there none. It is to be assumed that the programme of barbers and baseballs is coordinated not to coincide. What else is the hot line for? (Laughter.)

It is interesting that we find that funny. I suppose it is quite funny, as bomb jokes go.

It is not all that long ago since the first A-bomb was dropped on the capital of Honshu, in Japan – name of Hiroshima. That is to say thirty-eight years and eight months ago. That is to say that almost all the responsible people in government today were children at that deadly moment of truth, with the exception of the American President, who developed into childhood later. To the geriatric worthies of Russia it probably seems like yesterday.

Most politicians of today have grown up with the atomic age; they have known nothing other; they invoke the 'nuclear threat' as though it were some over-emphatic Act of God, like an earthquake in Ecuador: nothing to do with them, not really. Not to be *encouraged,* of course. While they encourage it every day.

I doubt if one could name anyone in political authority today who ever saw an atom bomb go off, and what it could do. I have seen three, and I saw Hiroshima. I admit that is the familiar conversation stopper of your friendly old neighbourhood atomic bomb-bore. It is none the less true, and I reckon to know more about this matter than, say, a dozen Mr Heseltines. Or a hundred Mr Reagans.

Once upon a time even the Harry Trumans and Clement Attlees regarded the thing with awe, and even more so the ones who really knew, the Oppenheimers and the Rotblatts. Today the world's cheap politicos speak of the nuclear nightmare as though it were some sort of trump in a card game – bingo, I win; now let us pause for a drink and wait for the Second Creation. Mine's a small plutonium, without ice. Here's to our descendants, a thousand years from now.

I am not in the least frightened of the nuclear bomb, or not if I can be sure of being exactly underneath it when it comes. I am frightened only of the powers who – seriously and without irony – accept the military-political principle of Mutually Assured Destruction, appropriately initialled as MAD.

For some time 'deterrence' was based on the acceptance of MAD; now it can be, and has been defined as a 'viable strategic option'. If Mrs Thatcher's boss, Ronald Reagan, can accept that, it is bad enough for me.

We have all of us, not the politicians, lived with and accepted it for so long that it is like the weather. My children – who have now their own children – have never known any other sort of world. 'Oh, let us not have another war', they hear their parents say, 'Rationing! Conscription! Utility clothes!' Let me assure them: there will be none of that, for there will not be time. 'We know,' they say, quite honestly. 'We have always known. That is the world *you* made for *us*.'

All this is not occasioned by a sudden attack of morbidity; on the contrary. It is just that for some days I have been in a cutting room watching old library film of the Hiroshima and Bikini bombs for some arcane television purpose shortly, I hope, to be revealed. After all these years it still brought the hint of tears, at least to me. Not everyone can revisit after thirty-odd years that thousandth part of a second that changed his life. And, of course, yours.

Mrs Margaret Thatcher cannot possibly be held responsible for that early atom age, having been but twenty at the time. But she is emotionally still at the age when war was, and I suppose still is, an extension of sport. When she announced the Falklands War she bade the nation 'Rejoice!' We might not have done so too vigorously had we known then what we know now.

On that sporting theme, and to get me out of my melancholy doldrums, let me ask a sincere and simple question. Mrs Thatcher goes on endlessly about 'batting for Britain'. I know virtually nothing whatever about the game, sorry, but is there a cricket team called 'Britain'?

I believe Mrs Thatcher.

17 April 1984

Peace Be, BBC

Peace is no longer a dirty word. It has officially been brought from behind the arras into the front TV stalls of everyone's home; true, not as a matter of hope but of regret, something not to be saluted but mourned, but at least publicly no longer behind the hands of the anointed ignorant.

Just as many years ago we rightly blamed the pusillanimous BBC for its crude suppression of Peter Watkins's *War Game*, we must salute it now – with heavy reservation – for its showing of *Threads* and *On the Eighth Day*, illustrating what will happen to Sheffield while, and after, the Bomb goes off.

It is strange, or I find it strange, even perversely encouraging in its gruesome way, that we can now talk of Armageddon, of nuclear disarmament, even of peace of any kind as to be preferred to war, of which there is now only one kind; talk of these things in serious discussion, without having to look over one's shoulder or make apologetic excuses ('it might as well be said'). The media's painful discretion about the no-go subject has come to an end, and about time too.

I am personally used to being much more on the defensive. I am reinforced by the *Guardian* leader of 28 September which asks in unexpectedly realistic terms: 'What happens if it's not a holocaust?' Thinking the unthinkable, it says, is decades overdue. Should we go in for civil defence, and if so, what? It defines the 'apocalyptic' school, including CND, which argues that civil defence against a nuclear onslaught is not only a waste of time, but actually counter-productive because it could seduce people into thinking that the thing is in fact survivable.

I suppose I must accept inclusion in this 'apocalyptic' school, because I was one of the handful of founder members of CND when it was a very different thing from what it has become. CND had a predecessor, with a jaw-breaking name: National Campaign Against Nuclear Weapons Tests, chaired by the Quaker, Arthur Goss. Then at the beginning of 1958 there was a gathering in the Amen Court home of John Collins, Canon of St Paul's, of which I wrote at the time: 'It may be accounted a punctuation mark in the democratic record, because on that evening was born the Campaign for Nuclear Disarmament.'

Nobody could be quite sure why I had been asked to this party. I had neither academic nor political credentials. It could be perhaps, and was, explained by the fact that of all that group – perhaps of any group that could have been raised in the country at the time – I was the only one who had actually seen three atom bombs go off, and who had seen Hiroshima.

The effect upon me was something I barely understood in the 1950s, but which became only too clear over the years. The obsession greatly bothered my work; just as eight years later I came to be overwhelmed by Vietnam, so was I then inextricably enmeshed with the Bomb. I gained the name of the very first and inescapable atom bomb-bore. In those days there seemed to me nothing of comparable importance. Looking back, I see no reason at all to change my mind.

Since the 1950s and 60s CND has gone through many vicissitudes, some caused by internal squabblings encouraged by an almost universally hostile press, which tried to do with derision what it could not do with debate, CND endured. It had its glories, the first Aldermaston Marches; and its errors, brought about mainly through the mutual detestation of its two leaders, the worthy, dedicated, almost saintly contenders for immortality, Bertrand Russell and Canon Collins. It was years before CND discovered its real leader in Bruce Kent, a monsignor of uncommon wisdom, common sense, and above all humour, who reckons that you can promote a cause of transcendental seriousness through not being obsessed with Mission at the expense of Man.

Even in our, days of CND, the Bomb was a fact; we did not try to uninvent it. All we argued, and still do, was that it was useless to confront a terrible threat with the old and empty responses of balance of power, of spread the risk, of diplomatic arrangement.

Only one thing, we argued in those days and now can argue much more freely, could break the endless procession of fruitless words and suspicion and mutual misunderstanding and accumulating fear – and that was an *act* that was totally unequivocal, incapable of misunderstanding. Such an act – in our view then and now the only one practical – was the formal renunciation of nuclear war by the one nation that was in the supreme position to do it: Britain.

Whether that attitude may be held too simplistic in these complex days is a valid question.

We were not in CND to save our skins. Neither did the campaign denigrate the value and authority of Britain, but strove to increase it. A Britain, we said, that publicly told a world still aware of its history that she was at last siding with the forces of reason, and sense and right, would rally behind her at least 1000 million people of the non-Communist, non-American world who had no bomb.

All this makes as much sense to me now as it did then. It has been a fraught, exciting and emotional week. Normal service will be resumed soon.

2 October 1984

Long Ago and
Far Away

The Doctor Versus the Wizard

The end of the century's longest and beastliest war got house room in the press for about a week; not a bad claim for an industry that grows fretful when a story wears out its welcome in a matter of days. At the same time it kept up its remorseless ear-bashing over the Market debate, which has now become a numbing bore to the point where it can only be infallible propaganda for the Don't-Give-a-Damn Faction. An acre of argument for Europe: a bleak so-long for Saigon.

If the end in Vietnam has sidled uneasily into history (except for the great Martin Woollacott, for whom the *Guardian* is owed as many cheers as yawns for its other obsessions) and if the end in Cambodia was marked by predictable horror stories from a lying French doctor who later recanted and of course from the egregious Dr Kissinger who wasn't there anyway, and by a final galvanic twitch from the Seventh Fleet – then the end in Laos was the end of the show, to an audience already reaching for its hats. Poor old Laos, always last on the bill, dutifully providing not climax but compromise.

This is in character. In its day Laos was by far the oddest calmest, most idiosyncratic of the Indo-China dominoes, a place of quite preposterous charm and lunacy, and, from all accounts, serene to the last. Even now there would seem to be an element of the reasonable in Laos, though of course it may be sloth.

Laotians are very slothful people. It is a decent quality among so much neurosis. The more jumpy my own domestic circumstances become, with everyone telling me to do something *now,* when manifestly there is nothing I can do any more than anyone else, the more I respect the position of tranquillity. *Pas trop de zèle* might be the national motto of Laos, and for all I know it is.

I can tell you about Laos, because I was once a mercenary there. That was a long time ago. Laos was one of my earlier landfalls in Southeast Asia. In one of the bizarre vicissitudes of a newspaperman's life I found myself momentarily attached to the Foreign Legion. (Those were the days when the French of course were the masters, and the war was run on more stylistic lines.) We were based in Hanoi, which then was a place of provincial elegance and not a congeries of air raid shelters. I understand it has greatly changed, but it was pleasant then, set around its quiet lakes. No matter, we were soon dispatched to Laos, which everybody said was Hell.

It was on the contrary completely delightful. Two names linger in the memory to give the place its savour. The King of Laos, for what it meant, was Sisavong Vong – it sounds like a temple bell. The royal capital (as distinct from the administrative centre Vientiane, which is simple French) was Luang Prabang, which sounds like a cymbal. Sisavong Vong in Luang Prabang – what better orchestration could you ask? I must say it sounds a little pretentious for what it was: a township on the great cocoa-coloured tepid Mekong River, over-come with what seemed like an unconquerable drowsiness. It had, however, a quite extravagant importance for what it was, since it was under siege – though we did not know it at the time – it was a simple and leisurely rehearsal for Dien Bien Phu. To be sure you would not have thought so. I doubt very much if you would think so now.

I say that at the time I was a *Légionnaire,* and so I suppose I was, in my foolish fashion. I have been briefly and lovelessly involved with all sorts of units of one kind or another on land or sea; it would be hard to think of a more unattractive lot than the company with whom I was defending the French colonial empire, mainly tipsy homosexual German war criminals, or so I deduced. It was difficult to reprove them since they were almost always drunk, and so I dare say was I.

The point is that we are talking of a country that is, or should be, very vigorously in the news just now. We know Laos has gone to the Communists. When will they catch on? I guess it will take some time.

We were dropped into Luang Prabang at a crisis in its destiny. In the mountains all around us were what were said to be 300,000 revolutionaries who in those days were called Viet Minh. Those of the staff who were sufficiently articulate to say anything, said that the guerrillas were invincible, ubiquitous, irresistible; all the adjectives that sound better in French, but they wouldn't take us out so we did nothing at all. This, I assure you, is how the greater part of the Vietnam War was waged, at the time.

Now here was Luang Prabang, the Second City, imminently

threatened with conquest from the Communist hordes. This was undeniable, since we were wholly surrounded. And the township slept in a long, relaxing siesta; an occasional eight-year-old monk would play a desultory hopscotch on the pagoda steps. Now and again one of our *Légionnaires* would reel up the road singing 'Lilli Marlene'. It was a pretty tranquil emergency.

Now the reason for all this is an oft-told story, worth repeating in the light of today. The serenity of Luang Prabang was rooted in total confidence. Certainly not in the French high command, certainly not in General Navarre, by no means, in our bunch of bums – but, of course, in the Wizard. This was the senior citizen of the royal capital, the head magician and necromancer and prophet to the court of King Sisavong Vong, a deeply entrenched courtier and chamberlain. He was immensely old and, it was said, totally blind, but he had been in the business for a long time, and had never been known to miss. Every day he told the beads and cast the chicken's entrails, and daily he announced that the approaching Viet Minh invaders would move in closer, closer, to exactly 11 kilometres from the town, and they would then pause and go away.

This was good enough for my friends in Luang Prabang. I was perhaps the only uneasy man there. Everyone else implicitly believed the Wizard, who daily examined the omens and reported the same form: the Viet Minh would advance, and in due season would withdraw. This being so, why exert oneself? I repeat that only I had what my Presbyterian grandfather would have called Doubts. What I wanted was a helicopter.

However, thus it came to pass, and for me not a moment too soon. Air Reconnaissance HQ in Hanoi reported the Communists within 11 kilometres of our town, engaged in some inscrutable activity. They hung around for a day or two, and then they shoved off. This understandably gained the Wizard even more face and put him in the top league of soothsayers. He died shortly thereafter, full of years and with a crafty wink.

This hoary anecdote has doubtless long since gone into the archive of the Quai d'Orsay, though not, I suspect, the Pentagon. Anyhow, the simple truth of the matter was that the wicked Communist Viet Minh armies had never had the least intention of invading us; they had been harvesting the opium crop.

It must be remembered that little old Laos was, and is, one of the major opium-growing states in Southeast Asia. Our poppy juice that fetched 500 piastres a kilo in Luang Prabang (where we certainly didn't need it) was worth 2000 in Hanoi or Haiphong, and probably 10,000 in Hong Kong. I have no doubt a similar ratio works today. Anyhow, while we bemused inhabitants of Luang Prabang slumbered incontinently away the Viet Minh made off with a million and a half pounds' worth of opium, and flogged it to the Chinese for guns with which, shortly afterwards and in rather more deadly earnest, they destroyed Dien Bien Phu.

The real point is about the dear old Wizard, rest his artful old soul: it turned out later beyond a peradventure that this great Merlin of the Royal Court had been on the Communist payroll for many a year and his information had been strictly kosher all along, since he had depended less on his hen's entrails and the stars than on his short-wave radio link with General Giap. Even in metaphysics things are not always what they seem.

This is perhaps an unforgivably frivolous aspect of what should be an elegiac state of affairs. I think I have a right to offer it, diffidently, because I have had off and on about thirty years of Indo-China conflict and – as Patrick O'Donovan put it long ago in a beautiful book – one smiles, for fear of weeping. I rejoice that – as far as any of us know so far – the last domino has gone in a sort of peace, or at least non-war, which is I suppose the best we can ask of anywhere these days. Laos was of course luckier than Vietnam, or Cambodia. There are no Americans to be dramatically chased out. The Americans left Laos almost a year ago, after ten years of what our great contemporary the *Times* newspaper last week called, I am sure without irony, 'heavy military bombing and ground fighting by American Advisers'. Nobody knows where the Hell Laos is, but who needs such Advisers?

All Indo-China is now Communist: that is ineluctable. In Cambodia it seems to have been unreasonably painful and cruel: in Vietnam it is enigmatic. In the US State Department it must be agony, and Dr Kissinger's Peace Prize must be turning in its grave, or wherever he keeps it. In Laos, the land of the dominoes (or is it?) goes, and I would guess they can rest easy. They are now used to a fragile coalition including the Pathet Lao, that is to say the Communists. I wonder who they are?

Washington has always worried itself grievously about the International Communist Menace. This is explicable to me, as a fairly innocent observer, only by assuming that its bureaucrats never go to Communist countries. As one who has done, quite a lot, I would respectfully suggest that there is in the whole world no such thing as international Communism. It might not be a bad idea if there were; it would ease things up, and make it simpler to take sides.

There is not even such a thing as Indo-China Communism. Who is to say what is the meeting point between a Maoist Khmer Rouge and a Marxist Vietcong? Who among us is qualified to say that 'Communism' – however it may be interpreted, whatever its variants might not be better for – as an example – Saigon than the corrupt and brutalized society it has known for years? I would not, personally, like to have to make that choice. Not, I would suppose, that there is much choice.

Let us assume that the Indo-Chinese peninsula is now in the Communist orbit. Is Dr Kissinger, that great Bismarckian student, going henceforth to mark it in his Red Book, beyond the pale? Could he perhaps be brought to realize that in every poor and hungry country there is *certain* to be born something that's called Communism, and which will take its form from the character and the traditions of where it grows, capable of infinite development and modification? What about Tito, what about Brezhnev, what about Mao? (Or, if you like what about Wilson, Ford and Giscard?) To polarize this sort of world is wholly ridiculous, yet that is what we do.

It might not be a bad idea to go back to the Wizard.

19 May 1975

Thoughts of Mao

At some point in every day I go down on my knees, with a little help from my friends, to give thanks that I am not in the business of politics. Oddly enough I am not thinking especially of Blackpool, although the suicidal antics of the Labour Party up there, at least as seen on television, gave an extra urgency to my thanksgiving. I was not even thinking of the United States, condemned next month to a presidential election whose huge importance is betrayed by the numbing mediocrity of the contestants. Nor strangely enough am I thinking of the cruelly pointless conflicts of the Gulf, the exact purposes of which nobody seems able to define.

No, I was thinking of something far more remote and unregarded, and in a way more pitiful. I don't know where one can think with accuracy of 'politics' in Peking; perhaps only of their aftermath in a place where symbolism is sometimes so stirring, sometimes so sad.

The other day was the thirty-first anniversary of Communist rule in China. It was from all accounts a colourless affair, with none of the familiar celebrations and parades and spectaculars. Except for one thing: on the previous day functionaries entered the Palace of Culture, seized the immense statue of Mao Tse-tung, cut it into huge blocks, and carted them off to oblivion. I wonder why. Chairman Mao is indeed no longer god. He is remembered today for his omissions rather than his triumphs – but he surely did the State some service. For three decades he was a symbol of almost supernatural reverence. Yet on the very eve of the fourth decade his image must be physically destroyed, lest even momentarily he should haunt the festival of the new regime.

This seems an inelegant, un-Chinese gesture, unworthy of a society that, whatever else it may be, is rarely crude. It seems to be the inescapable reflex of a second-generation, revolutionary administration to turn and rend the creators of the first one – without whom, after all, they would hardly have been around to criticize. Chairman Mao follows Comrade Stalin into the shadows; it will be an awkward moment when they meet.

I regret, too, to learn of the national anniversary being celebrated so drably, without the familiar colour and excitement, without bands and fairs and clamour; so flatly, as it were a bank holiday in Bootle. Apparently hardly anything happened at all. In the old days it was never thus, I assure you. Once upon a time it was the greatest show on earth.

My first memory of Peking is of this day many years ago, with the Glorious Dawn but four or five years old. It was the first day of my first visit to China, in the innocent days when October began with a phenomenon of matchless extravagance: the day of the Big Parade. It is not impossible that this was the biggest crowd of human beings ever assembled anywhere on earth. They marched, they danced, they played and sang; the actors laughed and the soldiers frowned; even the tiny Mongol ponies of the cavalry trotted precisely in step, like clockwork toys; the vivid kites soared and swooped in unison;

the fireworks – ah, the fireworks! This, after all, was where they were invented. For hour after hour they went off, as the beguiling pastel silks weaved in among the brutal steel-grey as the tanks and rocket launchers rumbled past the Tien An Men, the Gate of Heavenly Peace.

As one watched this incredible profusion passing by, there came a rather frightening flashback to the old childhood tale: that if all the living Chinese should march past a given spot, they would *never* stop, so endless is their number. There in Peking that day it came to me in alarm that this was exactly what was going to happen. So on and on they went, the sections of workers at this and that, federations and unions and associations. It may be hard to believe, but somewhere there appeared a section of Roman Catholic nuns, with a banner saying 'Christians for democracy!' Even more bizarre, there was a group among the Minorities labelled the 'New Chinese Capitalists' Association', with huge characters which read, 'Long live private enterprise in the Glorious Revolution!' At that point one surrendered one's grip on reality.

So there we were by the massive blood-red gate, beneath an enormous portrait of Chairman Mao, the Eternal Uncle of this strange new world. It did not improve the architecture, but it was this that everyone had come to see and cheer – not the elegance of the Forbidden City. Benign and bland, he looked impassively down on his revolutionary creation and, if he wondered where it might be going, he did not let on.

And so last week they took his statue in the Palace of Culture and chopped it to bits. For all I know they left a message saying whatever is the Chinese for *sic transit*. Maybe the image of the Palace of Culture will be the better for its going. Not, I think the image of the Chinese.

7 October 1980

183

Tea for Thieu

Looked in the other day for a cup of tea at the White House. Not exactly the one that springs to mind, though it is inhabited by a President – or rather a very much ex-President. The not especially lamtented Nguyen Van Thieu, former political and military boss-man of what used to be South Vietnam, now lives in exile and cultivates his garden in a rather dainty part of Surrey, and his very smart pad is indeed called The White House; it is written on the door.

This is paradoxical, since former President Thieu's bitterness at America and all its works goes very deep indeed, and he is not slow at expressing it once he gets going. It is understandable from his point of view. This rather eerie little ex-supremo, or US puppet as most might say, considers himself wholly betrayed and martyred by the patrons who let him down by losing the Vietnam War, and obliging him to run for his life four years ago.

Hitherto Thieu has steadfastly refused to talk to any journalists, especially Americans. He relented in the case of a friend and myself who sought him out to suggest he take part in a television pro-gramme on political refugees. Mr Thieu would have none of it. 'What I could say now is well known. For the rest, the time is not ready.' In our case, however, he was happy to go on and on. Or if not happy, at least willing. One found oneself thinking stupidly: tea for Thieu, and Thieu for tea, Kingston-on-Thames is the life for me.

The ex-President is a slight man, both physically and I would guess intellectually, but merry withal, except when he talks of Nixon or the dreaded Henry Kissinger, his former paymasters, now anathema. Like all Vietnamese he looks about twenty years younger than he is, which is fifty-six. The grey in his hair is alleged to come from his own hand, to give him the venerable gravitas admired in the East.

Mr Thieu, son of a small landowner, was educated in Hué, Vietnam's cultural capital in Annam beside the Perfumed River, that same tranquil town ravaged by the 1968 Tet offensive. As a young man he had a brief flirtation with the Viet Cong opposing the

French, until he realized that they were a Communist outfit, whereupon he moved over and joined the French. Similarly he moved over from Buddhism to Catholicism; he is a flexible man. He became a general and rose to high office. His anti-Communism became fanatical, and remains so.

After the assassination of Diem, therefore, he became an acceptable President of the South Vietnam American battleground and remained so for nearly ten years, longer than any leader in Saigon. It was probably the worst time in its history, corrupt and bloody. Richard Nixon defined Thieu as 'one of the best politicians I ever met in the world'. By their friends shall you judge them.

President Thieu fought furiously against the peace agreement reached by Kissinger and Le Duc Tho, and lost. With the Viet Cong at the doors of Saigon the US Ambassador fled frantically from the embassy roof, and Thieu took off bitterly for Taiwan. By and by he was granted permission to live in Britain, and here he is. He bought a cosy house in New Malden, then another one in Wimbledon. He moved around. He covered his tracks with care, using a variety of aliases. His present establishment, this White House of Coombe Park, Kingston, is not quite on the level of the Doc Lap Palace in Saigon, but it cannot have left Mr Thieu much change out of £250,000.

The funding of ex-Presidents in exile is always an intriguing matter. At the time of his escape Swissair was reported to have refused Mr Thieu's request to carry 16 tons of gold from Saigon to Europe. The present Vietnamese government insist that he nevertheless got away with $3\frac{1}{2}$ tons.

Today the ex-President's philosophy is straightforward, undiluted cold war doctrine circa 1960; one could be listening to Barry Goldwater. Totally simplistic hallmarked anti-Communism: China and/or Russia intend to master the world; to that end they must dominate Southeast Asia.

'But my people will resist,' says Mr Thieu. Even after four years the words 'my people' still come readily. 'I don't know how or when I shall return to Vietnam, but I shall. Today in Vietnam even the lamp-posts would leave if they could. Oppression, imprisonments. . . .'

But in his day was there not, shall we say, quite a lot of that?

'I imprisoned nobody. Some Communists it was necessary to neutralize. Captivate them, yes. Neutralize. A very different matter. It was my country.'

Surprisingly, he suggests that the French should have stayed on. 'There would have been a certain independence, autonomy. In the manner of your Commonwealth. How much better than this.'

But did he not once fight against the French?

'That was long ago.'

Indeed it was. And a long way between the once-so-elegant and then debased Saigon and the stockbroker-belt greenery of Kingston and The White House, where the present Mr Thieu, private citizen, lives with his wife, Nguyen Thi Mai Anh, and his son, born here. Another son is at boarding school in Hertfordshire, and there is a daughter.

Why did Nguyen Van Thieu, failed defender of democracy in Vietnam, decide to make his exile hermitage in England? His brother, an engineer, was already here; his son had grown up with his brother's children. He likes it here. The air is full of the anti-climax of exiles. The ex-President of 15 million baffled people reads his books in suburban Surrey, does his garden, and doubtless dreams. Everything is very long ago and far away.

I am fitfully reminded of the last time I talked to a big man in Vietnam; it was years ago in Hanoi, shaking with bombs, and the man was the late Uncle Ho Chi Minh. As I recall it, he gave me a Jack Daniels. In the circumstances, it was very civil of ex-President Thieu to have seen me at all.

21 May 1979

Victoria Falls

My heart lifts when I hear of something, *anything,* happening in the Seychelles, which I love like a long-lost child. The idea of a coup in the Seychelles is as quaint to me as that of a revolution in Bournemouth. The Seychelles is not a place where people have coups to overthrow governments; after all they only *got* a government the other day, or so it seems to me who once knew it well.

Coups are military, are they not, and the Seychelles does not even have an army. Or they are an Uprising of the People, and in my remembrance to get a Seychellois to uprise so much as off his backside was a rich and rare sight. I am far from sure that the whole thing has not been got up by the press to promote tourism, to introduce a touch of the Red Revels into what has for too long been trade-named an Island Paradise.

Hands up all those who have been to the Seychelles. As I thought, scores. In my day I do not suppose there were as many as three tourists a year, if that. How could there be more, with neither hotels nor airport? When I went there on an inscrutable mission the only way was to take the Bombay–Mombasa ship, which after three days or so would briefly pause and put you ashore in a small boat to Victoria, the main island. I intended to stay a week; what I overlooked was that the returning ship did not even stop, so I was stuck for some two months. Just two more days and I would have stayed forever, and gladly.

My reasons for going to the Seychelles in those halcyon days are too complicated to explain now, involving as they did a colonial shakeup initiated by a bemused Labour government that had never until then even heard of the Seychelles, and a nest of subsequent intrigues and comedies that could properly have been recorded only by Evelyn Waugh. For thirty years I have dreamed that if ever the divine afflatus descended upon me I would write the Great Novel about it, but since I have no talent for fiction, and since every single word of my newspaper story was killed by the lawyer, I fear the tale will forever go untold.

Nevertheless I was richly rewarded. The Seychelles is, or are –

there are ninety-odd islands, with lovely, haunting names like Praslin, Silhouette, Curieuse – beguilingly beautiful, endless ocean and soaring hills. (My acquaintance with Archbishop Makarios of Cyprus began when we learned that during his EOKA-time exile in the Seychelles he had been quartered, as I had briefly been, in the then Governor's hilltop house called, wouldn't you know it, Sans Souci). Yet chiefly I recall it as a fantasy.

No offence in the world to ex-President James Mancham or his successor-apparent Albert René, who were doubtless beardless boys in those days, but my most enduring and favourable impression of their country was that it was inhabited by a people in whom isolation, matchless climate and indolence had induced a state of wholly delightful dottiness. They were the barmiest lot of decent folk I ever met, and I readily fell into their ways. In all my time there I cannot remember meeting a single Rational Man, which was wonderfully refreshing.

Eccentric is not quite the word. From Government House down everybody was slightly, in varying degrees, off-centre. From the judge, who, having once been a lyric-writer for Charlot's revues, tended to offer his judgements in verse; from the charming lady who had retired from running a whore-house in Mombasa to start a private-enterprise nunnery; to my good friend who felt obliged to establish a private school of his own to accommodate his vast flock of illegitimate innocents. Even nature cooperates with the strange and eerie Black Parrot, which breeds nowhere else, and the extra-ordinary palm that produces the coco-de-mer, a huge nut of a shape so outrageously indecent that people use them as doorstops *pour épater les bourgeois*.

Today, now that the aeroplane and the package tour and so on have befallen the Seychelles (and why should one complain; the poor souls had little else before but copra and patchouli) things have clearly changed, as witness this new coup idea. I have to say that I have not the least notion of what the coup is all about, nor does the equivocal Mr René make it much easier to find out. I am depressed to read that Tanzanian troops are being flown out in case they need to repel the alleged mercenaries that Mr Mancham is said to be recruiting from goodness alone knows where. What on earth can this all this be about? In the *Seychelles*?

The Seychelles lie equidistantly about a thousand miles between India and Africa. The population is about that of a medium-sized English county town. The place has absolutely no history at all, and basically no indigenous population. It was nicked by the British from the French in the late eighteenth century, largely as a naval coaling station; it is now a fairly considerable C & W communications centre. For years there was nobody there except the French planters, the *grands blancs,* and their imported African workers. Even after the British colonials moved in everyone got on pretty well with one another, in a dozy sort of way. It is not for nothing that the national animal is the giant tortoise, which moves with extreme lethargy and lives forever. (I brought back two of them, to my cost.)

If, as is darkly rumoured, the Russians want to take the place over as a naval station, then let them be warned: they will be wooed by soporific sounds, like Circe's island. Let them go; they will never want to leave.

But it is a sad, sad day when the last nice place joins the rat race.

13 June 1977

The Merchants of Darkness

In the last generation the British Imperial system had to protect itself from time to time not from aggression from outside but from rebellions from within. The Falklands episode was unusual – indeed in our time unique – in that the islands were formally invaded by an outside power. Whether or not that foreign power, neighbouring Argentina, felt it had a more reasonable claim to the place than a fading colonial authority 8000 miles away is irrelevant. The fact is that for once the British went to war to repel an alien invasion and not, for once, an indigenous 'freedom' movement.

This to be sure was taking things back in time a long way; the British Army was much more accustomed to sending its forces overseas to protect, as they saw it, the colonials from themselves.

They were, technically, 'police actions'. Thus we fought Cypriots in Cyprus, Kenyans in Kenya, Malayans in Malaya. I am sure that history will shrug them off as fairly trifling. They did not seem so at the time. But then, probably, neither did Agincourt at the time, though as many died there as have just done in the Lebanon. Nobody reported it properly, except the late W. Shakespeare, and that at second hand.

Nobody will write a drama about Kenya. Probably the only one who might have done was Noël Coward, who would have detected its quality of the tragically preposterous. It is possible that he had colonial Kenya in mind with 'Mad dogs and Englishmen go out in the midday sun'. I went out there in the early 1950s when this essentially colonial – middle-class suburbia was suddenly enveloped by a higher organized African anti-European terrorist movement known – rather horribly – as Mau Mau. What did Mau Mau mean? To this day nobody actually knows. But it put the fear of God into the Colonial Office. And, quite often, me.

Every British colony developed its own popular character and image. Kenya's was that of a wonderfully beautiful and abundant country inhabited by what generally seemed to be regarded as the well-to-do and rather effete second sons of good family who could be shuffled off to a fairly affluent African obscurity. That was broadly true, though the picture changed when the snobocracy became diluted by random ex-officer pensioners of a lesser breed, thus complicating a simple society with an intrusive middle class. One had to live in an intensely divided and hierarchical African society to realize how even more tribal were the Brits. The accepted name of the place was Keenya; if you used the African pronunciation: Kenn-ya, that was eyebrow-lifting subversive. Like most coarse strangers. I knew no better. There was much I had to learn. I once referred to Kenya in an article as 'an Equatorial Ealing'. That indeed was what it was, but it did me little good among the paleface gentiles.

The Mau Mau period was among the eeriest times I remember. Mau Mau was almost wholly of the dominant Kikuyu tribe, the most literate and intelligent and pervasive. It was wholly stealthy. There was no front, no battlefield, no neutral zone. You could find yourself abruptly and silently done-in in a garden in Nyeri or at a street corner in downtown Nairobi. We had an army facing phantoms. Nobody could possibly believe that a loose congeries of individual ghosts could ever win; but of course they did; they had been there forever and we had not.

Nevertheless it was still difficult to see the Mau Mau as heroic.

The white settlers, as they were universally called, were pretty unendearing, but the militant Kikuyu were of another mental world. We once found a farmer slaughtered in his bath in the Highlands. Someone pulled the plug and most of the farmer slipped down the drain: he had become mincemeat. With every good will, therefore, it was not easy to identify this macabre technique with the normal values of a patriotic movement.

The Kenya emergency never, emotionally nor politically, involved the British homeland as did, for example, Cyprus or Suez. It was disorganized, barbaric and remote, without any romantic historical associations. It had not even any remotely Communist shadows that could be usefully exploited. Yet, inexplicably, it went on and on.

It was epitomized only in the name of its titular leader, the Kikuyu renegade Jomo Kenyatta. He was identifiable, and sinister in the picturesque way journalism loves. He could be, and was, defined as 'a merchant of darkness and death'. In white settler circles he was the irrefutable argument against allowing Africans into the London School of Economics, that traditional academy of revolution. He was also gifted with the mortal sins of being both attractive and articulate. Worst of all, one of his several wives was a respectable English lady in Sussex, where he had farmed for a while.

By any colonial standards Jomo was bad news. Yet it was difficult to cast him as the terrible mastermind of Mau Mau, since almost as soon as the Kenyan state of emergency was declared Kenyatta was sent to prison, technically for life, while the Mau Mau went on without him for another five years.

His trial, with half a dozen of his Mau Mau colleagues, sticks in my mind for curious reasons. For security reasons it took place not in Nairobi but in a schoolroom in a remote northern township called Kapenguria. During my long drive up there I was held up by a traffic accident, and arrived too late to find a seat in the tiny schoolroom-court. An accommodating policeman let me in, however. The only corner he could find for me was, in fact, in the back of the dock. Jomo Kenyatta on trial was given to making speeches of almost uncontrollable length. I sat through his last one cringing in a corner, fearful that everyone in the dock would be instantly hustled off to some nameless gaol forever.

As it turned out, Jomo was released six years later, and five years after that was President of the independent republic of Kenya. It is one of the recurrent ironies of the diminishing British Empire that very soon this 'merchant of darkness and death' was being acclaimed in Whitehall as the most moderate and reasonable of ex-colonial leaders; the erstwhile assassin was shortly being hailed as the best law-and-order man in Africa. There was a somewhat sad background to this.

Jomo Kenyatta had always been a hearty and convivial drinker. When he emerged from gaol he was an evident alcoholic, and nobody will persuade me that this had not been induced by his captors. I had known him before and after, and the change was obvious enough. This would have mattered little had it not corrupted his constitutional balance. He became not the leader of his nation, Kenya, but of his own predominant tribe, the Kikuyu. One does not always realize that even a small entity like Kenya has vicious racial divisions. His only rival was Gginga Odinga, or the Luo tribe. Kenyatta crushed him, and gaoled him. How the white settlers would have whooped in triumph. 'They hate us, but they hate each other more.' On that, of course, was the Empire built.

I knew Kenya for a long time, in good years and bad. A year or two ago I went back for a holiday on the coast. Already it was doing its best to look like Miami. I almost preferred the days when you drove at night with your lights out.

21 September 1982

High Society

'This is your captain speaking,' said the captain, if indeed it was he, and obligingly someone turned down the Muzak. If only airlines knew the torment their piped mock-music causes their captives they would have it banned by IATA.

'Your captain speaking,' he said, as though his name was Horatio Nelson. 'I am sorry to say that No. 1 port engine cannot be started, because the starter motor is not starting, which is necessary for the functioning of the No. 1 engine. In a word,' said he, 'we shall be delayed for an hour, during which time you are requested to observe the no-smoking sign, and the bar will open when we are airborne. Have a good time.'

Up surged the Muzak again, in case people should start growling, or even fighting. I developed a favourable attitude to hijacking, if only to get one's own back. You cannot, however, hijack, a 707 whose No. 1 port engine is lying on the tarmac, apparently ignored by the world.

'We are shortly landing in Frankfurt,' said the captain hours later, now sounding forlorn. 'There will be no disembarking, and you are requested to observe the no-smoking sign.' Up comes the inescapable music. They do not do this even to the customers in Wormwood Scrubs.

I return to *Catch 22,* my only aeroplane book, since it alone makes me feel comparatively sane. Mr Heller has saved my reason on many a long flight. Sometimes I vary it with a dip into the Safety Leaflet, which for so many years has instructed me on seventeen ways of escaping from an aircraft, provided the aircraft is intact, stationary, on the ground, and the right way up. It is reassuring to know there are ways of getting out of the thing, as one sits imprisoned there, smokeless and drinkless and listening to *Rose Marie* on its fourth trip round the tape.

By and by we were travelling at 27,000 feet over somewhere or other at 536 miles an hour, no more and no less. An absolutely ravishingly beautiful blonde air-lady piled my plate with caviar, stroking my hair lightly, bending provocatively over with the champagne, murmuring endearments. I woke up abruptly, and a stern games mistress was there admonishing me about my seatbelt, because we were now landing in Cairo, or Tripoli, or some such place on which we must not set foot, because the only times you are allowed out of a plane in transit these days is when it is on fire, or the doors fall off.

I often wonder how it is that aeroplane travel becomes less and less agreeable as it becomes more and more popular, indeed almost unavoidable. As a rule technical things, as they develop, become more acceptable; not so the flying machine.

I have been using commercial flight since the days of Imperial Airways, since the Croydon days of the Horsa and the Hannibal, when you went to Paris sitting in deckchairs, and if you had a headwind you could look down on the Brighton road and see the motor cars overtaking you. In those days they treated you almost as though you were a gentleman, or even a human being, not as though you were a package in Cricklewood sorting office.

No one who ever crossed the ocean on a Cunarder, when that was possible, ever regretted the passing of the windjammers, but I shall never stop ruing the disappearance of the now extinct flying boats. Oh, nostalgia. That for my money (though it was always someone else's money) was the way of all ways to get around the world. A couple of dozen of you in a thing the size of the Albert Hall, or so in retrospect it seems, droning along at 5000 feet, so that you were looking down not on limbo, but on real terrestrial scenery, setting down each sunset on some convenient lake or harbour for a night's sleep in a proper bed, a handful of airborne Jeeveses asking if you would care for another drink. For one brought up in converted Lancaster bombers or RAF Yorks the old flying boats were the deep, deep peace of the double bed of aviation.

True, they took about five days (as I recall loosely) to get to, for example, Hong Kong, but who the hell wanted it any quicker? On the Durban run you saw bits of Africa – unexpected lakes, broad reaches of the Nile – that one will almost certainly never see again, like long-abandoned branch lines on abandoned railways. You were not, as now, encapsulated in cylindrical sardine tins, battened below hatches, released by numbers. You were a passenger, not a projectile. So that is why the flying boats were phased out. They were uneconomic, as everything polite and civilized is uneconomic. Indeed it occurs to me that the human race is itself intrinsically uneconomic, especially me.

The other day I came back from Nairobi, a perfectly normal overnighter. Yet it put me in mind of many years ago in that same place, in the days when you had to get what they called a 'Priority' for a passage. I couldn't get a Priority, and I couldn't get a hotel room. I took my dilemma to the New Stanley Bar, where I fell in with a more-than-civil white settler-type Kenyan in a crepe-de-chine shirt. After half a dozen gins it turned out by chance that he owned a little Anson aircraft. He had had it in mind for some time to take it for a run back to the UK. Today was as good as any other, and he wouldn't mind the company. So off we went to the airfield and pointed north.

It must have taken us about a week. We had a range of about 350 miles, so it meant plenty of pit stops on the way. When the owner felt drowsy he let me drive, which I could then still do, just about. I cannot remember exactly how we navigated. Finally we came down somewhere in the freezing rain, which just had to be England. He said: 'I believe this is Southampton.'

I said: 'Pity it isn't Portsmouth,' because in those days I lived not far away.

'No sweat,' said he, and we flew for another ten minutes or so to Portsmouth, where I said: 'Many thanks for the lift, and cheers.'

11 July 1977

A Spy Story

What I know about the trade of espionage, or secret services, or intelligence, or what you call it, could be written in large type on the back of a large postage stamp; though I am quite sure that I have among my acquaintances many fully paid-up members of the International Union of Spies, on one side or another. Most of my knowledge of this interesting subject is derived from the absorbing works of John le Carré, whom I have the good fortune to know and at whose feet I only too infrequently sit and he very understandably keeps his sources under his hat.

I was glad therefore to be filled in the other day by Richard Norton-Taylor in his absorbing piece in the *Guardian* about the care and treatment of the British intelligence service. It was called incompetent by Sir Harold Wilson and indeed from all accounts it seems at the time to have been staffed largely by the Russians. This causes me no great concern, since for all I know the Pushkinskaya bureau in Moscow is equally manned by defecting Oxbridge dons. This would argue a wholesome enough situation, provided some mutual agreement is made for a balance of moles, as I believe they are called, one lot as it were cancelling the other out.

I doubt very much if it is as simple as that. Indeed I also doubt very much whether your actual spy is not an anachronism today, now that – from what I read, and I believe everything I read, which I sincerely pray you do not – electronics have taken over and every diplomatic telephone is tapped and every diplomatic wire is intercepted, and the post doesn't work anyhow. My colleague Richard N.-T. tells me that we have some seven hundred men working for MI6. For all I know you are one of them. What a pushover of a job!

It has always rather irked me that no one ever asked me to be a spy. I have every qualification: a devious nature, an inconspicuous personality, a used raincoat. This is of course pure vanity, since the whole business is preposterous and everyone engaged in it must in his heart feel a proper Charlie. In a world, however, of proper Charlies.

It is not quite true that no one ever asked me. I was once briefly but intensively cultivated by a member of the East German Trade Mission, which in those days stood in for an embassy. He was an amiable fellow, albeit rather thick and speaking English with some difficulty, but he bought me several awful lunches in order to pump me about affairs in the Middle East, where I had lately been.

I would read him the current *Guardian* leader on the matter, or perhaps the *Economist*, or indeed anything that came into my head; he would thank me profusely and take elaborate notes of what he could have bought that morning for a few bob in the open market. If that is being a secret agent then God grant that I get on the game. By and by he vanished, doubtless recalled to East Germany for his decent innocence. I was sorry to lose him, but I did not miss the melancholy luncheons.

It is an oft-told tale, but I cannot resist telling of the one occasion when I momentarily entered the John le Carré twilight world. It was in Delhi, shortly after Independence, during a big deal called the Pan-Asian Conference, which was a much more important affair than is remembered now, since the delegates did in fact represent something like half the population of the world. Everybody seemed to be there, but especially there was said to be a delegate of singularly secret and mysterious purpose whom nobody was allowed to meet; it was put about that he was the sole confidant and emissary of the legendary Ho Chi Minh, of Indo-China. He was said to carry with him secrets of astonishing importance. In no way whatever would he be seen by the press.

However, somehow or other I got an elaborate nudge that I might just possibly make contact with this impenetrably elusive bloke, using excruciating discretion. I had to be on the verandah of Maiden's Hotel at precisely a certain hour, wearing a certain kind of suit, and reading page two of the *Statesman*. I would then learn something to my advantage, and probably the world's.

I followed my instructions punctiliously, looking round corners as I went. At the appointed moment a waiter loudly paged my name, and there arrived a small Annamese-looking man with a huge briefcase. He joined me and drew from his wallet an absolutely enormous calling card, on which was printed in heavy type the words: Mr San Do Lau, Secret Agent. He had nothing to say whatever, except to ask how best to get his hands on four thousand rupees cash to buy a practically new second-hand Chrysler at the moment on offer down the road.

So one cannot say that I was never involved in the secret service. It has never been engagement as intimate as the 2000-odd people whom Richard Norton-Taylor informs me work in the Government Communications HQ in Cheltenham (where else?) which is in close liaison with the US National Security Agency: what bliss. But 'tis enough; 'twill serve. I once knew quite well the vanished Kim Philby, in Beirut; I would not wish to be him. I want nothing to do with secrets; I have troubles of my own.

1 August 1977

Crashing Out in Castro's Cha-Cha

Poor President Carter accumulates egg on his face thicker than any President since Eisenhower. He is now held responsible for everything from the energy crisis to the Middle East to Hurricane Harriet to the impending extinction of the snail-darter fish, imperilled by the building of the Tennessee Dam. I admit I know little of the snail-darter fish, nor specially care, but wherever it is going it looks like taking President Carter with it.

Now he is lumbered with Cuba once again. It is not exactly a re-run of October 1962 but there are some who would like to see it develop into a promising crisis, even graver than that of the snail-darter fish.

I cannot quite understand why it is so heinous for the Russians to keep their soldiers in Cuba while it is quite acceptable for Americans to keep theirs in Europe, including this semi-sceptred isle. That is to say, I think it is ridiculous and provocative for either of them to do it, and I could wish for both sides to get the hell home, but if it is all right for one I cannot see why it is otherwise for the other.

In any case it always seems to be forgotten in this context that the Russians have for years been openly maintaining a naval base at Cienfuegos in Cuba, and the Americans have had their military establishment at Guantanamo in Oriente province since 1903, no less. This produces the nice paradox that the two main actors in the cold war deal both retain quite powerful forces within the territory of a third nation, and only appear to notice the fact about every fifteen years.

This business of mutual electronic keyhole watching is, I suppose, inevitable and forever, but my, what a waste of time and money is this folk dance of the free-booters. Russian soldiers go to Cuba, Cuban soldiers go to Africa, American soldiers go to England, English soldiers to go Ireland hands down, turn about, follow round the middle, ring-a-roses and we all fall down.

I know it is very wrong of me, but I find it quite difficult to take Cuba seriously. The ghost of the musical comedy crook Batista still haunts Castro's Havana for me. For one thing, Cuba was the first People's Democracy I ever experienced in a decent, not to say lush, climate; hitherto I had always associated a somewhat cheerless Communist system with the somewhat cheerless conditions of East Europe, where it always seemed to be four o'clock on a November afternoon with everybody shutting up the bars.

Not so in Cuba. The inter-reaction of didactic socialism with Caribbean-Latin temperament was in the early days almost hilarious. I had known the place very slightly in the corrupt old days, when it had seemed rather like a West Indian Soho. After Castro I turned up again (to my great surprise one didn't need a visa; maybe you do now) in a terribly clapped-out old Constellation filled with slightly tipsy trades unionists from the North of England, I would suppose party members to a man, to whom this was the daddy of all outings.

Havana greeted them – and indeed me, since I was inextricably by now a TU groupie – in great style, with gallons of rum punch and a little guitar band playing in our honour what they must have supposed to be the British social-democratic hymn, 'The Red Flag'. After a shaky start the tune within a couple of bars turned into a cha-cha-cha. 'Let the cowards flinch – cha – and traitors sneer – cha – we'll keep the cha-cha flying here.' It was much better fun than Blackpool. Anyone who can turn that rather dismal melody into a cha-cha-cha, said I, has my vote.

I turned to find that my typewriter had been nicked before I ever got to the customs. Not that it mattered much; I got to do little work in Cuba. I was supposed to be interviewing Old Faithful, the great Fidel, for a rather stern American journal called the *Atlantic Monthly*. He gave me at least half a dozen appointments all over the island, and stood me up for every one. In the end I abandoned the project and turned in for my one and only early night in the Hotel Habana Libre, which had transformed itself from a Hilton into a sort of Gulag. At about three in the morning I awoke from a deep sleep to find the bedroom full of bearded bodyguards, and among them the great man himself. He sat on the end of the bed and said: 'We shall talk no? I have much to say.' And indeed he doubtless did, since Sr Fidel Castro has rarely been known to utter a sentence less than two hours long. But what it was I know not, since I had taken the precaution of swallowing two deep narcotics, and by the time I awoke again in the morning the audience was over and the room was empty. I have never seen Fidel Castro since, and I greatly doubt if I ever shall. One does not trifle with history.

As far as that goes, I feel a kinship with the snail-darter fish, about to be rendered extinct by President Carter's Tennessee Dam. Surely one day we shall all be reunited in that great Habana Hilton in the sky.

17 September 1979

Arrogance West of Suez

The episode of the Falklands has been compared, at least by its opponents, with the politico-military debacle of Suez in 1956. In my opinion the analogy is somewhat false, and the only common factor between Falklands and Suez is impetuous arrogance, and the fact that both operations were conceived and dominated by uneasy and obsessed Prime Ministers.

Even that comparison is not wholly accurate because while Mrs Margaret Thatcher is vain and obdurate and diplomatically a novice, Anthony Eden at the time of his Suez debacle was clearly and probably clinically paranoiac, and experienced enough in foreign affairs to have known better.

Mrs Thatcher, moreover, appeared to carry the country, or at least its *lumpen-mass,* with her in her maiden fumble into warfare – and indeed the mass of her opposition. Eden on the other hand split British public opinion over Suez as it had probably never been divided since the Boer War. Furthermore Eden was opposing not just the Egyptians but, far more importantly, the Americans, and it was not Gamel Nasser who brought him low but John Foster Dulles.

I was not in London – I rarely was in those days – to see

Parliament tearing itself to furious pieces, to hear Nye Bevan's most memorable of speeches in Trafalgar Square, to see friends and even families divided in incurable bitterness over the impending war. 'Everyone in London,' wrote the American reporter Joe Alsop to his paper, 'is itching for a wog-shoot.' Of all this I read much later, and too late for me, because I was in a sort of workaday tangle not unusual to my trade.

I never took holidays, except from time to time to go home, since travel had long ago become a chore and not a treat, but in that autumn of 1956 I found myself with an unexpected fortnight to spare. I learned this in an Athens bar with the poet Laurie Lee, also at a sudden loose end. We said we could go on a little Aegean cruise. We would pay our way by some gentle busking: Laurie was a fine fiddler; I strummed an indifferent guitar. We did this as far as Crete. I was getting off the boat at Heraklion when I was met at the gangway by a telegram. It was from my newspaper, the late *News Chronicle,* and couched in its leisurely and well-mannered style. It said that rumours were afloat that something or other, no one knew quite what, was going on in Hungary – a Russian invasion, perhaps? Anyway, since I was not on anything special would I nip up to Budapest and have a look?

I do not know if you have ever tried to get in a hurry from Crete to Hungary. It is probably the most impossibly intricate journey in the world. Somehow or other it had to start in Athens. I abandoned Crete, and Laurie Lee, and my abortive holiday.

The cruise ship had by now gone its ways. I found a little freighter bound for the Piraeus that night. There was of course no berth; I had to pass that night on deck in unspeakable company. For some curious reason a great part of Greek inter-island commercial traffic consists of sacks of, to put no fine point on it, human excrement. There must be an excellent reason for this, but until then it had never obsessed me enough to investigate. That night I spent almost enveloped by this stuff. The sea was terribly rough. I reached Greece with my journalistic enthusiasm at its lowest point in my life.

From Athens, then, to Hungary. All the air services had been stopped. I was condemned to a railway train to the Balkans – but where? Two points of access offered: Vienna and Belgrade. This was where I made my truly amateur mistake. Obviously if the Russians had entered Hungary Vienna would be closed off as a capitalist vassal. So I embarked for Belgrade: a ride of total nightmare. The train was crowded to suffocation. For something like thirty hours I stood in the corridor jammed like a pilchard, dreaming of death. In Belgrade I hired an ancient motor car from the State agency Putnik and made course for Budapest. Over the border at Subotica they spotted the Yugoslav number plates and kicked me out. Meanwhile the smarties from London who had chosen Austria from the map were heading in and out of Budapest like commuters.

I crawled back to the Metropol in Belgrade. I had not been able even to lie down for three days and nights. There was waiting another courteous newspaper service telegram. Never mind Hungary, it said; story's over; seems the new world war's starting in Suez. Suggest repair to Cyprus, British Army HQ, soonest; don't acknowledge. So back on that inexpressibly bloody Balkan train to Athens; plane ferry to Nicosia, crawling on hands and knees into the Ledra Palace, by now nearly eighty hours unbathed, unslept, undrunk.

It can cause no surprise that politics aside, international morality aside, Eden and Nasser aside, I viewed the Anthony Eden Suez operation with but modified enthusiasm. Even so, enthusiasm diminished daily. The 'Suez Caper', as everyone, even the soldiers, called it, seemed to me about the dottiest and most doomed operation. We could capture the Canal, but how to keep it? The Americans were dead against us. True, we had the French and the Israelis, but everyone knew what they were. Everyone in London, said Joe Alsop, may have been longing for a wog-shoot. All I asked for was a small snort and about three days' sleep.

My troubles began quite soon. Telegraphic communications from Cyprus in the ordinary way were about the best in the world, but things had changed. Suddenly there was censorship. I have grown fairly used to censorships here and there, but the past masters of obtuse and obstinate obstruction are the British military, as of course my poor colleagues found out in the Falklands.

There were exceptions to the rule, but it always seemed to me that the main qualifications for military men charged with the supervision of journalists' copy were (a) never in any circumstances to have had personal experience in the newspaper trade; (b) to nourish an instinctive mistrust of those obliged to describe the act of fighting while themselves bearing no arms; (c) an aversion to the study of the printed word other than a quick whip through the *Mirror*, as far as possible avoiding the words.

I say there have been honourable exceptions to this formula, but I recall meeting none in the Suez operation. Curious and arbitrary rules appeared, the oddest of which was the banning of the use of the word 'war'. This was a troublesome limitation for those who were supposed to be describing the armed invasion of one sovereign state by another. The other novelty was that, if you transgressed, the offending word was not simply cut but the whole message was held up.

I found myself in a simultaneous position of liberty and confinement. I had confirmed at the outset that my newspaper shared my distaste for this non-war, so I was not inhibited editorially. On the other hand every time I suggested a hint of criticism meant a rough deal from the Army. It became increasingly clear that whatever handful of reporters would physically be allowed on the operation it would not include me. I sought a meeting with the general and respectfully explained my problem. 'I can't reasonably work here, so I'm going home tomorrow.'

'Well . . . ' said the general. 'Maybe.'

That afternoon orders were posted that from then on anyone seeking airline passage out of the island would have to obtain a military laisser-passer. I got mine a week later, when the Suez operation was good and dead, as were my two photographer friends who had penetrated the Canal. Operation Anthony Eden came to a sudden and humiliating collapse, under the implacable pressure from Secretary of State John Foster Dulles. It was the one good thing that that sick and obstinate old American ever did.

Everyone packed up and went home, and none so fast as I. And thus I came to an end of my almost wars, or non-wars, in three weeks. International enemies should employ me more often. I bet I could have stopped the Falklands business before a shot was fired.

But ahead lay Vietnam. None of us were so lucky there.

23 September 1982

Bertie's Booster

Now that most of the clotted cream and treacle has dripped off the eulogies to the Queen Mother for her eightieth birthday, I feel able at last to reveal the story of my brief association with the gracious lady many years ago. The indiscretion is unlikely to figure greatly in the official royal biographies, so it might as well figure momentarily in mine.

At the time the lady was on the throne, and I was in Sussex. Very late at night, I got a phone call from the foreign desk of a newspaper, which was not the *Guardian*. It was to this effect: would I go to India, and there was a plane booked at six next morning. Reasonably enough, it seemed to me, I asked why. The man on the phone said he had no idea; the Foreign Editor had gone home, leaving this urgent requirement.

Had it occurred to the Foreign Editor, I asked, that I had only that very morning got *back* from India, and I knew damn well there was no story? The hireling replied: 'All I know is it says here, "Get the 6 a.m. tomorrow".'

So, obedient to a fault, as I always am, I got it. In those days there was no question of 747s and soft seats; you travelled on horrible converted Yorks or Lancaster bombers; it was Hell, and it took forever. A lifetime later I decanted at Karachi, and found a feeder to Delhi. I cabled back asking, with respect, what the Hell I was supposed to do?

To which, in the fullness of time, my master gave reply. (He is still a friend of mine, or I would tell you his name.) 'Most sorriest,' he said. 'Didn't mean India, meant South Africa stop proceed Capetown soonest accompany royal tour.'

Anyhow, that is how I came for the first and last time to be part of a royal party. Never having been what you might call an over-enthusiastic monarchist, such a thing had not occurred to me. In the event, it turned out to be rather fun. We travelled in what was called the White Train, and in a style to which I have always vainly hoped to become accustomed. We went all over the place. South Africa is, mostly unfairly, a vividly beautiful country, and we were fed and watered profusely. There was practically nothing to do.

No two personalities could have been more different than those of the King and Queen. She was, then as now, composed, eager, on top of every situation; he was tense, unbearably nervous, alternating diffidence with bursts of temper. At the time there was a frightful cold spell in Britain; the papers were full of snowdrifts and power failures and freeze-ups; he kept saying he should be at home and not lolling about in the summer sun; never was a man so jumpy. The Queen kept smiling through.

Three or four times a day the White Train stopped at some wayside halt, where everyone was formally lined up. The King would stand shaking at the door of the train, dreading the inevitable encounters. The Queen would appear beside him, looking (the word is inescapable) radiant, or at any rate full of beans.

'Oh, Bertie, do you see, this is Hicksdorp! You know we've always so wanted to see Hicksdorp! Those people there with the bouquets – they must be the local councillors. *How* kind! And those people at the far, far end of the platform, behind that little fence – I expect they are the Bantu choir. How kind! We must wave, Bertie.'

And with a little nudge, the King found himself on terra firma, clearly wishing he were anywhere else on earth, with his wife just as clearly having waited all her life to see Hicksdorp.

One evening he called some of us press people along to his dining car, ostensibly because he had a communication to make, but more probably to relieve the deadly boredom of the Hicksdorps and the Bantu choirs. I believe it to have been the only royal press conference ever. We found him behind a table covered with bottles of all sorts of things, with which it would seem he had been experimenting, with some dedication.

'We must not f-forget the purpose of this t-tour,' he said, bravely, because his stammer was troublesome for him, 'trade and so on. Empire cooperation. For example, South African brandy. I have been trying it. It is of course m-magnificent, except that it is not very nice.' (It was in those days quite dreadful.) 'But,' he said triumphantly, 'there is this South African liqueur called V-Van der Humm. Perhaps a little sweet for most. *But,* now, if you mix half of brandy with half of Van der Humm. . . . Please try.'

The South African journalists were ecstatic. They, and their fathers, before them, had used this brandy–Humm mix for generations; nevertheless they applauded the King for having stumbled on something as familiar to them as gin and tonic. Their stories could have done the South African liquor trade no harm.

We arrived one day at a place called Outshoorn. This was a centre of the ostrich feather trade, and ostrich feathers had suffered a sad decline since, I imagine, the days of Queen Alexandra. Our passage through this empty place was, I supposed, to stimulate it – to which end the King was detailed to nip a tail feather off a sacrificial ostrich for the cameras, presumably to create a renaissance of feather boas. The King was understandably more nervous than usual – the ostrich even more so, its head and neck buried in a long stocking-like thing, as if it were for an execution. The King fumbled the operation, and his tweezers nicked a quarter-inch off the ostrich's backside, at which the unlucky bird made a fearsome screeching hullabaloo, from which we all retreated in terror.

Enter the Queen, stage right, as usual in total smiling command. She took the clippers from her husband, and there and then did an absolutely expert featherectomy – snip. She spoke to the nearest bystander, who happened by chance to be me.

'We do a lot of gardening at home, in the Palace,' said the Queen. 'The King is good at the digging and the weeding. It is I who concentrate on the secateurs.'

Here endeth the first and last of my Monarchical Memoirs. Let me be the last to wish the old lady a happy birthday. The ostrich can look after itself.

5 August 1980

Point of Departure

Jerry's Way

My friendly neighbourhood doctor died suddenly the other day. For once both the adjectives are accurate: he was my dear friend and he lived round the corner. There is something very grievous and wrong when a doctor dies unaccountably and unexpectedly, especially when it is the doctor who twice saved me from the same thing, at great pains to himself. He rescued me; when the time came, I could not rescue him. There was one moment when he was having dinner quietly at home, and the next he was gone. I shall miss him very much, and not I alone.

There cannot be many in our North London bailiwick who did not know Jerry Slattery, or were not part of the entourage of which he and his wife Johnny were the nucleus. He was probably one of the best-known family doctors in London, and loved for a great deal more than his medicine. And probably by hundreds of people who had never been ill in their lives but who tried to be, in order to have a private word with Jerry.

Dr Slattery was Irish, therefore convivial; he was a doctor, therefore skilled; he was kind, and therefore loyal. I should know, since I forced catastrophic complaints on him that were not to be dealt with by pills. I think this originally brought Jerry Slattery and me together: that a man in such a mess as I was in could not only be brought together but bounce back as good as new.

'Come, me boy,' he would say calling at the hospital bed, 'we'll have a small one on the survival of your living soul, and we'll get the Sister in.' Thus I lived, and Jerry died.

I am making this piece about Dr Jerry Slattery because to me he represents something the medical profession could ill afford to lose, lost it though it has. He was a celebrity, in his way. In another age I suppose he would have been called a 'fashionable doctor', which in a sense was true, since he created his own fashion. He ran something between a surgery and a salon. If you called in at one of Jerry and Johnny's almost innumerable parties you were almost certain to find yourself in the midst of the Dr Slattery Repertory – a very miscellaneous and rewarding company, since Dr Jerry Slattery rejoiced in the company of actors and writers and professors and comic singers and lunatics.

It might be Peter O'Toole, Olivia Manning, Michael and Jill Foot, T. P. McKenna, Llew Gardner, everyone you can think of, even me. In some way or another all of us had been preserved by the ministrations and comradeship of this extraordinarily versatile man. And throughout these occasions Jerry was always on the line: he was a doctor, and went where a doctor was needed. Once, I remember, I called in in the middle of the festivities with a rather bad pain; instantly he broke away and summoned an expert to give me a cortisone injection, which was totally horrible, and then soothed me by saying: 'Now we'll have a small one to make it better.' As it happened it made it worse, but it was well intentioned.

I am writing about Dr Jerry Slattery not as a local GP but as almost a national figure. He was passionately interested in politics, which made him a pleasure to talk to for me at least. We met long years ago on one of the early Aldermaston marches, so we had much in common from the start. Thereafter we in consultation abandoned the symptoms very quickly, and got down to the nitty-gritty.

One time he came to see me on what we supposed, without much rancour, to be my deathbed, since I was frankly in a pretty poor way. 'You're somewhat down,' said Jerry. 'In fact, we'd better get you to hospital right away, without delay.' (Which he did.) 'But while we're waiting,' said my beloved doctor, 'by the way, what did you think of that *Times* leader today? Was it not an outrage? Now I'll tell what I feel about that situation, the *Times* should be ashamed of itself. . . .'

And thus I drifted into consoling oblivion and thus my life was saved.

My doctor was unusual in his profession in that he did not accept sickness as a thing in itself; he argued that there were only sick people. Many doctors argue that illness is a condition to be found in this patient or that; Jerry argued that there were patients who happened to be ill, and that their emotions and circumstances were as important as their temperatures or their blood count or their ECG. Not more so, but equally so. Several eminent consultants have told me that they have been obliged, or even forced, to listen to a brief life history of the customer before they knew whether they had a paroxysmal haemoglobinuria or an in-growing toenail.

This may have exasperated the consultant gods, but it did the sufferers much good, as well I know. As I say, Jerry Slattery believed that illness was something that happened to people, not something to be examined by itself. This is not as common as you might think.

This is such a wholly personal memoir that I am sorry to have inflicted it on those who were not friends or patients (it was hard to be one without being the other) of the archetypal family doctor, a dying race. I do not use doctors very much, but when I do, by gum, I stretch them. My creed is that I believe in the Holy Ghost, if you insist, but I worship at the shrine of the National Health Service, and I shall not forget Dr Jerry Slattery.

You cannot really say less for someone who saved your life, and who lost his.

28 November 1977

Patient Merit

Limbo is a lovely land. I clung to it as long as I could. I have lived there, sort of, for nearly three months, hitched to an electrical machine that claimed to be, at least for a while, better than a body. And so indeed it was. Now it is returning to the real thing that is unnerving. Who wants life when there is limbo? No one who ever had the choice.

I am told it was a pleasant sunny summer. I saw it, occasionally and indifferently, through a hospital window in south London. I could have asked no more, nor did I. Apparently they thought it was worth spending our money on the huge ray apparatus. It was flattering, but time-wasting, since the end is the same anyhow.

Perhaps it worked. In this context one doesn't talk of Cure, but of Arrest. The paradox is that Arrest means Liberation. So they sent me home, where if you want a prison you must make your own. This is not simple when you also have to make a living. Much easier to make a dying.

The huge advantage of a tolerant newspaper is the privilege of using it, once in a lifetime, not to entertain others but to discover oneself. Time, as they say, will tell. In the meantime one scribbles at random, grateful when even a sentence comes out right. I am trying desperately to remember the thing I used to do. I use this space and your time to practise my lines again, groping to recall what I am supposed to be all about, because, until I discover that, there is no point in doing, or being, anything. Maybe there will be, maybe not.

In three short months, though they were long for me, I changed a lot, but the world changed more. In hospital it is not only difficult to keep abreast of what goes on outside, but the need to do so fades. More immediate things intervene. The Threat to Democracy means a lot less than what is, quite literally, a Pain in the Neck.

Anyhow, newspapers were all I ever knew. They have no meaning without context. Context now is the occasional reference to something before last spring. I study them now as a sort of practice ground for memory, an attempt to make a context of my own.

The friendly schoolboy who distributes our ward's newspapers tells me that he sells twenty *Suns* and one *Guardian*: mine. He looks at me curiously.

'Were you a reporter?'

I say: yes, used to be.

'Could I be one?'

Sure, if you hurry up. And then by and by you'll be in this bed and I'll be selling papers to you, and we'll all be out of work but Robert Maxwell.

Newspapers must be therapeutic; I am beginning, though only just, to feel better. All those weeks ago, the more I groused and complained about the government the stronger it got; it needed my big mouth to be shut for a month or two for Thatcherism to start its collapse. Should I perhaps retire?

When I went to bed, Mrs Thatcher was invulnerable and her arrogance proclaimed it. Surrounded by her coterie of nervous nobodies, she had only to mention 'Falklands' to cue in the inane applause. Now three months have reduced her from sermons to squeaks, derided even by the pop press which only yesterday was a crew of crawling yes-men. Her day is done and perhaps theirs too.

'Mrs Thatcher's post-Falklands halo has finally worn thin. She is seen as a callous authoritarian. In fact she was widely hated. . . .' In what paper was that? *The Daily Telegraph*, if you can believe me. There must be a creeping plague of sanity infecting the press. Even the *Economist* joined in gibes 'though putting its fingers before its lips.

Mrs Thatcher apart, there must be public figures other than Arthur Scargill, but from the papers and the TV news one would never know it. The miners' case seems to me just and proper; I feel just occasionally regretful that the whole debate, or non-debate, must be symbolized by two gentlemen as resolutely unattractive as Mr Scargill and Mr MacGregor, so wholly obsessed with their personal considerations that I realize (perhaps for the first time) how easy it is to become disenchanted with public men, of any kind.

One retreats, erratically, to reading. Someone gave me a book by Francis Pym that said nothing while claiming to be 'forthright'. The day Mr Pym becomes forthright will be the day when Lord Whitelaw becomes dynamic, or Michael Foot becomes unkind.

Apropos – three times Michael Foot has come all the way to the South Bank briefly to redeem my loneliness. Even for Michael Foot, this is a singular kindness. I am only regretful that in his new political solitude he has the time to spare on mine. Why is the Labour Party so sinfully ungrateful to its most honourable men?

For the rest, one cultivates one's own introspections. The face I see in the mirror – rarely now, since I no longer shave – is not what I remember, but more and more resembles an amateur Dracula. No wonder how totally unimportant one has always been to one's closest people. After the motions of regret (poor James, but he had it coming), absence becomes the norm and reappearance a chore.

Anyhow – hello world; remember me?

24 July 1984

A Pain in the Neck

There are two wholly exact and irreversible punctuation marks in everyone's life that can be exactly defined: the day you are born and the day you die. No one has any control whatever of the first, and only a troubled minority claim the right to decide on the second.

For some people, indeed many, there comes a third chapter heading, always uninvited. Using the punctuation mark analogy again, it could be described as the semi-colon situation, suggesting something tentative between the opening phrase and the full stop. Most writers use the device when they cannot make up their minds whether they have finished with one thought, or whether it needs a sort of PS, a compromise.

Clinging to this whimsy, I would suggest that this semi-colon arrives when the customer is told on absolute authority that he, or she, is ill of a condition once considered grave, but that in this enlightened world is unlikely to send him to kingdom come today or tomorrow, or next week, or even with luck this year, and which can be postponed by accepting some tiresome and painful disciplines. In a word – which is unfortunately not mine – it is the moment of truth.

At least for himself; he will of course continue to lie to everyone else.

We may stop being coy about it. A man learns quite suddenly, though after a fairly long suspicion, that he has an established malignancy in this or that part of him. The doctors have hedged and fiddled about with the definition, since the thing can be described in arcane technical terms that they, usually correctly, assume are unintelligible to the layman. Eventually, however, they are obliged to come clean, or cleanish, and tell the poor sod that this or that part of him has got cancer and has got to be fixed, or else. If the patient is lucky this has happened somewhere that can be chopped off and forgotten. But the chances are, since cancer is cruelly crafty, it usually takes over some awkward and inaccessible organ that the unlucky customer cannot readily do without. Both cases are fairly determinable: you chop it off or you leave it to the painkillers.

Sometimes, fortunately, there is a third option: the thing can grab you somewhere that is fairly accessible but nevertheless essential, requiring much complicated and expensive machinery and demanding a fair chunk out of the customer's daily life, and a lot of hitherto inexperienced pain.

Some people flatly refuse to accept it. This bloke didn't; he realized what was up from the start; indeed he provided the hospital with much of his own diagnosis. Privately, of course, he continued to kid himself, and others, insisting on calling his little trouble by the name of its zodiacal mate: I got a touch of Capricorn.

This provided the additional satisfaction of leaving the questioners uneasy or bothered: should we have known of this Capricorn business? Sure you should; if you had worked in the South Pacific you would have seen it all the time. Just call it, as this chap does, a tropical disease.

Remember Arthur Clough. 'Thou shalt not kill, but needst not strive, officiously to keep alive.' However, the customer cannot so strive, officiously or otherwise. The others must strive; he must submit.

Once the chips, as they say, are down there is something quite soothing about this submission. From now on the buck is passed to the experts. If it doesn't work it is not his fault. Or – dare we say – not entirely. The medics talk a lot about the 'will to live'. This particular customer didn't have too much of that. In his trade he had seen a fair amount of death, mostly violent. The process itself was clearly unpleasant, but the end product seemed restful enough. Indeed, as the psychological depression (which he had been warned was to be a clinical part of this illness) deepened, the end product came to seem quite desirable. The electric rays and lasers and things did not do anything about that.

When alone at night this chap would frequently grizzle and weep to himself, but only because it hurt. It did not do the least good, but it got something off his chest. Not, unfortunately, off his throat.

Family and friends had to be considered. As this customer quickly realized, few of us are beloved enough to be missed for more than a couple of days or so. Meanwhile their reaction is either embarassment or resentment. Initially everyone feels that the selfish bastard has cooked up the situation to attract consideration or create a drama. Some are even frank enough to ask one to hurry it up a bit.

Useless for him to say that this wasn't his idea, that the scenario came from total strangers whose concern was wholly clinical, and sometimes not especially even that. It will be blamed on him, as everything is blamed on him.

This patient's regard for the National Health Service had always been totally steadfast; it had saved his life before. He began to invent fantasies – which was higher on Mrs Thatcher's hit list: him or the NHS? He mused on this for hours in the radio-therapy machine; it passed the time well.

Regarding this situation objectively, forgetting personal pain and fear, this unimportant personal crisis had come at a strange time. This customer (and it is becoming affected and pedantic to disguise his identity now) has lived for almost two score years with the dread of my wife and children being caught up in the Holocaust that was made possible by my generation, in my generation, and probably for my generation, and for which I have always felt an absurd and wholly illogical responsibility, if only for the silly reason that I personally witnessed the explosion of atom bombs, and did nothing about it, and could do nothing except protest, tiresomely and uselessly, and finally boringly.

Paradoxically, and I suppose romantically, I hoped that I would be there again, with them, to share the real thing, hands in hands. I still refuse to surrender that, which means the obligation of getting well. I can truthfully think of no other reason.

Before the hospital business even began, the doctors, who had done this often before, said that an inescapable concomitant of this treatment was depression, a lowering of the spirits inexperienced before. I said: You should have known me years ago. They said: You don't know nothing yet, and they were right.

Anyhow, we shall see.

Before you slip, inconspicuously and guiltily, out of the room, let me tell you about my operation. . . .

28 January 1985

James Cameron died in the early hours of Sunday, 27 January 1985, at his home. 'A Pain in the Neck' had been written three months before, but not printed at that time. Letters of regret flooded in, from friends, colleagues, acquaintances, and from hundreds of ordinary people who had never met James but who had come to know and value him from his writings.